FROM C

Ramachandra Sharma was born on 20 November 1925, in Bangalore. He completed a B.Sc. and a B.Ed. at the University of Mysore, and a B.Sc. (Honours) and a Ph.D. in psychology at the University of London. He has worked as a secondary school teacher and as a psychologist in India, England and Africa. He has been the head of the Psychological Service in Zambia, and an educational psychology expert for the UNESCO. Sharma is regarded as one of the pioneers of Kannada literature's Modern movement, and his poems and short stories have been translated into several languages.

Ramachandra Sharma is married and lives in Bangalore.

E.D. GALGOTIA & SONS
BOOK SELLERS
17-B, CONNAUGHT PLACE
NEW DELHI-1

PENGUIN BOOKS
FROM CAUVERY TO GODAVARI

Ramachandra Sharma was born on 28 November 1925 in Bangalore. He completed a B.Sc. and a B.Ed. at the University of Mysore, and a B.Sc. (Honours) and a Ph.D. in psychology at the University of London. He has worked as a secondary school teacher, and as a psychologist in India, England and Africa. He has been the head of the Psychological Service in Zambia, and an educational psychology expert for the UNESCO. Sharma is regarded as one of the pioneers of Kannada literature's Modern movement, and his poems and short stories have been translated into several languages.

Ramachandra Sharma is married and lives in Bangalore.

From CAUVERY To GODAVARI

Modern Kannada Short Stories

Edited by

Ramachandra Sharma

PENGUIN BOOKS

Penguin Books India (P) Ltd., B4/246 Safdarjung Enclave,
New Delhi 110 029, India
Penguin Books Ltd., 27, Wrights Lane, W8 5TZ, London, UK
Penguin Books USA Inc., 375 Hudson Street, New York, New York 10014, USA
Penguin Books Australia Ltd., Ringwood, Victoria, Australia
Penguin Books Canada Ltd., 10 Alcorn Avenue, Suite 300, Toronto, Ontario M4V 3B2, Canada
Penguin Books (NZ) Ltd., 182-190 Wairau Road, Auckland 10, New Zealand

This collection first published by Penguin Books India (P) Ltd. 1992

Copyright ©Ramachandra Sharma, 1991, 1992

Page v is an extension of the copyright page

All rights reserved

Typeset in New Baskerville by Digital Technologies and Printing Solutions, New Delhi
Made in India by Ananda Offset Private Ltd., Calcutta

This book is sold subject to the conditions that it shall not, by way of trade or otherwise, be lent, hired out, or otherwise circulated without the publisher's prior written consent in any form of binding or cover other than that in which it is published and without a similar condition including this condition being imposed on the subsequent purchaser and without limiting the rights under copyright reserved above, no part of this publication may be reproduced, stored in or introduced into a retrieval system, or transmitted in any form or by any means (electronic, mechanical, photocopying, recording or otherwise), without the prior written permission of both the copyright owner and the above mentioned publisher of this book.

Acknowledgements

The editor wishes to thank and acknowledge the following authors, translators and copyright holders for permission to use the stories in this volume:

Smt Vijayalakshmi Rao, for the late Bagalodi Devaraya's story, 'The Lord of the Earthenware,' published in *Rudrappana Roudra Mattu Itara Kathegalu*, 1986; Yashwant Chittal, for his story, 'The Girl Who Became a Story,' published in the collection *Katheyadalu Hudugi*, 1980; Shantinath Desai, for his story, 'Bharamya Becomes Nikhil,' published in *Koormavatara Mattu Itara Kathegalu*, 1988, and for the translation of the same story; A.K. Ramanujan and Manohar Granthamala, for the story, 'Annayya's Anthropology,' published in *Innashtu Hosa Kathegalu*, 1972; U.R. Anantha Murthy, for his story, 'Stallion of the Sun,' published in the Diwali Number of *Udayavani*, 1983; Raghavendra Khasaneesa, for his story, 'Orphans,' published in *Hosa Kshitija*, 1966; K.S. Sharat, for the late K. Sadashiva's story, 'Rama Rides to the Fair,' published in *Hanneradu Kathegalu*, 1985; P. Lankesh, for his story, 'Not Me,' published in the collection *Nanalla*, 1970; Poorna Chandra Tejasvi, for his story, 'Tabara's Story,' published in *Poorna Chandra Tejasvi Avara Ella Kathegalu*, 1987; Veena Shanteshwar, for her story, 'A Story Like This,' published in *Sanna Kathegalu*, 1987; S. Diwakar, for his story, 'Cruelty,' published in *Itihasa*, 1981; Vaidehi, for her story, 'Akku,' published in *Antarangada Putagalu*, 1984; Ramachandra Deva, for his story, 'A Revolutionary Incident,' published in his collection of the same name, 1983; and Devanoor Mahadeva, for his story, 'Tar Arrives,' published in his collection, *Dyavanooru*, 1973.

The editor also thanks:

Padma Ramachandra Sharma, for her translations of the stories by Yashwant Chittal and P. Lankesh; Narayan Hegde, for his translations of the stories by U.R. Anantha Murthy, A. K. Ramanujan and K. P. Poorna Chandra Tejasvi; P. Sreenivasa Rao, for his translations of the stories by Bagalodi Devaraya and K. Sadashiva; Basavaraj Urs, for his translations of the stories by Veena Shanteshwar and Ramachandra Deva; Manu Shetty and A. K. Ramanujan, for their translations of the stories by Raghavendra Khasaneesa and Devanoor Mahadeva; and Shantinath Desai, for his translation of the story by S. Diwakar.

Contents

Preface

Though Kannada literature has known story-telling for over a thousand years, as is evident from *Vaddaradhane,* a tenth-century prose work of religious tales, the short story as a literary genre was born in the first two decades of this century. It may be said that the official registration of the birth took place when Masti Venkatesha Iyengar published a slim volume of his short stories in the year 1920, though there is evidence to believe that experiments in this genre had been going on for some years before that.

It was at about the same time that B.M. Srikantia, a pioneer of Kannada literature as we know it today, was engaged in translating some sixty poems, mostly of the Romantic period, from English. The influence of English on the resurgence of Kannada literature can be seen both in poetry and the short story. Masti himself went on record saying that he was inspired to write his stories after coming across some published in *Strand* magazine. There must have been a tremendous excitement along with expressions of apprehension when mythological heroes like Rama and Krishna were replaced on the centre stage of literature by ordinary folk, when kings and queens were replaced by neighbours and their wives.

The form of the short story proved to be eminently suited to the genius of Masti, a born story-teller. Though there was no form of literature which he did not employ with distinction, it is as a short story-teller that he is cherished by the people of Karnataka. Telling a story was his forte as is proved by the hundred stories he has left behind, along with two novels and a large number of narrative poems. The method he adopts is that of a sentient witness who observes life and comments on it while keeping faith in the value system inherited by the whole community.

Though there were many talented writers who followed him,

Masti is undoubtedly the best exemplar of the Masti tradition. One can, of course, list a dozen stories written by his followers which are good by any standards, but finds it difficult to say that any of them added significantly to the development of the short story as a literary form. Masti's followers were more influenced by the poets of the Navodaya period than by Masti himself, and so took the road to the usual Romantic excesses and forgot Masti's sense of realism and detachment. The only writer who came close to the master was Bagalodi Devaraya, who shows a remarkably modern sensibility though his story-telling is traditional. His death, soon after retirement from the Indian Foreign Service in 1985, followed by Masti's own death the following year, were great losses to the world of short stories.

The Progressive school of writers, very active during the '40s and the first couple of years of the '50s, also contributed very little to the development of the form. They were basically Romantic in their attitude in spite of a shift of emphasis in the theme of the short story. Barring a few exceptions, the stories written during those years suffer from idealization and oversimplification, both of events and characters.

*

Kannada literature had to wait till the middle of the '50s before it made a radical departure which affected all the forms, including the short story. The Navya, or the Modern, movement, which originated with poetry, had a telling effect on the way one perceived and communicated experience. The change that took place was not just a matter of technique, as opponents of the Modern movement would have us believe, but of vision. The new vision of the writer seemed to demand a new mode of expression, whatever the genre he chose. It is no coincidence that those who led the modern movement through poetry, like the editor of this anthology, also wrote the first modern short stories.

The Navya writers used the form of the short story not just to narrate an experience but to explore it for its significance. They took a calculated risk in using tools traditionally associated with poetry, like symbols and images, to achieve the fullest possible expression for what they had to say. Wanting to capture experience in all its complexity, writing a short story for the Navya writer was no different from writing a poem. It was both art and craft and the writer was prepared to exploit all the resources of the language in order to attain his end.

It is no wonder that there was a reaction to this mode of writing as the years passed. Though there were signs of an incipient revolt by the end of the '60s, it was in 1971 that Lankesh, one of the important writers of the Navya school, expressed his disaffection saying that the Navya writer would never produce a perfect story because of his desire to stay aloof from society as such. Tejasvi came out with a clearer and louder statement in 1973, asking writers to turn their backs on the prevailing mode of writing. Here is an excerpt from the preface he wrote to a collection of short stories published that year. It became a manifesto of sorts for him and a number of other younger writers in the following years:

> 'We have to jettison the Navya movement in its entirety
> and seek a new direction. It is time that a writer is seen
> in his writing only because he is an honest witness to life.
>
> There is no longer any vigour in the Navya literature. It
> is incapable of bearing the responsibilities which the
> changed circumstances of our life impose on us, because
> of the mechanical nature of the symbolic style and
> techniques that it employs. Other reasons for its rundown
> state are that most of the writers of that school are
> teachers and that all its revolutionary fervour is confined
> to literature *per se*. . . .'

Though Tejasvi's call seems to ask the writers to return to the days of Masti and his brand of realism, the stories that have come out from him and his admirers are unlike the ones written during the Masti era. The differences are not only in the thematic content of the stories but also in the use of language and the authenticity of the details which form the body of the narration. One can clearly see that these writers have not been able to 'jettison the Navya movement in its entirety'.

There are two aspects of the development of the short story

during the '80s which need to be mentioned. One is the reincarnation of the Progressive movement of the '40s in the form of the Bandaya, or the Protest, school. The second is the increased number of women writers who are taking to the form. The two aspects are related to each other in that both are protests against the oppression and exploitation of the weaker sections of society by those that wield power. A close study of the output of the '80s reveals an interesting side to it. While the best of the women writers seem to have given up the strident feminism of the earlier years in favour of a more mature understanding of the man-woman relationship, the best Bandaya stories have been produced not by the hardcore champions of the Protest school but by others who had had their apprenticeship in the Navya school.

A novel feature of the present day may prove to be of greater significance in the coming years. More and more of the oppressed and underprivileged classes are taking to writing about their experiences. The universe of human experience coming into literature had expanded considerably as a result. There has also been a concomitant experimentation with the language used for fictional purposes, which is sure to prove to be of immense worth to Kannada literature.

*

In conclusion, a few words about this anthology.

Modernism, in the context of Kannada literature, has been a complex phenomenon involving a radical departure from the aesthetic strategies adopted by the best of the Navodaya school, like Masti. It has, in a conscious fashion, negated the transcendence of human experience and called for a return to the real. The lessons learnt by writers, thanks to the Modern movement, have stayed with them even though some have struck postures indicating that they have turned their back on it.

This anthology of fifteen stories, the editor hopes, represents the best of the movement. It is a very young anthology, in a sense, as no story in it is older than twenty-five years of age. The editor has, in most of the cases, looked for one of the recent stories of a living writer instead of picking a well-known one from the distant past.

Finally, a word about the title of the anthology. There was a time when the Kannada land stretched from the Cauvery to the Godavari, reference to which can be seen in *Kavirajamarga*, a work of the ninth century, more or less contemporaneous with *Vaddaradhane*. Therefore, the editor hopes, the title of this book suggests to the reader the glorious past in which the present-day Kannada writer has his roots.

Thanks are due to the writers (or the copyright holders) who readily granted permission to include their stories in the anthology, and the translators for a job well done.

July 1991   *Ramachandra Sharma*
Bangalore

The Passage

Ramachandra Sharma

He was perplexed to see the orphan eyes watching him from the bed of dry leaves under the jackfruit tree. He smiled at his own fancy that his marbles were those eyes. There was no fear in them. Moving its flat, soft, fur-covered face from left to right, the baby-bird investigated the boy's body.

'Ho, ho, hoy,' he cupped his mouth with his hands and called like the hero of an English film he had seen a while ago.

There was absolutely no need for that loud call. Amase would have heard the boy even if he had called as usual. He was only a few feet away, past the banana grove, on the way to the stream. This boy from Bangalore who had come to the village for two months during the summer break was strange, Amase thought. It had been his first contact with a village and he was excited by the quotidian things of village life, things which Amase would have ignored if Diwakar had not drawn his attention to them, *Ragi* balls, cow's milk of the first week after bearing a calf, *chiguli*, the water-snakes which swam with them when they plunged into the well by the garden, the stream near Madehalli and the fish that held up their undersides to the sun to shine like silver when they dived into the water—Amase was about to give up his attempt to list them as he traced his way back to Diwakar.

'Hurry up. Come and see. What on earth is this?'

Amase looked at the thing. It was an owlet. He was happy that he knew something which the clever boy from the city did not know. There was no trace of the usual subservience when he spoke: 'An owlet, *ayya*. Must have tumbled out of the nest.'

Amase was right and there was proof enough when they looked up. There was a vertical light-filled hollow in the tree from the bottom to the top as if someone had carved it. One could see at a height of about twenty-five feet a pan-shaped nest made of twigs. They heard a sound from it suggesting the presence of a couple of young ones.

The owlet on the bed of leaves looked at them from top to toe wanting to know what they had in mind for it.

Amase found words for what was passing through Diwakar's mind: 'Let's leave it there. A kite or a cat will account for it. Anyway, *ayya*, Subbiah will take you to task if you were to take it home. Remember, it's only a few days old. . . . Won't survive.'

Diwakar got down to his knees and gently scooped up the bird along with some leaves, as if he had not heard Amase's words or as if they did not merit comment. The bird sat in the hollow of his palm, looked up and squeaked. By the time he stood up, he had made up his mind. Unbuttoning his shirt right down to the belt on his waist, he put the bird inside his shirt. As the shirt was tucked in, the bird could not slip out. He felt its soft nails scratch his belly, tickling him.

He started climbing the tree, taking care that the trunk did not graze his belly. Amase was filled with admiration mixed with anxiety for the city boy. If, by chance he slipped, he would have scratches all over even if his bones stayed intact. His shirt would be smeared with blood here and there. . . . Subbiah, who had left the boy in his care, would thrash him. So would his own father. He broke into a sweat.

'Get down, *ayya*, get down. Give it to me. It's nothing much for village lads to clamber up jackfruit trees.'

Diwakar replied even as he climbed: 'Where will you keep the bird? Don't you need both hands to climb the tree?'

Amase flinched as he remembered his outfit of shorts and a short vest that could not be tucked in. He decided to play the overseer. 'Take the branch to the right, *ayya*, it's strong. Be careful. . . .'

Diwakar had almost reached the nest. He could even hear one or two young ones stirring in the nest which was nestled in a spot where two branches met. He held a branch firmly with his left hand and was about to put his right hand into his shirt to take out the bird when. . .

Nobody knew where the mother-bird came from. Flapping its wings it flew about a foot above the nest, screaming wildly. The target of its round eyes, which had grown rounder, seemed to be

Diwakar's eyes as it flew towards him without caring for the branches in its way. The hand which had gone into the shirt came out. The sweating hand made him think that he was fast losing his grip of the branch. Before the bird could return to attack, he had started climbing down.

'Damn it. There she was, a moment ago, sitting quietly on the tamarind tree . . . ,' Amase said.

As Diwakar reached safety, Amase was lost in thought. The ghost of Basavalinga, who had fallen from the tree while picking fruit, stirred in his head. He was not sure he should mention it to Diwakar. The city boy, who had made fun of him when he touched the coconut tree and pressed his hands to his eyes before climbing it, would surely laugh at his mention of ghosts.

'A ghost-like bird. Maybe a real ghost,' he said instead. 'Wise to leave the owlet under the tree,' he added.

Diwakar seemed to agree with him. He took the bird out, held it in his palm and looked at it. It was likely the mother-bird would come and pick it up. He searched the sky for it. When his eyes wandered toward the smoke rising from the village, he sighted two mongrels chasing each other to the place where the two boys stood. He changed his mind when he saw a kite circling leisurely above. They would have to keep watch till evening after placing the bird under the tree hoping that the mother-bird would gather the young one. He told Amase that under no circumstances would he allow the bird to be eaten by the kite or the dogs. . . .

The owlet did not open its eyes when he placed it again on its bed of leaves. The boys went and sat under the tamarind tree. Amase started talking of all sorts of things, mainly to forget the ghost in his head. His younger sister, Lakki, had grown up a few days ago, he said. He was fed up of eating all that *chiguli,* he added. Their young cow was in heat, they should drive it soon to Madehalli to have a bull mount it, he said. . . .

Diwakar failed to grasp fully what Amase was saying and so only half his mind was on it. . . . The girl was his own age and the same size. What was the meaning of Amase saying that she had grown up only a few days ago? And what had the business of growing up got do with *chiguli*? Confused, he decided to keep quiet. The business of the young cow needing a bull to mount tickled him. But, before he could question Amase about it, he saw the mother-owl circle above and he forgot to ask.

It was not the gyrating mother-owl but dusk that eventually descended to the earth. By the time the cattle, which had gone to graze beyond the stream, returned with the cowherds shouting 'hoy, hoy' and the dogs barking, it was dark. When flocks of crows flew towards Bommanayakanahalli, Diwakar went to the jackfruit tree, picked up the bird and started walking towards the village.

Amase was about ten yards behind him. The owlet was squeaking all the way and he was nervous about what would happen.

*

There were quite a few in the village who were scared of Subbiah's moods, his wild temper and the words of abuse that seemed to be waiting at the tip of his tongue. Though Diwakar had been spared all that because he was the apple of his childless uncle's eye, he knew about his being a latter-day Durvasa and so was naturally nervous about taking the bird to his own house. He was as nervous about it as Amase himself. It did not even occur to him to seek his uncle's permission to keep the bird and so the bird went with Amase. It was neither an altruistic love for life as such, nor an unusual fondness for his son, that persuaded Amase's father, Karigowda, to keep the bird. He had his eye on the wet lands of Dyavayya who had died childless barely a month earlier, and so allowed the bird into the house. Dyavayya's wife had already sold most of the property of the deceased, except for the wet lands, and had gone to Mysore to live with her brother. Subbiah and Dyavayya were of the same stock and were fond of each other. There was no possibility of Dyavayya's wife not heeding Subbiah's advice. Besides, Subbiah was extremely attached to Diwakar, his dead brother's child. Karigowda reckoned that Subbiah would be pleased if the boy was made happy. The bird found a sanctuary in his house because his calculations ran all the way from the bird to Diwakar, Subbiah, Dyavayya's wife and to the wet lands of the dead man. Besides, he had seen tears in Lakki's eyes as her brother stood on the threshold of the house, trembling uncontrollably, stuttering and holding the bird in his hand to the light of the lantern. Just as he told himself that the girl would be particularly vulnerable after the onset of menstruation, the old woman in the corner had got up as if she had smelt an unusual happening and crawled towards the door shouting, 'What is the matter, Kariya?' The mention of Diwakar's name by Amase had been enough for her to decide to play a major role in favour of the orphan bird. At that point, her speech became incoherent as usual. Her reference to Chandrappa, his father and breast milk meant nothing to Lakki and Amase. They did not mind because she had come to their help on the matter of the bird. Karigowda had already made up his mind but he chose to make it look as if he was saying yes to please his mother. 'Let the bird stay, Mother. Did I say anything against the idea?' As he went back to the veranda for another beedi, the children engaged themselves in attending to the bird.

Karigowda's mind travelled back in time. Diwakar's father, Chandrappa, and he had been born within a week of each other. He sighed as he recalled how unlucky his childhood friend, who visited the village every summer, had been. Having lost his mother within a month of his birth, Chandrappa had survived because Karigowda's mother had given him her breast. It had looked as if she was more attached to the foster child than to the one she had borne. Karigowda had come to hear what people whispered amongst themselves but that had not affected his love for Chandrappa. At the age of one, Chandrappa had been adopted by his maternal uncle in Mysore. He had even gone to the college there, and later to Bombay for a job. His visit to the village once a year had continued till his death at the age of thirty-two. Diwakar had gone to his grandfather's on his mother's side in Bangalore after Chandrappa's death. The friendship between him and Chandrappa had been reborn as friendship between his son and Diwakar. . . .

Karigowda did not exactly like recalling Chandrappa's father. There was something more than mere friendship between him and Karigowda's mother, and that was the reason for her attachment to Chandrappa, was what people had been saying. He had known about the rumours. He would never come to know the truth, he told himself. As youngsters, they might have been very fond of each other. His mother, who had been perfectly all right till about ten years ago, had grown senile. She would be talking rationally one moment, and the very next her mind would start wandering as if someone had snapped the thread of her thought. No one could hope to stay with her when she went on these lone journeys to an unknown destination. . . . It had been no use repeatedly reminding her that this boy was not Chandrappa but his son. As far as she was concerned, Diwakar was Chandrappa . . . her shapeless breasts had filled up with overflowing milk and Chandrappa had been reborn in the form of his son. . . . Karigowda started on another beedi.

Diwakar joined Amase after dinner that night. His reckoning that something would have been settled by then was right. Lakki and Amase were caressing the little bird and the old woman looked happy.

'Come, son, come. This bird has come here just like you used to come for my breast-milk. Let it also become big like you, poor thing.'

She started guffawing even before her words, which drew a parallel between him and the bird, had sunk into Diwakar. 'Owl . . . owl . . . Chandrappa . . . here, child . . . take my breast. . . .' She dropped the *pallu* from the shoulder and held up her breasts and started caressing them. The children were aghast. Lakki's eyes, as they turned towards Diwakar, grew bigger and bigger. Was growing up the same as the eyes growing big? The old woman was back to her normal self even as he played with the thought.

'Kariya, make a nest for the bird here. Amase, bring some straw for the nest. Kariya, let the nest be high so that the bird does not get out. Lakki, fetch my other saree from the backyard. . . .'

The bird lay in her bed with eyes closed while the nest was being prepared.

The bird thrived on the tablets of meat that Lakki prepared from what the boys begged or borrowed from the Harijans' huts. It was fun to watch it open its mouth wide to swallow the ever-so-tiny pieces of meat. Placing the bird on the lowest branch of the guava tree, they took turns at rolling meat balls and feeding it. The bird would shake its head each time it got a piece so that it would go straight in. Within a fortnight its sides darkened. Once in a while, the old woman would come out and watch it, while sunning herself. She would get excited when the bird hopped along the branch. One day, she clapped at its antics and called out:

'Chandrappa, look! It's getting big like you, isn't it? You watch my words. Someday it will also fly away like you. . . . '

Her health took a turn for the worse that evening. Karigowda, who had gone for the day to Nagamangala to buy a pair of bullocks, had not come back. The old woman had refused even the porridge that Lakki had made for her and starved the whole day. Amase had come to Subbiah's house that evening and asked Diwakar to go with him.

'Come, come, my love. Where had you gone till now? Come.' The old woman recovered a bit.

'Eh, Lakki, you have grown up for nothing. It's dark and you haven't given me anything to eat. Do you know that I was already married at your age? Chandrappa's father and I. . . . '

What would have followed was anybody's guess. Lakki had got up, gone into the kitchen and come out with some rice and *esaru* in a plate. The old woman had insisted that Diwakar feed her. Obviously she ate with relish and everyone was happy. Lakki wiped the spittle off the sides of her mouth as she ate.

'You just can't imagine what I was like at her age.' The old woman looked at Lakki closely as if she was inspecting her.

'I was much fairer. Even before I had grown up, I had breasts which looked like two tops. Your father would be walking to and fro in front of the hut wanting to catch my eye. . . . I was so amused. He was good-looking even though his face was covered with pimples. . . . ' Who knows what particular memory haunted her at that moment! She pulled off the *pallu* and cupped her breasts to hold them up. Lakki ran into the kitchen and Amase tried to bring his grandmother back to the present.

'He is not Chandrappa, *ajji*, he is Chandrappa's son. Didn't Chandrappa die a few years ago, *ajji?*'

'So, you think you know what I don't know, do you? Idiot, listen to me and remember what I'm going to tell you. This is no son of Chandrappa. This is Chandrappa's father. He is to Lakki what . . . eh, Lakki. . . . '

Just as Lakki came out, Karigowda came in with Subbiah who had decided to look for Diwakar. The bird, which had been lying quietly till then in the basket, jumped out, beat its still tender wings and followed Diwakar. Even Subbiah had to laugh at the sight.

The old woman did not laugh. She lay curled up in her bed sobbing.

*

When Karigowda and Amase went to Madehalli with their cow to have a bull mount it, Diwakar went with them. Lakki was in the backyard feeding the bird. Lakki blushed when the boy seemed to look at her as never before.

Neither had noticed the little frog as they searched each other's eyes intermittently, not knowing how to verbalize what was vaguely bothering them. But the owlet on the guava tree had noticed it. After staring at it for a little while, it had swooped on it. Not having done any such thing before, it had landed a foot away from the frog and had sat there dazed, looking intently at the jumping frog. Diwakar had caught the frog and placed it in the centre of the yard while Lakki had taken the bird back to its perch. The bird had more or less landed on the frog on the second attempt and gulped it down.

With that, they started catching frogs for their bird. And then mice. They were amazed that the bird learned so fast the skill to direct its wings and claws to follow the eye. Karigowda compared his son's learning with the bird's and made fun of the boy. The claws which had tickled Diwakar whenever the bird landed on his finger had now grown to be an inch long. Their grip, which had been like a caress when Lakki passed the bird to him, so that it perched on his fingers, now hurt him like a vice. A foot high, it would look into his eyes wanting to find out about its future.

The boys thought of letting it free so that it could find its natural habitat. It was getting close to the end of the summer vacation when Diwakar had to return to Bangalore. They knew the bird had to go, but it saddened them whenever it landed without warning on either the shoulder or the head, gave a light kiss with its beak and made gurgling noises of contentment. It was now a competent flier taking all the trees in the yard in its flight.

The boys had gone somewhere that evening, leaving Lakki behind with the old woman. The bird had left its perch on a raft and landed on the woman's chest. She had opened her eyes and while she was mumbling some words, all the while caressing the bird, Lakki had come out. The old woman's hands might have tightened round its neck, perhaps, even as Lakki thought of picking it up to return it to its nest. The bird had flapped its wings wildly and the old woman had let it go. It had gone up to its usual perch and had looked alternately at Lakki and the old woman.

Nobody could be blamed for what happened next. After having looked at them both a dozen or more times, it might have concluded that it was the old woman who had tried to strangle it. Her eyes might have even looked like a jumping frog's or a scuttling mouse's. Anyway, it had swooped on to her face. It must have been a mysterious wisdom hidden in the embers of her lingering life that had made the old woman turn her face away at the very last moment. The bird's claws had hit the wrinkled face and not the eyes. She had not cried out in pain but whimpered as the blood that oozed out of the wound had flowed down to her chin, neck and then to the bedclothes. When Lakki cried out in terror, the owlet had returned to its perch and started cleaning its feathers as if nothing had happened.

The boys had eventually returned to hear about what happened. Amase went out to get the pandit to attend to the old woman. There was no need for any words as the boys made their decision.

It was long after the boys' return that Karigowda came home. He had taken a look at the bandage on his mother's face and thrashed his son soundly. When Lakki sobbed, he had called her a flirt. Sitting on the veranda, he had finished smoking a whole bundle of beedis.

When someone knocked on the door at an hour when the whole village was asleep, Diwakar, who had been making an entry in his diary, opened the door to find Amase sobbing. The bird was in his arms and Diwakar knew what had happened. The bird flew to his head and perched on it, playing with his hair. It was excited—as if it had found a long lost friend.

It was obvious that his uncle had not been disturbed in his sleep, judging by the rhythmic snoring that could be heard. He went to the cowshed, brought a basket to keep by his bed, made a bed of his blanket and turned off the lantern to sleep. . . .

He woke up even before the cock had a dream. He remembered the bird and sat up with alacrity. He heard a dog bark in the distance in that hour of twilight. Even as he thought of getting up to take the bird away, he heard his uncle come down from the attic. The bird had not stirred as he lay back pretending to be still asleep. His uncle opened the door. A little light had peeped in before he closed the door shut.

He knew that Subbiah would be on his way to the stream for his morning ablutions. He got up before the bird could ask him a question from inside the basket, neatly folded the blanket, gathered the basket and walked out of the door in the opposite direction. There was an urgency in his steps as he headed for the woods by the Hucchakere waters.

He crossed his uncle's fields on the other side of the tank, and reached the foot of the hills that rose and fell all the way to Melkote. He wandered among the trees of the woods till he spotted a jackfruit tree. He caressed the bird from head to tail and threw it up in the air. The bird was shocked by this unexpected development. It did not fly away but sat on the nearest branch and looked at him intently. He traced his way back to the tank frequently turning to look at the bird. It had not moved at all.

Unable to bear the sense of vacuousness in him, he went looking for Amase. They did not say much to each other as they sat on the veranda. Even Karigowda, who had paced between the backyard and the main door without any apparent reason, had not said a word. Lakki had shown her face once—she had gone in after bringing them some guavas to eat.

It was twilight when Karigowda left the house telling Lakki that he would be going to Narasa's. Before leaving, he warned Amase without looking at him: 'Don't step out of the house. Remember, the pandit is supposed to call. I want you here when he comes, understand?'

It was obvious that the real target for his anger was Diwakar. After making sure that he had gone, Amase went in with Diwakar. Lakki was beside the old woman's bed. Diwakar thought that she was looking for something in his eyes.

The old woman rolled to her side, opened her eyes and spoke as if she was still sleeping: 'Come, Chandrappa, come. Have you come for milk, my child?' She turned to Lakki. 'Eh, girl, what have you done with my bird? Out with it. . . . ' Before she said another word, the bird had flown in through the open backdoor and perched on her chest. The old woman caressed it as she cooed, 'So, you have come back, have you, my life? Come. . . .' Diwakar had not noticed that Lakki's hand had come to rest in his own, like a bird, as they stood listening to the old woman groan in contentment.

*

His heart was heavy as the day for his departure drew near. He had hardly two days in which he had to find a solution. He was haunted by the grief in Lakki's bird-like eyes and found it difficult to sleep that night. He woke up at dawn after a disturbed night to hear Karigowda's voice as his uncle opened the door. Perhaps, he had been waiting outside. One could hear what he was saying even though the door was closed. He was telling Subbiah about his mother's —obsession she would fret even if the bird went out of sight for a second, he said. What was to happen to the bird—an ill-omen—he wanted to know.

'The boy is leaving the day after, Kariya . . .,' his uncle drawled.

'Does it mean that I've to keep the bird, Subbiah? It's not fair.'

'Have you already been to the stream?' It was obvious that Subbiah was out to pacify him. 'Otherwise, come with me. Let's put our heads together and work out something. . . .'

At breakfast, his uncle talked to Diwakar about the fair in Chunchanagiri the following day. He spoke about the thousand peacocks that thronged the place, the *math* and the temple. He could visit them, he said. A cart would be leaving for Chunchanagiri in an hour and would be coming back after the fair. Would the boy like to go? Among the sight-seeing places there were the hill and the forest, he said.

'Yes, Uncle. I would like to go. I'll take the bird with me and leave it behind,' the boy said. His uncle was taken by surprise.

For the first time, Subbiah, not given to any form of demonstration, had held him close and caressed his head.

'Get ready then. I'll give you a letter. You stay with Narasimha Joisa for the night. He is our kinsman.' He removed the towel from his shoulder and blew his nose into it though it was dry.

*

It was night when the party returned from Chunchanagiri. Diwakar put down the empty basket by the bag of wheat as he wondered whether the village had already retired for the night. He curbed his desire to call on Amase as he thought of Karigowda and the old woman, had a glass of milk and went to bed. His uncle had come down the steps from the attic a couple of times during the night. He was aware of it but had not stirred.

Morning broke as usual. All that was left was to pack and walk to the market-place to catch the Krishnarajapet-Mysore bus. While he was eating the rice-roti, Subbiah, who already had put a shawl round him, said, 'It seems the old woman died some time in the night. Nobody knows when; they came to know about it only in the early hours of the morning.'

He rushed to the street with the knapsack on his back. His uncle had shouted, 'All right. I'll be going to the market-place via the temple. You take the road in front of the village and meet me there.'

There were people in front of Karigowda's place. Karigowda started crying when he saw the boy.

When he went in, Diwakar turned to look at the corner where the old woman had her bed. She was lying there as usual, curled up. Lakki and Amase, who were on either side of her, stared at him.

He did not say a word, but ran out of the house. When he passed the peepul tree and turned towards the market-place, he saw his uncle at a distance walking briskly.

The boy tripped. When he looked down at his feet, he thought he had grown big, so big indeed, that he could not see the dust he had kicked up when he tripped.

—*Translated by the Author*

The Lord of Earthenware

Bagalodi Devaraya

Potter Chandrappa was incensed. 'Where has your son vanished? He can't stay a moment at home after finishing work. A complete stray bull! You gave birth to a single child. Can't you keep that only son disciplined? Your fondness for him has become excessive. He is a total nincompoop. You have brought him up as a free spirit. . . .'

Poovamma said, 'Why are you shouting away? You said yourself that he had finished the day's work. You have praised him often for being so skilled at pottery at such a young age. You have rejoiced over his brightness. Is he a bonded servant to stay home after work? Is it wrong for children to run around and play? God has blessed us with a golden child. You are cursing him unjustly.'

'Now I understand. He is a product of your misguided thinking. Women's foolishness. Our family has a long history. We have respect in a hundred towns. Earthen pots and pails made in our workshop are revered as being equal to vessels made of gold and silver. This house supplies the earthenware to the Ballalas of Beedu, the Savanthas of Moolki, the Ajilas of Aladangadi, the Bairas of Karkala and the Jatas of Ullala. That is our heritage. How do you think I got this gold bracelet? It did not come from a goldsmith's shop! It came from King Kadamba of Udyavara. Our clan has great fame. How can hand-craftsmanship prevail if your son runs away so soon after every day's work? Our profession is not easy. It needs constant practice. I checked in our neighbourhood. He is not anywhere. Where is he? At a cockfight? Gambling joint? Liquor shop?'

'What a foul mouth you have! Alas! Why do you speak such ominous words? Do you think your son belongs to such a crowd? Don't you know him? Most probably he has gone to Dharanayya's house. He likes to go there.'

'Why does he go to a Brahmin's house? What business does he have there? Has he been seduced by Brahmin sweets? That Brahmin is clever. He will get his plants watered for free by feeding your son some silly jaggery dish! He may even get his cattle washed. All right. I will have to find a cure for this myself.' Chandrappa reached Dharanendrayya's house, thundering and muttering all the way.

Dharanendrayya's house was a conventional building. Towering walls. Inside, an inner yard and an outer yard. In between, the huge house. A big garden behind the backyard.

The potter swallowed his anger and saluted formally. The Brahmin asked politely, 'Headman potter! What news? Everything all right? What brought you so far?'

'Our son, Eithu, Poovamma thought he might be here. What is that wandering bull doing? Are you getting some free work done by him?'

Dharanayya was provoked for a second, but he controlled his anger soon. He noticed that the potter was indignant and so he spoke patiently with mockingly respectful words: 'Master, please step in. You are most welcome. Come and see for yourself what sort of free work your good son is doing.' He took the potter to the garden past the backyard.

Three boys were sitting there. There was soft sand neatly arranged in front of them. Some palm-leaf books and a carving pen were next to them.

All three children were practising writing with concentration. They did not become aware of Potter Chandrappa's arrival at all. A little distance away, there were four swords and four bows and arrows.

Dharanayya and Chandrappa went back silently. Potter Chandrappa's face showed surprise, fear and agitation.

'Master, what have you done? You have placed me in grave danger. Is it all right to teach language skills and weaponing to the son of a potter? I may be ostracized from my caste. Am I a Brahmin? A Brahmin's profession is fit only for Brahmins.'

Dharanayya said with a smile: 'Master Potter, stop harping on the Brahmin. Who is a Brahmin? Whoever has gained knowledge of the Brahman is the real Brahmin. One who studies the Vedas is the real "*Vipra*". I haven't gained knowledge of the

Brahman, the Creator. I am not truly a Brahmin. You call me a Brahmin. That is your illusion. I read the Vedas now and then. Therefore, it wouldn't be absurd to call me a *"Vipra"* .... The state of a Brahmin or Kshatriya is the product of a human being's self-worth, genius, skills and labour. Krishna; Badarayana; Vyasarishi, the son of a fisherwoman. Sage Valmiki was the son of a hunter.'

'Master Brahmin, you are a scholar, but please don't make me mad by lecturing to me. Keep your mystery to yourself. My family's work is not mean. As leader of the potters, Chandrappa commands respect in this whole province. My son should enhance the fame of our family. My father earned a silver bracelet. I got a gold one. He should earn the privilege of wearing gold inlaid headwear in the midst of ten peers. We don't need your books. We don't need your bows and arrows and swords. Please don't weave your magic spell around my son. You have absolutely no authority over my son.'

'Master, don't be angry. Please listen to me patiently. I will tell you the background to this happening. I should have told you earlier. It is my fault. But I made this mistake thinking that you would not accept it and feel provoked.

'Your son, Eithappa, and my two sons, Sushista and Sumantha, became friends on their own; in a sense, naturally. They met somewhere at a fair or a folk play. Your son, Eithu, is sharp both in play and in study. Always with a pleasant smile! Once one of our calves fell into an abandoned well. When others merely groaned "Rama! Rama!" Eithu descended into the well, made a hundred heroic attempts and saved the calf's life. Another time, when Chikka Ballal's mischievous horse ran amuck, your Eithu, having no experience of horse-riding whatsoever, caught it and brought it under control. When Upadhyaksha's little child fell into the river while playing, everyone just screamed, "Oh, my God!" But your son jumped into the river and swam ashore with the child alive and well. Therefore, my two sons have not only love but tremendous respect for your son. He is a hero to them. A mother's concern for caste is one thing, but curbing the enthusiasm of a child is quite another story. One day, my wife got very angry when these three kids snatched bananas from the garden without permission. I caned the palms of my boys. Then I told your son, "Your father

is a leader. I'll tell him about your mistake. Let him punish you."
Eithappa immediately pushed his palm in front of me and insisted,
"You punished these two. You should punish me too." When he
held out his right palm, my eyes fell on the lines on it accidentally.
I was stunned. I have some knowledge of palmistry. I felt I saw in
Eithappa's palm-lines indications of "Veerasaraswathi Yoga"
and "Rajalakshmi Yoga" in his future. I told you already, I am
not an expert. But I did feel that God had blessed this kid with an
unusually great future. His nature and behaviour are in
consonance with this projected future. Should we ignore an uncut
diamond in a river, accidentally found when bathing? Isn't it
sensible to get it cut and carved systematically and safely into a
gem? Eithappa, just like my children, has shown a rare zeal in
learning language and weaponry. Actually, without taking my
permission, my sons had already taught him enough. I thought
there must be divine will in all this. Time, place and persons have
come together ideally. I have not engineered any of this. If this
young man's future is going to be brilliant, why not contribute my
little share to it? Wouldn't it fulfil my life's purpose too? Becoming
a famous man is an extraordinary event. Helping this process is
not only a great task but a pious one too.'

'Master Brahmin, I am perplexed by your words. My eyes are
blacking out. Isn't it enough for Eithu to be a master potter? Why
should we fall into this mysterious trap of temptation?'

'Master Potter, listen. What if he is to become a leader of
leaders? What if his future holds kingship for him? Are you so
arrogant as to refuse God's gift?'

'Master, don't confound me. Eithu is not a Kshatriya. Nor a
Brahmin. How can he become a king?'

'Master Potter, you don't know history. I know the roots of
royal families. The origins of great rivers are small water-holes:
water that springs from rocks skirting a hill. Do you know the
beginnings of the Shathavahana and Shathakarani royal families?
Do you know the roots of the Chandela clan? I told you earlier. A
sage is not born. Ability, genius, practice, hard work, soul-power
and brain-power are involved in the making of a sage. The same
holds true for a king. Genius, heroism and diligence are all needed
to become a king. Now, a word of wisdom to you: you should tell
none about your son, because if the now-ruling kings, squires and

chieftains were to find out about your son's possible future, your son might become a victim of their jealousy and hate. He might even be sentenced to death. Be careful.'

'Acharya, pardon me. But I am going to speak from the guts. You are a pandit. It's true. But you have subjected my son to great danger. You have committed a sin.'

'Master Potter, danger exists for me too. If kings and their governors come to know about your son, won't they punish me too? Whatever that be, Eithu is your son. I have not a bit of power over him. You think for yourself and decide. I have told you all that I know in detail. The rest is God's will.'

Potter Chandrappa went home with a heavy heart. In the evening, after a ritual bath, he went to the temple and prayed. He sat for a long time with his hands folded in prayer.

Next morning, he went over to Dharanendrayya's house and said: 'Master Brahmin, you are a learned man. I now believe what you are doing is in the interest of my son. How can I say no? Let your wish be carried.'

'Master Potter, no, not my wish! Let God's will come to pass.'

*

Thirty years later, King Adityavarma was sitting on his throne and holding court. Royal Teacher Sushista was seated high up near the king. Prime Minister Sumantha was sitting just beneath the throne. Lieges, small kings, chieftains, a chief justice, a treasurer, commanders, encomiasts, etc were all present. A short distance from the palace the cupolas and spines of the temple of Ghatabhandeshwara, the Lord of Earthenware, shone brightly.

After a few formalities, King Adityavarma asked each one whether he had anything special in his department to report.

Justice Hiranyadama's turn came. Hands folded in respect, he said: 'May Your Highness listen! We have arrested three young fishermen and a Brahmin youth. This Brahmin belongs to an illustrious family. He is renowned as a great scholar. Some people are unhappy over his arrest. A few present at this court have also debated this issue with me.'

'Why? What crimes have these four committed?'

'Your Highness! Listen. We have heard from our spies that

this Brahmin has secretly educated the fishermen in the use of language. The spies also suspect that he has taught them the Gayatri hymn.'

'Language teaching for fishermen? Weapons-training? This is a horrendous crime. I will not tolerate such crimes in my state. All four sinners deserve capital punishment. It is such ambitious heretics who start revolutions and become traitors.'

'Death sentence even for the Brahmin?'

'That Brahmin is the chief protagonist of this crime. But for his ineptitude, there would have been no language or weapon-training for the fishermen. The kingdom itself would be endangered by such evil. I know the nature of such ambitious men. First, language. Then, weapons. Soon after, their eagle eyes covet the throne!'

'But, Your Highness, capital punishment for a Brahmin is forbidden. How can we order it?'

'Make that heretic a non-Brahmin. Force-feed him meat. Push it down his throat. Hold his nose down and make him drink liquor. His Brahmin-ness will be destroyed. Then give him the punishment his crime deserves: the death sentence!'

The royal teacher opened his mouth softly: 'Your Highness, blessed with a long life, don't be hasty! Clamping down capital punishment after a minute's reflection does not become your well-deserved fame.'

'All right. I'll accept the royal teacher's suggestion. I'll announce my decision tomorrow.'

After all the members of the court had left, the king, the royal teacher and the prime minister sat alone.

Prime Minister Sumantha said: 'Your Highness' attention please. Pardon, Your Highness, to this slow-witted slave. The transgression committed by these four doesn't seem to be an unpardonable, heinous crime. If the young fishermen have the potential, why shouldn't they get educated? Education is Kamadhenu, the Plentiful Cow; it is Kalpavriksha, the Tree of Desire. Education can grant fulfilment of desires. But genius is God-given.'

'Minister, I don't want your metaphor-ridden lectures on this case. This is a royal decree.'

Then the royal teacher said gently and with dignity: 'Aditya, it seems you have forgotten. We are childhood friends, playmates and fellow-students. You are not a Kshatriya by birth, you are a potter. Your father was the famous potter, Master Chandrappa. Your real name is Eithappa. You know that your father in his old age, remembering his old profession, got the temple of Ghatabhandeshwara built. A big earthen pot and an earthen water vessel are right in front of the temple's sanctorum. You know this precisely.'

Adityavarma's eyes turned to stone. 'Scholar's son, listen. We were childhood friends, yes. Playmates, yes. Fellow students, yes. But now, I am the king. You are my subject. It is dangerous to say unpleasant things to the face of a king, whether they be truth or falsehood.'

Adityavarma continued: 'Listen with attentive ears. I am a Kshatriya by birth. I belong to the great Chandra (Moon) family line. My Father's name is King Chandravarma. My mother's name is Queen Pushpambe. The founder of my family line is King Chandradityavarma. Sage Kavera offered the sacred water from the Ganga in an earthen pot, and the sacred water from the Kaveri in an earthen water vessel to celebrate the coronation of Chandradityavarma. The same earthen pot and earthen vessel are still found in front of the sanctorum of Ghatabhandeshwara temple. This historical act has been proclaimed throughout the kingdom. This edict has been engraved in stone in the temples and on the ten demarcating pillars of the kingdom's ten provinces. Your father himself composed the hymns for the occasion. Your deceased father, the previous royal teacher, was a dedicated king's man, wise and intelligent. At no time did the irrelevant forgotten words of the long past escape from his mouth.'

The king concluded: 'Listen—death sentence for all those four heretics, traitors. This is a king's order. Pay attention. If a single improper word about that long past, long forgotten matter were to come from your mouths, you too will receive the same punishment. This too is a king's order. This conversation is now over. You may go home.'

—Translated by P. Sreenivasa Rao

The Girl Who Became a Story

Yashwant Chittal

> 'Yet if nothing else, each time a new baby is born there
> is a possibility of reprieve. Each child is a new being, a
> potential prophet, a new spiritual prince, a new spark of
> light, precipitated into the outer darkness. Who are we
> to decide that it is hopeless?'
>
> —*R. D. Laing*
> *Politics of Experience*

Come. Sit down. I shall tell you a story. I don't know why I should.
Maybe because you want to hear it. I begin here only because I
could begin from anywhere.

Thirteen-year-old Janaki passed away—she had blood can-
cer—just after thirteen days in Bombay Hospital. She died very
early one morning when the morning light was yet struggling to
emerge. What bothers me to suffocation is a simple request, as yet
not understood, made by naïve Janaki: '*Anna,* will you write a story
about me?' Why this request of all? Why that very day? Even while
smiling and spreading cheer around, was she aware of something
even the doctor did not know? Even as I think of it now, what I see
before me is her smiling face. Her pearl-like teeth. Her dimpled
cheeks. There was a moist lustre in her eyes when she smiled. Her
soft, pencilled lips had opened just enough to ask the little question
which was nothing but crystallized innocence: 'Will you put me in
your story?' When my eyes widened with surprise, she added, 'I
want Mary in that story and Dr Anand too.' Mary was the nurse
who looked after Janaki. Both the doctor and the nurse had taken
her to heart. Not knowing the end was so near, I had said yes
without thinking. She could come home and tell me what to write.
The story would be published in her name. I must have said that

not really knowing what to say at that moment. Janaki didn't speak again. She smiled very weakly but beautifully. It was only very much later, when I sat actually writing the story, that I realized they were her last words and it was her last smile. The end must have been very sudden, even for the doctor. He seemed to have faith in a new medicine brought from Germany even though it was known that the disease was incurable. He wanted to start using it soon after the clinical tests in progress were over. Despair was written large on his face. When the white cloth was drawn over the innocent peaceful face there were tears even in those eyes which were accustomed to death. Mary and her friends had cried unashamedly. Janaki, who was an intimate part of my existence for thirteen years, had come very close to these people in days. The covered body lay in the shape of a question mark, as if questioning the relevance of everything. Dr Anand had laid his hand on my shoulder and said, 'Be brave. She was a brave girl.' He had walked away as if he didn't want his eyes filled with tears to be seen.

Don't be afraid. I am not going to tell you a story about my Janaki. In the stories you have learnt to admire, I know there is no place for Janaki, or for her death and the courage she had shown in facing it. I haven't forgotten the clever ones who made us wise by teaching us that there is no social relevance in this type of death and this type of sorrow. Why should I be irresponsible enough to write about the death of an innocent Janaki when the valiant call of those who believe in writing with relevance is still ringing in my ears?

But then, if you too had seen Janaki, who would bring to mind the mango tree breaking out red-leafed in spring, the sea dancing with abandon, waves flashing surf in the sun, the quiet liveliness of a rose making a bloom of its inner joy . . .! If you too had heard the questions she had asked the doctor . . .! You are bored, I know. There is no mention of these things in the list provided by the learned. Moreover, I am aware of the philosophical and intellectual concerns that worry the faces of those who set us thinking about big questions. Why should I, then, speak of the questions Janaki asked the doctor about life and death as she lay dying, or of the doctor's exclamation: 'Will these questions ever touch the evil vanity of those who are scared of death but breed death nevertheless?' You don't want all that? You must be scared too. After all it is so much more soothing to our egos to believe in the permanence of what we possess!

That's why I started writing the story keeping in mind these fears and the index provided by the learned. Even before I was aware of it, Janaki had become a slum girl. The story started with the description of slums in Bandra, those on either side of the highway connecting Mahim Causeway to the airport. Just when I was getting thrilled by the way the story was coming to grips with the 'present' and the 'relevant', my hand stopped all of a sudden. Only when the familiar landscape, that appeared and disappeared as images on my retina as I travelled to and from the office everyday, began to take shape in highly poetic prose revealing all its inner tragedy, did I realize the true meaning of what I was engaged in and I was suddenly faced with a question I had hitherto not asked: what is it that I want to achieve from all this? What am I doing by spending nights in using this tragic reality as raw material for a work of art knowing fully well that it would alter nothing? Publication in a well-known magazine, my name in bold print! Credit for pioneering a revolutionary trend in Kannada literature! Praise from the clever ones who sit waiting just for such things, praise for bringing to literature material never before written about, praise for a picturesque, transparent, crystal clear style! Should I really bother about these questions relating to the creative process when no one bothers about more fundamental questions relating to life and death? As if to pacify my uneasy conscience, I decided to dedicate the story to the memory of Marx, M.N. Roy or JP and felt more uneasy by the decision. Why all this flamboyance of self-justification for writing a story to fulfil Janaki's last wish? After all I was writing it for Janaki's sake. Enough of this useless brooding. I shall not think of anything like this again until I finish. . . .

I felt like laughing and crying at the same time the moment I saw Janaki come alive in words. The ridiculous manner in which the poor innocent thirteen-year-old had dressed up just to make her death touching made me terribly sad. For the helpless body that lay on the hospital bed, wrapped in hospital clothes, name was unimportant. Caste, tribe, beliefs—all useless—at least at that moment. Just one intention for coming to hospital: must live! The question 'why live' would not arise. The question 'how to live' was irrelevant to the tender age. God knows how many of the same age had used those clothes. They too must have thought like Janaki that to be alive meant to receive the warmth of love of mother, father, sister, friend, teacher, doctor, nurse. They too must have trembled, imagining the possibility of the known warmth turning into something unknown and ice cold! On this side of this philosophical anxiety to comprehend the meaning of life against the merciless background of death, however, there was petrified terror: a small girl in a torn skirt stood before me, the waist so thin, I thought I could span it with my hand. Dishevelled, matted hair, unwashed for months. . . . Shiny, oily, black face. Sparkling unblinking eyes. A questioning look . . . out of this world. Her parents couldn't be pictured by me no matter how hard I tried. She stood alone before a hut made of rusty metal sheets, torn mats and cardboard.

The sun had set long ago. The stench of Mahim Khadi had filled the air. There was an incessant rush of traffic on the highway. The signal light turned to red and the traffic towards the airport came to a sudden halt. As if waiting for this very moment, two young men drove up and parked their scooter near the huge water pipe that ran along the road. They got down, climbed over the pipe and ran straight down to the hut and stood at the door. The girl stood engrossed in looking seemingly skyward, with just her feet on the ground. Even before she could see the two strangers who suddenly appeared before her, one of them covered her mouth with his hands and she felt faint. As she collapsed someone lifted her off her feet and carried her into the hut. Her hands were tied and so were her eyes and mouth. The torn skirt was pulled off and the legs bared. . . .

'Amma. . . . Janaki. . . .'

'What happened? What's the matter? You've slept off on the chair. Did you dream of Janaki? Come and lie down in bed. You've broken into a sweat.'

I was unable to answer my wife as she dried me with a towel. I myself hadn't realized the full meaning of that experience. It was impossible for me not to believe that Janaki had died just then, just five minutes ago. I shuddered when I remembered how she had died. I saw the pain in my wife's sympathetic eyes and she too remembered the dead child. Then I asked for some coffee. 'Of course, I will make coffee, but what made you so pale?' she asked with make-believe courage, her voice almost breaking into a cry.

My whole being shuddered as the new shape Janaki's death had taken began to take hold of my mind, a shape that would now shake the cramped conscience of those who were prepared to be touched by human suffering only if it came in certain specified forms. The scooter riders had come as if their bestial attack on the helpless body had been planned before. As if that was not enough, they had stabbed the child who had fainted, before getting away. It was then that I had woken up crying out 'Amma', when I saw the child lying in a pool of blood. . . . I couldn't stop trembling even after the coffee. I couldn't face my wife who sat before me anxiously wanting for me to say something. 'Come, it's late. I must have dozed off as I sat writing. . . . I'll tell you in the morning.' I consoled her, stroking her gently. When I lay in bed after switching off the light, I found it impossible to close my eyes. The helpless body kicking out over and over again. . . . I could not erase the image from my mind. I ran to the bathroom afraid that I would be sick. Not wanting my wife to hear anything, I closed the door and vomitted. I felt a little better but it was impossible to sleep. I took out a tablet of Calmpose from the drawer as I did occasionally and swallowed it with water.

It was quite late when I woke up in the morning. I didn't feel like getting up, though. My wife must have been in the kitchen. I could hear the pots and pans. There was a six-storey building coming up at the back. A few workers lived on the ground floor. They must have got up too. Among them was Saraswati who was Janaki's friend. I then realized that Saraswati too had merged with Janaki in the child I had portrayed in the story: in the large eyes made even larger, there was grief filled with unknown fear. What if we adopt Saraswati as a daughter? My hair stood on end as the thought was forming itself in my mind. They were poor all right, but would they give up their child just for that reason? What about getting a child from an orphanage? The house was empty without a child. But the next moment, the thought that this adoption might not be good for the child filled my mind with sadness. The orphan might grow as my daughter no doubt, but would she not have to carry on her forehead the curse of a thousand years' history? I was so agitated that I sat up in bed. I wanted to call my wife from the kitchen, I was that scared. I had planned to write about the rape in the Mahim Khadi slum right after breakfast. But now an altogether new question stared at me. Would the brutal rape and the death of the innocent girl by themselves attain social significance? Would we be moved to tears before knowing the caste, religion, class and the status of the killed and the killers? And if we did get moved, would we not feel that it was just stupidity born of a lack of philosophical and intellectual concern? Then to what caste or religion or class should they belong to make this 'brutality' socially significant? My fingers felt cramped even before I sat down to write. It was then, even while I was losing the very zest to write, that my famous story 'Chasnala' was born, a story which shook you all so profoundly!

Janaki had suddenly been born as the daughter of a coalminer at Chasnala! Chasnala: the whole nation knew of the tragedy through newspapers, which had vied with one another to present the tragedy in pictures across their front pages. The heartbreaking incident of over 300 miners losing their lives in a watery grave. A horrible incident which, most of us accustomed to consuming such news in the morning, had savoured at breakfast. I had forgotten where exactly Chasnala was. Bihar? Orissa? West Bengal? I didn't even know what coalmines looked like. I wanted to look at old editions of *The Times of India*, but then it seemed difficult to look back so many years—I had even forgotten how many. The thought of the slums where the mine labourers lived brought to mind the Bandra slums, which I had earlier described. I decided not to make any changes in my description. The familiar landscape I had described in words in two nights of uninterrupted work had come alive, vividly. I called the very landscape 'Chasnala' and lo, the lustre of relevance it took on! I was amazed at the transformation: details which I had not thought of before just came along naturally.

A mine, disused for many years, had filled up with water. There was digging going on in a mine right next to it. Three-hundred-and-sixty people (figure supplied by a colleague, proud of his extraordinary memory) had gone down the mine as usual. Water was already seeping in from a crack in the wall between the two mines. Even before they could scream for help the wall had collapsed filling their own mine with water and they had all drowned. I was amazed at the way in which the details dovetailed into one another opening up a new meaningful world. Even the icon of death which had inspired the act of creation, crumbled to powder and began to crystallize gradually into a new shape: the evening in Chasnala was similar to the one in Bandra. Could anyone have survived? Could they suddenly come up one by one? Torn by this excruciating anxiety, the whole labour colony had waited near the mines without food and water on that fateful evening. Janaki was alone in the hut. Her mother had gone to the mines with her three children leaving behind a three-month-old baby in Janaki's care. As Janaki stood at the door of the hut desperately waiting for her parents to return, the tragedy from which the story was born struck—the scooter riders had arrived. We know what happened next. The class difference between the raped and the rapists had now become clear.

A disaster unparalleled in the mining history of Chasnala had occurred one evening and simultaneously another tragedy had come into being in words, fulfilling all the conditions set down for it to become a touching story. The dead girl was a miner's daughter. The young beasts that killed her were the sons of mine owners. The death of the young girl had now acquired undisputed social significance and would make anyone weep.

At last my sweet Janaki had become a story—'Chasnala'!

I didn't even know what I had written. I only knew I had to send it off for publication before losing the courage to do so. I didn't even read it again before sending it off. How well it was written, I came to know only when I got a commending letter from the editor. Later, one morning, three of my long lost friends rushed into the house excitedly waving the magazine in which the story was printed. On entering, they embraced me one by one. 'Congratulations. A tremendous story. We must celebrate this big event and we have brought the stuff. . . .' So saying, they showed me the bag they had brought with them. The clinking as the bag was lifted announced the presence of beer bottles inside. Janaki had died just three months ago. The sense of loss was still all-pervading. None of them seemed to know about her death. I didn't feel like telling them now. One of them went straight to the kitchen after leaving the bottles on the table. Not finding my wife there, he called out in the usual familiar tone, 'Vahini, where are you?' There was movement in the bedroom. She must have been resting after cooking. She came out, not wanting to dampen their spirits by showing her inner turmoil. Eagerly they announced the reason for their coming. They wanted something to eat with the beer. Since they had come without prior intimation they would not press for a meal. My wife went into the kitchen promising to fry *pakodas* for them. 'Great,' they said and turned to the beer. 'Vahini, we want four glasses.' They had included me in the beer drinking. I went into the kitchen and brought out three glasses. 'I don't think you know about my health,' I said. 'I'm under medical observation. There might even be an ECG, if necessary. You please carry on. I will enjoy myself vicariously.' The mention of an ECG raised their eyebrows. 'Don't tell me'; 'hope nothing serious'; 'you worry too much'—the glasses were filled as they exclaimed.

'Cheers,' they said and the talk turned to literature and by the time my wife brought the *pakodas,* it had come to my story.

'Well, well . . . at last you've written a story that will open up a new trail. There is death in this story as in your other stories. But it is meaningful here because it is born out of a concrete, social situation; it is not there just to shock.'

'This story doesn't stand apart only for its artistic tidiness. The misery of the labourers, the inhuman dealings of the mine owners—the description is unique . . . significant.'

'Particularly the description of the inundated mine, the terrible helplessness of those caught inside—struggling, dying of suffocation. Even as you think of it, you feel breathless, choked. . . .'

'And that is the difference between journalism and creative literature. I just can't imagine how you could conceive this story at all.'

'As far as I'm concerned, the peak of artistic achievement in the story is the rape of the little child. It is frightening. Only a genius could have achieved it. This is not just lip service. You've accomplished something great again.'

The beer was being consumed at the same speed as their talk. I was so disgusted at the smell of beer that I swore I would never touch it again. I prayed that my wife would not hear their lively talk. She knew I had written about Janaki. But she did not know what I had written, for I hadn't read the story to her. My friends' words seemed so ready-made that the story itself seemed superfluous. Their eager, inebriated talk, the cleverness of one word giving birth to another, the way they relished the sweet sobriety of their own voices—I felt disgusted at my story for the first time. They all knew Janaki. Running around in the house, smiling, her teeth shining, dimples in her cheeks, she was a friend to all. Maybe they thought she wasn't at home or they didn't remember her at all in the midst of their talk, nobody enquired about her. No one came to know of her death. I somehow felt that my child was dying now, for the first time. My stomach turned when I remembered the last day and the last night at the hospital. The voices of the 'significance seekers' and their mechanical words became meaningless noise and started scaring me. '*Anna*, will you put me in your story?' A small question without any special significance had been stifled into non-existence and along with it the moist lustre of the eyes, the innocent smile on the lips when the question was asked. . . .

As the bottles were emptied, the conversation also lagged. Politics flowing from Karl Marx to Jayaprakash Narayan, Ram Manohar Lohia to Sanjay Gandhi, traversing across Africa, Israel, Egypt, America, Cuba . . . The talk was now sharpening its beak on the whetstone of relevance and shining meaningfully: it was challenging literature to show its ability to capture the shine.

'Vahini, we're leaving now.' 'Next time we come, we must have your patent chicken biryani. . . .' 'You never came out today. . . . The *pakodas* were excellent.' 'Make this fool write ten more stories like this. We'll bring out a collection. . . . Kannada literature. . . .' They had got off the front steps before finishing the sentence. After closing the door behind them, I came in and sank into a chair. I didn't have the courage to face my wife in the bedroom. It was past one o' clock. I was very hungry. . . . I was overcome by feeling. 'My Janaki died this morning. My three friends who came to the crematorium have just left. . . .' When I couldn't get rid of this feeling, tears which hadn't flown all these days rushed out and I wept like a child. I don't know how long I sat like that. When I heard the bedroom door open, I jumped up and I rushed to the bathroom and washed my face.

When I came out, I was stunned at the sight of my wife. She had turned pale, as if from a bad dream. She staggered straight on to me like a sleepwalker. 'You said you'd written a story about our child. How is it that none of your friends even remembered her, or, is it the way they are? I don't know how you portrayed your child's death that they could drink beer, eat *pakodas* and feel happy. To hell with your writing . . . burn it; don't you ever write another story. Swear on the child's name . . .' She collapsed on the chair, teeth chattering as if in an epileptic fit. The doctor had to be sent for because her limbs went stiff. 'She is terribly angry with someone. Don't say anything that will excite her.' He gave her an injection and a tablet which looked like a tranquillizer to be taken at bedtime. . . .

As I lay beside my drugged wife at night, I began to remember what had happened that afternoon. I remembered her wrath which stopped her speech before it struck me. What had livened up my description of the choking, struggling dying miners was my own feeling of suffocation at my inability to write directly about Janaki. The mine in Chasnala came into being when I visualized the clever people who had made writing impossible for me, as also the long water pipe which ran along the Bandra highway. I sat up alarmed when another thought came to me: Janaki's strange request at the last moment—was it the result of a desire to live on in our memory? Was the child afraid we would forget her?

As I sat in bed, I put my hands together and prayed as never before: God, give us all food, clothes, shelter, education, wisdom and jobs. Let a happy society without castes and classes and without exploitation of any kind be born. In it, let there be people, too, who will write a story about our little Janaki and people who will read it with love.

Our Janaki who used to call me her father, '*Anna*,' smiled sweetly in my dream that night, for the first time. Even as I woke up, my mind was enveloped in a feeling of warmth, amazed at its own being, wanting to trace its own source—her smile was so sweet. My wife was not in bed; must be in the kitchen. All that had happened yesterday came to mind and I became aware of my mind making a big decision. I suspected this was what had spurred me on to write the story, to prepare me for this decision. I sprang up and without even washing my face rushed into the kitchen to look for my wife. . . . The moment I saw her, I blurted out: 'You had mentioned this once before and I am ready for it now. Let's have breakfast and go.' My wife stared at me not comprehending my childlike prattle. I just went off to wash not bothering to satisfy her curiosity. 'Let's go to the orphanage and bring home a child,' I said as I sat for breakfast. I couldn't say any more. There was a lump in my throat. I just sat and looked at her. The same thought must have been in her mind too. Her gentle smile said yes. Neither of us spoke as we went towards Parel in a taxi. My wife had suggested it ten years ago when Janaki was just three. I had an operation since the doctor had said that she shouldn't have any more babies. She wanted a boy in the family. But then, I wasn't brave enough to agree to this suggestion born from her maternal instinct. I did not want the adopted child to become another link in the three-thousand-year rusty chain. The very thought of its prospective suffering scared me into saying no then. I didn't feel like hesitating now. If a child came into our home as a result of a spontaneous action and suffered only because it grew up as our child, there was no need to be afraid. The human spirit has the courage to fight any injustice and hold its head high even in the most difficult circumstances.

As the taxi reached Shivaji Park I was pondering over how to tell my wife that I wanted a baby girl. Just then she herself asked me, 'Are we bringing home a girl or a boy? You haven't told me.' I was flabbergasted. My wife didn't notice it. 'Let's bring a girl home and call her Janaki,' she said without looking at me. I suspected there were tears in her eyes.

In the end, we did bring home a baby girl. A six-day-old life, a small bundle wrapped in white, lay on my wife's lap on the way back in the taxi; the picture is still fresh in my mind. I still remember what the old nurse who made us take that particular child had said: 'You are a Godsend. Look at this innocent bundle of life. Someone had left it by the water pipe near the Mahim Khadi slums. We cannot look after so tender an infant here. Maybe it'll die. Take it home and give it life. God willing it will grow up to be great.' These words could have been said by force of habit to everyone who came to the ashram. But they shook us completely. At that moment at least I was not in a state to notice the coincidence that the Mahim Khadi in my story had got entangled with a real event in my life.

Janaki is a year old. Next Sunday is her birthday. Dr Anand and nurse Mary have very happily agreed to come over. You come too and see the lively little being that brought us both back to life. Wanting to sit up from where she is lying down, wanting to stand up from where she sits, her tiny hands reaching out to the four corners and wanting to hold them–come and listen to her joyful shouts. . . . I had also asked the three clever people who had praised my 'Chasnala' to the skies. But you won't see them. They got out of it on some pretext. They were very angry because I haven't written any more stories. When I telephoned, one of them, admiring the irony in his own voice, had said, 'Please accept greeting number twenty-one' instead of, 'Wishing the function every success.' He was supposed to be on night shift that day. The other two had to see Tendulkar's *Ghasiram Kotwal* that very evening. They had seen the play before. But Tendulkar had admired a critical paper they had presented in a seminar. It had shown the social significance of the play and the wonderful way in which a theme from the womb of history had thrown new light on the present and become meaningful to contemporaries when dramatized. He had sent them two complimentary passes for a new production of the play. They were very excited. 'Tell you what,' they said as if they didn't realize I was disappointed, 'make this new experience into a story. It'll be a wonderful sequel to "Chasnala". Then we'll come.'

But you mustn't stay away. You can see the sequel to my 'Chasnala' smiling in our cradle. Our house is small. That doesn't matter. You know the post office on Linking Road in Santa Cruz? Right next to it there is an old two-storeyed house. We live on the ground floor. Anyone will direct you if you ask for the insurance agent's house. There are trees in front—drumstick, banana, custard apple. In the veranda there are two flower pots, roses planted by Janaki herself. But enough of this. Just step into the courtyard. You can hear our Janaki's shouts of delight, coming from her cradle. Do come.

—*Translated by Padma Ramchandra Sharma*

Bharamya Becomes Nikhil

Shantinath Desai

That was the time when Dadasaheb Patil had always had some servant or the other to do all the chores at home. Dadasaheb and his wife, Padmavati, had absolutely no problem with servants for the simple reason that Kademani Nagappa, cultivated his sons, one or the other, to do the chores. As long as there was one boy or the other, Kallappa or Mallappa, aged about thirteen or fourteen, always at their beck and call, they had nothing to worry about. When summoned, the boy—Kallappa or Mallappa—would appear from nowhere, saying, 'I'm coming, sir,' or 'Coming, madam,' and if he happened to go wrong by any chance, he would be ready to get a beating from his master and fall at his feet saying, 'Sorry, sir, I made a mistake. Please forgive me for once, I'll never make such a mistake again.'

Their son, Nikhil (Padmavati had got the name from one of the Bengali novels she used to read on the sly, without letting her husband know anything about her passion for stories, or else how could the name 'Nikhil' get into the family tree of the Patils?), enjoyed himself at home by making either Kallya or Mallya do all his work: 'Eh, Kallya, get me my satchel of books . . . go and get my shirts and trousers from Krishna, that good-for-nothing tailor, immediately. Look sharp, go. . . . ' 'Eh, Mallya, who has taken the rupee from my pocket? Bastard, give it back to me immediately or else I'll tell Father and get him to peel your bums.' 'What? What do you mean, son of a bitch, by putting such a hot cup of milk in my hands? Burning hot. If my hand gets burnt, I'll take your leg off and put it your hand!' Nikhil, always sadistic towards Kallya or Mallya, loved shouting at the top of his voice. If, by any chance, his Raleigh cycle did not shine bright and beautiful, he would pounce upon one of the boys and pound him on the back till it shone with red swellings. Nikhil grew up like this, happy and carefree, and pursued, willy nilly, his educational career in the high school.

By 1940, before the Second World War affected India even distantly, Kademani Nagappa died of typhoid. Kallappa, who was then nineteen or twenty, started cultivating the Motikere land with the help of his widowed mother, Ningi. Mallappa ran away to Hubli and took up a job in some Shetji's shop. It was then that Dadasaheb, Padmavati and Nikhil encountered a real problem. For a while, Gouri, the fifteen- or sixteen-year-old daughter of Nagappa, younger than Kallappa but older than Mallappa, was brought to do the daily chores. But in that huge house of Dadasaheb Patil's—an ancient giant house with many dark and semi-dark corners—poor Gouri got totally perplexed. Seems that Nikhil, by then sixteen or seventeen, stood hiding behind a door and frightened her out of her wits. Gouri ran out screaming madly and sat weeping and sobbing. Padmavati, and the neighbour Seetakka, did their best to pacify her and squeeze the truth out of her. But Gouri kept totally mum and didn't answer any of their persistent questions. The next day Ningi, Gouri's mother, came, wept at the sight of Gouri who was sitting all the time in the butter-milk room, as though possessed by a spirit, and took her home.

How could Dadasaheb's house remain without a servant even for a day? Dadasaheb summoned Kallappa to come and ordered him: 'Kallya, go and get someone to do the routine chores on your behalf. Or else, I'll snatch the land from you, or, at least I'll see that you get a smaller portion of the yield than what you do now. I'll keep four or five extra bags of rice for myself. Go, do as I have told you. Look sharp.' Kallappa folded his hands and said, 'Sir, my lord, I'll certainly fetch someone. Please don't have any worry, sir.' 'Kallappa,' said Padmavati with tender sympathy, 'poor Mallya must be awfully miserable in that evil city of Hubli. It is your duty, you know, as an elder brother to fetch him back and put him on the right path, I wonder what he lacked here, poor boy, and why he had to go away.' 'No, madam, they say he is quite happy there,' said Kallappa with brotherly pride and overflowing enthusiasm. 'They say he will never return to our place now. He will get into business, they say, and make pots of money. He might even build a bungalow, they say.' Dadasaheb could not control his anger, 'How did you lose your control over Mallya? How did you allow him to go away like this?' he roared. 'Now, you go yourself to Hubli and fetch him here. Or else give up our land. You are getting sullen in the head. He is going, is he, to build a bungalow in Hubli?' 'No, sir, I shall get someone to work for you,' said Kallappa with tears in his eyes. 'If Father were alive we wouldn't be in such a mess. You are our father and lord. If only it were possible for me to do the work in the field as well as in the house.' Dadasaheb looked at him sternly and said in a serious tone, 'I am not going to listen to all this nonsense. You must come here yourself, and do the household chores until you get us somebody. Do you think, you son of an ass, that I should do the housework?'

Kallappa started working in Dadasaheb's house for two hours in the morning and two hours in the evening. Poor Nikhilkumar was greatly disturbed since he had to do most of his work himself: he had to clean his own bike; he had to go himself and get his clothes from the washerman. Once his mother said in as gentle a tone as possible, 'Nikhil darling, Kallappa hasn't yet come. You see, there are absolutely no vegetables at home. Could you please go on your bike to the market and bring some vegetables? And, while returning, could you please drop in at the doctor's and get medicine for my stomach-ache? The doctor knows about the kind of stomach-ache I have. . . . ' Nikhil was beyond himself with rage. 'Go, go, what do you think I am,' he thundered. The same evening Dadasaheb asked, 'Will you please go and get me a packet of Capstan, Nikhil?' and gave him a fiver. Nikhil took the fiver, rode to the market on the bike, bought four packs and returned in a jiffy. Handing over two packs to his father, he went up to his room and kept the other two packs and the remaining rupee in his sports jacket.

At last, when Kallappa brought his maternal uncle's son, Bharamya, to work at Dadasaheb's house, everyone was extremely happy.

Bharamya was, in a way, a very smart boy. Sixteen or seventeen years of age, wheat-coloured; the boy was not exactly handsome, but his energy-filled body, his small sharp eyes, his lips curved in mischief, lent him a special charm. Dressed in a pair of trousers, and a shirt, he carried on the tip of his nose city glamour and city pride. In Londa, he had done his first year in a high school—what we call the fifth standard now—and therefore knew a bit of English, all the alphabets and some words. He had also learnt the skill of making some money at the Londa junction by helping the Goan passengers to get seats in the Bangalore–Poona express trains. He knew the taste of feni from bottles kept in the baskets of the Goans, as well as the taste of the thrown-away butts of foreign cigarettes.

Bangarappa, Bharamya's father, was keen on marrying his daughter Chandri to Kallappa, who was now a tenant with a future; he was hard-working and capable of feeding his wife and children. He journeyed, therefore, to Kallappa's place and made the proposal of marriage. Kallappa was not to be so easily won over. Clever as he was, he asked him, 'First, send Bharamya to work at my master's. I'll think of marriage later.' Bharamya, who loved his sister Chandri very much, agreed to come and work in Dadasaheb's house.

Bharamya was extremely happy for the first seven or eight days. Everyone pampered him. Padmavati gave him Nikhil's old, but still usable, trousers and shirts. She sent him to the market often with a view to satisfying his roving impulse. If he spent a few annas more than she had expected, she didn't ask him about it, thinking that the poor chap must have had a cup of tea or something. Dadasaheb asked him to sleep not on the open space in the outer hall but in the butter-milk room near the kitchen, and gave him an old, slightly tattered mattress. Nikhilkumar, too, was a little more careful than what he used to be, and gave Bharamya fewer chores than he had given Kallappa and Mallappa earlier. He himself continued to clean, for instance, his Raleigh bicycle before he went out. . . .

Bharamya's wistful eye, fell, slowly and steadily, on the Raleigh bicycle. One day, soon after he got up in the morning, he cleaned the bike with a lot of water and rubbed it with a piece of cloth till it shone, bright and beautiful. The keen interest that flashed from his small sharp eyes caught Padmavati's attention.

'Bharama, do you know cycling?' she asked. Right from the day he came, she always called him 'Bharama' and not 'Bharamya' in order to keep him pleased.

'Cycling? Of course, I know cycling,' he said. I learnt it when I was little. Vahini, may I take it out whenever I go to the market?'

'Nikhil loves his cycle as if it is his own life. He doesn't, therefore, allow anybody to touch it. But do clean it everyday the way you have done today. . . . '

'Vahini, I know everything about cycle repairs.'

'Whatever it is, please don't ask Nikhil for his bike—at least for the time being. Do you understand, Bharama? What is the use of your asking and his refusing and getting angry? Why create any trouble at all?'

'Don't you worry, Vahini, I shall not ask . . . ,' said Bharamya, pouting his lips a little.

'Bharama, why don't you call me "madam" or "mamma"? Why do you call me "Vahini"?'

'They say "Vahini" in Londa or Belgaum, and it sounds very modern, doesn't it?' Bharamya laughed.

Seven or eight days later— no one knows what spell Bharamya cast on Dadasaheb— Dadasaheb called Bharamya in the presence of Nikhil and said, 'Bharama, take the cycle and go and ask Katti teacher to come as soon as possible. On your way back, fetch two packs of Capstan cigarettes.' Soon he turned towards Nikhil and said, 'Nikhil, this is your second year in the matriculation class. Don't you think you must pass the exam this year? Or else, how will you go to college? That is why I have asked Katti teacher to come.' Suddenly punctured, Nikhil didn't say a word and placed the cycle key in the hands of Bharamya. From that day Bharamya started using the bike for all the home chores.

A few months went by and Bharamya started growing a little jealous of Nikhil. He thought: what is the difference between Nikhil and him? Why should he lie sleepless on a tattered mattress in the butter-milk room, and why should Nikhil roll about like a prince on a soft mattress spread on a spring-cot which often made a sweet creaking sound? If he were educated, he could have passed the matriculation, the intermediate, the B.A. and what-not and become a big officer, a saheb. This dull Nikhil can't even pass the matric, but he is so stuck up he acts as though he was born into the family of Jawaharlal Nehru and has gone round the entire universe; does he think that his Raleigh bike is a Blue Bird racing car or what?

'Bharamya,' Nikhil shouted, 'go quickly and get my clothes from the laundry. I have to go and watch the badminton matches.

Look sharp and run and come back quickly with my clothes.'

Bharamya stopped where he was. 'Don't call me "Bharamya", Nikhil saheb, call me "Bharama". Both the big saheb and Vahini always call me "Bharama".' Bharamya's voice was thick and serious.

'What if you are called "Bharamya"? Does it bore holes in your body, you rascal?' said Nikhil sharply. 'You ask me not to call you "Bharama", you, son of a bitch? Then should I address you as "Mr Brahmakumar"?'

'Don't you call me "son of a bitch", said Bharamya. 'If you want, call me "Bharamya". And remember, "Brahmakumar" is not my name. My name is Bharama.'

'You conceited fellow, if you are so proud of yourself. . . . '

'You shouldn't stay as a servant in others' houses—that's what you mean, don't you? I am willing to go, you see. Ask your mother, and if she wants me to go, I'll certainly scoot. I can get any number of jobs, you know,' Bharamya said, keeping his anger under control.

'You are here to do us a favour or what?'

'I haven't come here to do a favour for you or anybody else. And you haven't kept me here to do a favour for me. You have a need, and I have a need. I work and you feed me and pay me my wages. But you don't have the right to insult me. . . . '

'What do you mean by "insult", you son of a bitch?'

'If you call me "son of a bitch", you are insulting my mother, you are abusing her. Beware, if you call me that, I may be forced to call you that also. I am just warning you.'

'Look, control your tongue. Or else I'll kill you, I will.' Actually Nikhil's anger was ebbing.

'Go ahead, kill me,' said Bharamya and stood before him his neck thrown back, 'come, take a knife . . . should I go and bring the knife myself? Go ahead and chop off my head.'

'Don't play the fool with me, Bharamya. Go, take the cycle and go—and bring me a pack of Capstan, will you?'

'Give me the money, please,' said Bharamya who, too, had cooled down.

'Hope you haven't told anyone that I smoke and all that.'

'How can I tell that, sir? I, too, smoke, you see—mostly beedis. If I get a cigarette, I smoke a cigarette.'

Both stared at each other, hard and long. Each knew that a war was on between them.

Now Nikhil had great difficulty in protecting his Raleigh cycle and Capstan packs. It became quite a job for him. If Nikhil went out to play football, Bharamya would take the cycle out for a ride in the town under the pretext of some housework or the other. These were the days of the Second World War—one had to queue up for everything, for kerosene, rice, jawar, wheat and so on. There was no dearth of chores for Bharamya. Nikhil lost patience and shouted at his mother, but that didn't diminish Bharamya's power. There seemed to be some understanding—a treaty, between his mother and Bharamya.

'Nikhil, what's wrong in his using your cycle for an hour or so?' asked his mother. 'And that too for household chores? You shouldn't behave like a small child now. You see, times have changed—and we'll have to leave the bicycles for servants. Do you know that your father has secured the agency of Vimco matchboxes? It won't be long before we have plenty of money to play with, and soon we'll have a car.' Padmavati knew how to work upon her son's mind.

'Car! Great.' Nikhil's mouth watered. 'But then, will you make Bharamya a driver?'

'What's wrong with that? I don't think you will be that—a driver?'

In the course of time a second hand Ford arrived from Belgaum. It brought with it a Muslim driver named Kasim, who, during the five or six months that he stayed with Dadasaheb, taught Bharamya a bit of driving, and a bit of car-repairing. Once he went back to Belgaum promising to return in seven or eight day's time, and never returned. On enquiring it was learnt that he had joined the military as a driver, driving huge trucks and jeeps. . . . Bharamya, inevitably, became Dadasaheb's driver. . . .

The winds of Gandhiji's satyagraha had started blowing intensely everywhere, and our small town, too, woke up to the call of the nation. Dadasaheb put on the Gandhi cap. Bharamya, donning a Gandhi cap, started participating in the *prabhat-pheris*. Nikhil did not wear the Gandhi cap, but he decorated his first-floor bedroom with the pictures of Gandhi, Nehru and Subhash Chandra Bose. Bharamya kept in the niche of the wall of his butter-milk room a small picture of Bhagat Singh, whose hat and pointed moustaches were his new sources of inspiration. . . .

As the position of Bharamya became stronger and firmer in Dadasaheb's house, there was a change in the style of his behaviour. He grew his hair long, like Nikhil did, parted it in the middle and kept it well combed. He washed his two pairs of trousers and shirts, white and bright, in Tinopal, and whenever he went upstairs to iron them, he slipped into Nikhil's room to powder his face and sprinkle rose water all over his clothes. Whenever he went out on the bike, he took out his red silk scarf—he had borrowed it from Kallappa, who, when he had gone to Hubli, had pinched it from Mallappa—and tied it round his neck. He fished out some old shoes of Dadasaheb's, got them repaired and polished, put them on and strutted out with increasing self-confidence. Whenever Nikhil went out for a long time, he would slip up to his room and roll about on his bed and listen to the creaking of the spring cot. He would lie down, pick up the magazines and comics from the teapoy and enjoy looking at the pictures. Even a little sound—say, of a cat walking—would make him jump up and rush to the window, where he would pretend to do some cleaning work. He would take out the cigarettes from Nikhil's sports jacket and stand smoking in front of the mirror. Sometimes he would put on the jacket, tie the tie round his neck and speak to the reflection in the mirror: 'Hello, Nikhil, good-morning!' and play-act a handshake. In all his daydreams Bharamya became Nikhilkumar, at least half of Nikhil.

Padmavati was always pleased with Bharamya, who knew well where the key to the happiness of Dadasaheb's house lay. He did all her chores with implicit obedience; he supplied her with all the gossip of the town; he drove her in the car to her relatives' places whenever she wanted . . . and so on. Bharamya's smiling willingness kept her always happy. To keep Dadasaheb pleased was quite easy: get him a pack of Capstan whenever he asked for it, massage him with oil everyday and arrange for a hot water bath, sometimes get a bottle of whisky from Rustumji's shop with the utmost secrecy, take him in the car to whatever place he wished to visit and wait for him in the car for any length of time. Bharamya didn't find the work heavy at all. . . .

Bharamya was bored with the daydreams which filled his

butter-milk room. He wondered sometimes about the extent of power he had in Dadasaheb's house, and he often felt like testing it, though he knew that it was rather strange and odd to do so. For instance, he once broke four or five spokes of Nikhil's cycle and took it to the repair shop where he kept it for six of seven days, and, whenever he wanted, used it with a sense of possession. Once he removed a nut from the car's engine and told Dadasaheb that the car was out of order. Dadasaheb, who had to go to Belgaum that day, went by bus. An hour after he left, Bharamya repaired the car and took Padmavati around the town for visits to relatives. The moment he returned home, Nikhil, who was by now an accomplished driver, drove away in the car. . . . As Bharamya became increasingly aware of his strength and power, he also became aware of his weaknesses and limitations, of his essential status of the 'dalit', of the oppressed and exploited. Bharamya was consumed with an intense feeling of jealousy towards Nikhil, sometimes his jealousy flared up into hatred. Bharamya had often hit in anger the ancient walls of the butter-milk room and peeled off the plaster, taking care, of course, to throw away the mess in the gutter outside.

Nikhil was as usual flirting with a pretty girl in his class. Her name was Shalini Gotekar. She was the daughter of a cook whom the Deshpandes had brought from Goa, and she was a little free with the boys. Nikhil was the only one who succeeded in the competition to win her attention. True, Nikhil had attained mastery over the art of flirting and its techniques—like, say, meeting her by chance near the Hanuman temple, talking to her suggestively and making her laugh, lending her books and guides though she hadn't asked for them—but his main attraction was his car. He would take Shalini and her friends for car rides, sometimes even up to Dharwad, at least once a week. Nikhil was such a central figure during picnics and social gatherings that things wouldn't move without him in the school. Though Nikhil's friendship with Shalini was still on a platonic level, people had already started making stories about it. A story doing the rounds was that Nikhil took her on his Raleigh cycle to Ramanagudda on a Sunday; they also had a story about how Shalini slipped into Nikhil's house by the backdoor early one morning and spent two or three hours with him before returning though a small lane behind the Hanuman temple.... People asked Bharamya about the truth of such stories. His hatred for Nikhil flared up and he added a dimension to their imagination. 'Yes, it is I who open the backdoor everyday,' he said. 'It is I who take them in the car.' And so on. In this way Bharamya's imagination caught fire.... The result was he started hating his butter-milk room, which now looked to him extremely ugly and disgusting. In fact, he was disgusted with his own life—two trousers, three shirts, of all Nikhil's old clothes, a foul-smelling bedsheet, a chuddar with multiple holes, a razor with rusted blades. He was fed up with the entire world.

One day Dadasaheb was to go to Dharwad with his family to attend the wedding of the fourth daughter of his brother-in-law. Since Nikhil was going with him, there was no need for Bharamya to go with them as a driver, and it was necessary that somebody stayed behind to look after the house. Dadasaheb gave proper orders to all members of the family and went out for his morning walk. Before he returned from his walk, Bharamya had taken off the fanbelt of the engine and replaced it with an old, dilapidated one. Just when they were about to leave, Bharamya lifted the bonnet and said, 'Saheb, the fan belt is broken, sir.' He looked at Dadasaheb's face and Nikhil's alternately with profound seriousness. 'Don't you worry,' he said. 'I'll go to Badekhan's garage and see whether I can get a new fan belt.' He zoomed out on the Raleigh, took a long round through the town and returned after a while, saying, 'Sorry, sir, the belt isn't available.' Dadasaheb exploded with anger and called Nikhil a fool. Nikhil threatened that he wouldn't go with them to the wedding. In the end father, son and mother went to Dharwad by bus. No sooner did they get on the bus than Bharamya returned home, put the original fan belt into the engine, drove the car to Kallappa's cottage, put the entire family into it and went on a trip to Marewwa's Temple on the hill. On their way back they had tiffin in the railway canteen at Alnavar, and by the time Bharamya was home after leaving Kallappa and family at their cottage, it was three o'clock in the afternoon. He closed the outer door of that giant house and went upstairs. Since he was very tired, the moment he lay down on Nikhil's bed he went to sleep. When he woke up there was a sort of queer restlessness in his mind, and for a moment he felt like hanging himself. Frightened by his own wish, he got out of the house, locked it and went for another drive in the car.

On the way he met Shalini who was hurrying home after a visit to her friend, Manda.

'Shalinitai!' Bharamya said as he stopped the car.

'Yes?'

'Nikhil saheb has asked me to fetch you home,' Bharamya almost stuttered. 'There's a party or something. . . . Come, I'll leave you back in half-an-hour's time.'

'But I must tell my mother.'

'Don't you worry. . . . It's just for a short while.' Shalini sat mesmerized in the back seat of the car.

As Bharamya led her upstairs, Shalini realized that there was no one in the entire house besides Bharamya. She screamed with all the strength in her body, which was already in the tight grip of Bharamya's hands.

'Please, Bharama, leave me. . . . Take my gold chain and gold bangles if you like, leave me . . . ,' she started weeping.

'You wouldn't have minded if I were Nikhil, would you?'

'No, no, I am not that kind of girl. Please leave me alone.'

'How many times have you gone with Nikhil.'

'Alone? Never! Please, leave me, reach me home,' Shalini begged piteously.

Bharamya was totally confused. 'Get thee gone, bitch,' he shouted. 'Who am I, after all? I am not Nikhil, am I?' He didn't know how Shalini slipped down the stairs and got out of the house, but he realized that she had disappeared. He rushed up the stairs again and sank into Nikhil's bed.

When he woke up in the morning and went down, he heard noises outside the front door. With trembling hands he opened it and saw Kallappa and Chandri sitting on the stone platform.

'Bharamya, are you mad or something? We have been knocking on the door for a long time. . . . Is this the way to sleep?' Kallappa thundered at Bharamya.

'Please sit inside, Uncle,' said Bharamya. I'll go to the bathroom and will be back in a minute.

Bharamya went inside, rushed to the backdoor which was still half open, went out and sat in the car. He drove like mad in the direction of Belgaum. By the time he reached Khanapur, the petrol in the car was exhausted. He left the car by the side of a road and caught a bus to Belgaum. As soon as he got off the bus, he took a tonga, went straight to the camp and asked for the Recruiting Office.

'I want to join the military,' he told the jawan at the office gate.

He stood in a long queue and waited for his turn. When he found himself in front of an officer, he blurted out, 'Please let me join the army,' and fell down unconscious.

A jawan got some water and poured it on his head. 'Come, get up, drink this water,' he said.

The officer-in-charge shouted, 'Get up, you rascal, stand up—straight!'

Bharamya stood up, straight-backed.

'Salute!' shouted the officer.

'What's your name, you son of a bitch?' the officer asked.

'My name . . . my name is . . . Nikhil Patil.' Bharamya's head reeled. . . .

In his mind he was flying high above in the sky in a military aeroplane. When he looked down at the ground, he saw Dadasaheb's house—old, huge and solid. No sooner did he catch sight of the house, than he aimed at it and flung the bomb which he had kept ready in his hand. He peered down: in the house that lay in shambles, there were two people sitting still—Kallappa and Chandri!

—Translated by the Author

Annayya's Anthropology

A. K. Ramanujan

Annayya couldn't help but marvel at the American anthropologist. 'Look at this Fergusson,' he thought, 'he has not only read Manu, our ancient law-giver, but knows all about our ritual pollutions. Here I am, a Brahmin myself, yet I don't know a thing about such things.'

You want self-knowledge? You should come to America. Just as the Mahatma had to go to jail and sit behind bars to write his autobiography. Or as Nehru had to go to England to discover India. Things are clear only when looked at from a distance.

> Oily exudations, semen, blood, the fatty substance of the brain, urine, faeces, the mucus of the nose, ear wax, phlegm, tears, the rheum of the eyes, and sweat are the twelve impurities of human bodies.

(Manu 5.135)

He counted. Though he had been living in Chicago for years, he still counted in Kannada. One, two, three, four, five, six, seven, eight, nine, ten, eleven . . . eleven . . . eleven. . . . At first, he could count only eleven body-wastes. When he counted again, he could count twelve. Yes, exactly twelve. Of these twelve, he already knew about spittle, urine and faeces. He had been told as a child not to spit, to clean himself after a bowel movement and after urinating. Whenever his aunt went to the outhouse, she took with her a handful of clay. She cleaned herself with a pinch of clay. As long as she lived, there used to be a clay pit in the backyard.

In the southern regions of the country, wind instruments like the *nagaswara* were considered unclean because they came in contact with the player's spittle. And so, only Untouchables could touch or play them. Thus, the *vina*, the stringed instrument, was for the Brahmins; and the rest, the wind instruments, were for the low castes.

Silverware is cleaner than earthenware; silk is purer than cotton. The reason was that they are not easily tainted by the twelve kinds of body-wastes. Silk, which is the bodily secretion of the silkworm, is nonetheless pure for human beings. Think of that!

What a lot of things these Americans know! Whether it means wearing out the steps of libraries or sitting at the feet of saucy pundits or blowing the dust off old palm-leaf manuscripts, they spare no effort in collecting their materials and distilling the essence of scholarship. Annayya found all this amazing. Simply amazing!

If you want to learn things about India, you should come to places like Philadelphia, Berkeley, Chicago. Where in India do we have such dedication to learning? Even Swami Vivekananda came to Chicago, didn't he? And it is here that he made his first speech on our religion.

> Of the three kinds of bodily functions that bring impurity, the first one is menstruation. Parturition/childbirth causes a higher degree of impurity. The highest and the most severe impurity is, of course, on account of death. Even the slightest contact with death will bring some impurity. Even if the smoke from a cremation fire touches a Brahmin, he has to take a bath and purify himself. No one, except the lowest cast *holeya*, can wear the clothes removed from the dead body.
>
> (Manu 10.39)

> The cow being the most sacred of all the animals, only the people of the lowest of the castes eat the flesh of the cow's cadaver. For this very reason, the crow and the scavenger kite are considered the lowest among birds. The relationship between death and Untouchability is sometimes very subtle. In Bengal, for instance, there are two subcastes of the people in the oil profession: those who only sell oil are of a higher caste, whereas those who actually work the oilpress are of a lower caste. The reason

is that the latter destroy life by crushing the oil-seeds and therefore are contaminated by death.

(Hutton 1946: 77–78)

He had known none of this.

Not that he hadn't read a lot. Many a pair of sandals had he worn out walking every day to and from the university library in Mysore. The five or six library clerks there were all known to him. Especially Shetty, who had sat with him in the economics class. He had failed the previous year, and he had taken the library job. Whenever Annayya went to the library, Shetty would hand him the whole bunch of keys to the stacks so that Annayya could open any book-case and look for whatever book he wanted.

The bunch of keys was heavy because of the many keys in it. There were iron keys which, with much handling, had become smooth and shiny. Ensconced amidst them were tiny, bright, brass keys. Brass keys for brass locks. Male keys for female locks. Female keys for male locks. Big keys for the big locks. Small keys for the small locks. And there were also a few small keys for big locks and some big keys for small locks. So many combinations like the varieties of marriage which Manu talks about in his book. Some locks were simply too big for their cupboards and so they were left unlocked. Others were nearly impossible to unlock. You would have to break open the cupboard if you wanted to get at the one book that beckoned you tantalizingly. Who knew what social-science-related nude pictures that one book contained!

When he was in Mysore, much of what he read had to do with Western subjects, and they were almost always in English. If he read anything at all in Kannada, rare as it was, it would probably be a translation of *Anna Karenina* or a book on Shakespeare by Murthy Rao, or ethnographic studies done by scholars who were trained overseas, in America. But, now, he himself was in America.

The knowledge of Brahman austerities, fire, holy food, earth, restraint of the internal organs, water, smearing with cow dung, the wind, sacred rites, the sun and time are the purifiers of corporeal beings.

(Manu 5: 105)

To learn about these things, Annayya, himself the son of Annayya Shrotry, after crossing ten thousand miles and many waters, lands and climes, had to come to this cold, stinking Chicago. How did these white men learn all our dark secrets? Who whispered the sacred chants into their ears? Take, for instance, Max Mueller of Germany who had mastered Sanskrit so well that he came to be known among Indian pundits as 'Moksha Mula Bhatta'. He, in turn, taught the Vedas to the Indians themselves!

When he lived in India, Annayya was obsessed with things American, English or European. Once here in America, he began reading more and more about India; began talking more and more about India to anyone who would listen. Made the Americans drink his coffee; drank their beer with them. Talked about palmistry and held the hands of white women while pretending to read their palms.

Annayya pursued anthropology like a lecher pursuing the object of his desire—with no fear, no shame, as they say in Sanskrit. He became obsessed with the desire to know everything about his Indian tradition; read any anthropological book on the subject which he could lay his hands on. On the second floor of the Chicago library were stacks and stacks of those books which had to be reached by climbing the ladders and holding on to the wooden railings. Library call number PK 321. The East had at last found itself a niche in the West.

'Why do your women wear that red dot on their forehead?' the white girls he befriended at the International House would ask him. He had to read and search in order to satisfy their curiosity. He read the *Gita*. In Mysore, he had made his father angry by refusing to read it. Here he drank beer and whisky, ate beef, used toilet paper instead of washing himself with water, lapped up the *Playboy* magazines with their pictures of naked breasts, thighs, and some navels as big as rupee coins. But in the midst of all that, he found time to read. He read about the Hindu tradition when he should have been reading economics; he found time to prepare a list of books published by the Ramakrishna Mission while working on mathematics and statistics. 'This is where you come, to America, if you want to learn about Hindu civilization,' he thought to himself. He found himself saying to fellow-Indians, 'Do you know that our library in Chicago gets even Kannada newspapers, even *Prajavani*?' He had found the key, the American key, to open the many closed doors of Hindu civilization. He had found the entire bunch of keys.

That day, while browsing in the Chicago stacks, he chanced upon a new book, a thick one with a blue hardcover. Written on the spine in golden letters was the title: *Hinduism: Custom and Ritual.* Author, Steven Fergusson. Published, quite recently. The information gathered in it was all fresh. Dozens of rituals and ceremonies: ceremony for a woman's first pregnancy; ceremonies for naming a child, for cutting the child's hair for the first time, for feeding the child solid food for the first time; for wearing the sacred thread; the marriage vows taken while walking the seven steps; the partaking of fruit and almond milk by the newly-weds on their wedding night. (He remembered someone making a lewd joke: 'Do you know what the chap is going to do on his wedding night? He is going to ply his bride with cardamoms and almonds, and he himself will drink almond milk in preparation for you know what!') The Sanskrit chant on love-making which the husband recites to the wife. The ritual celebrating a man's sixtieth birthday. Rituals for propitiation, for giving charity; purification rituals, obsequial rituals, and so on. Everything was explained in great detail in this book.

Page 163. A detailed description of the cremation rites among Brahmins, with illustrations. What amazing information this Fergusson chap had given! There was a quotation from Manu on every page. The formulae for offering sacrifices to the ancestors; which ancestral line can be considered your own and which not. The impurity that comes from death does not affect a *sanyasi* and a baby that hasn't started teething yet. If a baby dies after teething, the impurity resulting from it remains for one day; if it is from the death of a child who has had his first haircutting ceremony, the impurity is for three days. The ritual concerning a death anniversary involves seven generations: the son, the grandson, and his son who perform the death anniversary; the father, the grandfather, and the great-grandfather for whom the anniversary is performed. Three generations above, three generations below, yourself in the middle. The book was crammed with such details. It even had a table that listed the number of days to show how different castes are affected by death-related impurities. Moreover, if a patrilineal relative dies in a distant land, you are not subject to the impurity as long as you have not heard the news of the death. But the impurity begins as soon as you have heard the news. You have to then calculate the number of days of impurity accordingly and at the end take the bath of purification. The more Annayya read on through the book, the more fascinated he became.

Sitting between two stacks, he went on reading the book. All the four aspects of the funeral ritual were explained in it. All these years, Annayya had not really seen a death. Once or twice, he had seen the people of the washerman's caste, a few streets from his own, carry in a procession the dead body of a relative all decked up. That was the closest he had ever come to witnessing a death. When his uncle died, Annayya was away in Bombay. When he left for America, his father was suffering form a mild form of diabetes. But the doctor had assured him it was not life-threatening as long as his father was careful with his diet. His father had suffered a stroke a year-and-a-half ago. It had left his hands and the left side of his face paralyzed. Still, he was all right, according to the letters his mother routinely wrote in a shaky hand once every two weeks. In her letters, she would keep reminding him that every Saturday he should massage himself with oil before his bath or else he would suffer from excessive heat. In cold countries you have to be careful about body heat. Would he like her to send him some soap-nut for his oil baths?

When a Brahmin is nearing his death, he is lifted up from the bed and is placed on a layer of sacred grass spread on the floor, his feet toward the South. The bed or the cot prevents the dying person's body from remaining in contact with the elemental earth and the sky. The grass, however, is part of the elements, having drawn its sap from the earth. It is dear to the fire. The South is the direction of Yama, the God of Death; it is also the direction of the ancestral world.

Next, the Vedic chants are uttered in the dying person's ear. And *panchagavya*—a sacred mixture made from cow's milk, curds, ghee, urine and dung—is poured into his mouth. A dead human being is unclean. But the urine and dung of a living cow are purifying. Think of that!

Then there were the ten different items; sesame seed, a cow, a piece of land, ghee, gold, silver, salt cloth, grains and sugar. These ten have to be given away as charity. When a man dies, all his sons have to take baths. The eldest son has to wear his sacred thread reversed as a sign of the inauspicious time. The dead body is washed and sacred ashes are smeared on it. Hymns invoking the Earth Goddess are sung.

Facing the page, on glossy paper, there was a photograph. The front veranda of a house in the style of houses you would see in Mysore. The wall in the background had a window with an iron grill. On the floor of the veranda lay a corpse that had been prepared for the funeral.

The dead man is God. His body is Lord Vishnu himself. If it is that of a woman, then it is Goddess Lakshmi. You circumambulate it just as you would a god and you offer worship to it.

Then Agni, the sacred fire, is lit and in it ghee is poured as libation. The dead body gets connected to the fire with a single thread of cotton. The big toes of the corpse are tied together and the body is then covered with a new white cloth.

There was a photograph of this also in the book. There was that same Mysore-style house. But in this photoghraph there were a few Brahmins, with stripes of sacred ash on their foreheads and arms. The Brahmins even looked vaguely familiar. But then, from this distance, all ash-covered Brahmins of Mysore would look alike.

Four men carry the dead body on their shoulders. After tying the corpse to the bier, the corpse's face turned away from the house, the funeral procession starts.

The corpse is then taken to the cremation grounds for cremation. Once there, it is placed, head toward the South, on a pile made out of firewood. The toes are untied. The white cloth covering the body is removed and is given away to the low-caste caretaker of the cremation grounds. The son and other relatives put grains of rice soaked in water into the mouth of the corpse and close the mouth with a gold coin. Excepting a piece of cloth or a banana leaf over the crotch, the corpse is now naked as a newborn baby.

Where would they get a gold coin? These days who has got so much gold? Would fourteen-carat gold do? Do the scriptures approve it? he wondered.

The eldest son, then, carries on his shoulder an earthen pitcher filled with water. A hole is made on the side of the pitcher. Carrying it on his shoulder, the son trickles the water around the corpse three times. Afterwards, he throws the pitcher over his back, breaking it.

There was a photograph of the cremation too. Looking at it, Annayya became a little uneasy because it looked somewhat familiar to him. The photograph was taken with a good camera. The pile of wood built for the cremation; the corpse; and a middle-aged man, the front of his head shaved in a crescent, on his shoulder a pitcher with water spouting from it; trees at a distance; and people.

Wait a minute! The face of the middle-aged man was known to him! It was the face of his cousin, Sundararaya. He had a photographic studio in Hunsur. How did this picture come to be here in this book? How did this man come to be here?

On the next page, it was a photograph of a blazing cremation fire. At the bottom of the photograph were printed the hymns addressed to Agni, the God of Fire.

O Agni! Do not consume this man's body. Do not burn
this man's skin. Only consign him to the world of his
ancestors. O Agni, you were born in the sacrificial fire
built by this householder. Now, let him be born again
through you.

Annayya stopped in the middle of the hymn and turned the pages back to look again at cousin Sundararaya's face. He had no spectacles on. Instead of his usual cropped grey hair fully covering the head, the front half of the head was tonsured into a crescent just for this ritual occasion. Even the hair on his chest had been shaved off. He wore a special Melukote dhoti below his bulging navel. But why was he here in this book?

Annayya turned to the foreword. It said that this Fergusson chap had been in Mysore during 1966–68, on a Ford Foundation fellowship. It also said that, in Mysore, Mr Sundararaya and his family had helped him a great deal in collecting material for the book. That is how the photographs of the Mysore houses came to be in the book. Once again, he flipped through the photographs.

The window with the iron grill—it was the window of his neighbour Gopi's house, and the one next to it was the vacant house that belonged to Champak-tree Gangamma. Those were houses on his own street. And that veranda was the veranda of his own house. The corpse could be his father's. The face was not clearly visible. It was a paralysed face, like a face he might see under running water. The body was covered in white. The Brahmins looked very familiar.

The author had acknowledged his gratitude to Sundararaya, his cousin: he had taken the author to the homes of his relatives for ritual occasions such as a wedding, a thread-wearing, a first pregnancy and a funeral. He had helped him take photographs of the rituals, interview the people, and tape-record the sacred hymn. He had arranged for Fergusson to be invited to their feasts. And so, the author, this outcaste foreigner, was very grateful to Sundararaya.

Now it was becoming clear. Annayya's father had died. Cousin Sundararaya had performed the funeral rites, because the son was abroad, in a foreign land. Mother must have asked people not to inform him of his father's death. He is all alone in a distant land; the poor boy should not be troubled with the bad news. Let him come back after finishing his studies. We can tell him then. Bad news can wait. Probably all this was done on the advice of this Sundaru, as always. If Sundaru had asked her to jump, Mother would have even jumped into a well. Three months after Annayya came to the States, two years ago, Mother had written to him that Father couldn't write any more letters because his arms had been paralysed. Who knows what those orthodox people have done now to his widowed mother! They might even have had her head shaven in the name of tradition. Widows of his caste cannot wear long hair. He became furious, thinking about Sundararaya. The scoundrel! The low-caste *chandala*! He looked at the picture of the cremation again. The window with the iron grill. The corpse. Sundararaya's head shaved in a crescent. His navel. He read the captions under the pictures again.

He turned the pages backwards and forwards. In his agitation, the book fell flop on the library floor. The pages got folded. He picked up the book and nervously straightened the pages. The silence there until now had been broken by the roaring sound of a waterfall, a toilet being flushed in the American lavatory down the corridor. As the flushing subsided, everthing was calm again.

He turned the pages. In the chapter on *simantha,* the ceremony for a pregnant woman, decked up like Princess Sita in the epic, wearing a crown on her head, his cousin's daughter Damayanti sat awkwardly among many married matrons. It was her first pregnancy and the bulge around her waist showed that the pregnancy was quite advanced. Her father, Sundararaya, must have arranged the ceremony conveniently to coincide with the American's visit so that he could take photographs of the ceremony. He must have scouted around to show the American a cremation as well. And he got it, conveniently, in his own uncle's house. 'How much did the Fergusson chap pay him?' wondered Annayya.

He looked for his mother's face among the women in the picture, but didn't find it. Instead, he found there others whom he knew: Champak-tree Gangamma and Embroidery Lachchamma. The faces were familiar, the bulb noses were familiar; the ear ornaments, the nose studs, the vermilion mark on the foreheads as wide as a penny, were all familiar.

Hurriedly, he turned to the index page. Looked under V: Veddas, Vedas, Vestments. Then under W: Weber, Westermarck, West Coast . . . at last he found Widowhood. There was an entire chapter on Widowhood. Naturally. In that chapter, facing page 233, was a fine photograph of a Hindu widow; her head clean-shaven according to the Shaivite custom, explained the caption. Acknowledgements: Sundararao Studio, Hunsur. Could this be his own mother in the photograph? A very familiar face, but quite unrecognizable because of the shaven head and the edge of the saree drawn over the face. Though it was a black and white photograph, he knew at once the saree was red. A faded one. The kind of saree only widows wear.

Sundararaya survived that day, only because he lived 10,000 miles away, across the whole Pacific Ocean, in a street behind the Cheluvamba Agrahara in Hunsur.

— Translated by Narayan Hegde

Stallion of the Sun

U. R. Anantha Murthy

I am writing this about Simpleton Venkata—Venkatakrishna Joysa is his real name—whom I had not seen in fourteen years. He turned up before me in the market-place that day. He didn't recognize me because I had left the town a long time ago. But how could I ever forget my boyhood friend, this Venkata with *kumkum* smeared between his eyebrows, the front half of his head shaved in a crescent shape, his gap-toothed mouth that grinned in a broad smile? With a burlap bag tucked under his arm, he stood gazing at the vegetable stall like a boy in front of a toy shop. His eyes, which were scanning the mounds of *tondekaayi* and *alasande* peas and the banana bunches that hung from the ceiling, shifted the next moment to the cross-eyed Konkani shopkeeper who was watching him with the same indifference with which he watched the vagrant cattle in the street. I stood there eyeing him as though I had found a stream of cool water on a sweltering day. He too looked at me briefly, but it was a blank look. We were the only two in that market-place who were not carrying umbrellas. While all others were playing it safe, he, the professional astrologer that he was, was probably flaunting his ability to forecast the weather by showing that although it was the month of July, it wasn't going to rain that day. As for myself, I was someone who had left the place long ago to live in the city and had been to foreign countries, and so, seeing me in my city attire, no one was going to be surprised that I didn't carry an umbrella. Venkata, on the other hand, for all appearances unprepared for any downpour, stood there smiling to himself in his secret knowledge, as it were, of the atmospheric phenomena, and looked at the vegetables that had come to the market from the neighbouring districts as if none of them was really edible. Oh, the thrill that I felt on seeing Simpleton Venkata! Would it have ebbed away if he hadn't recognized me? I wonder.

Memories tend to dry up if they are not nurtured.

Though older than me by at least five or six years, this Venkata had been my closest friend when we were growing up. With him around, one's body and mind were at ease. Suddenly, an incident comes to mind: I must have been eight or nine years old then. I used to be quite afraid of water. Once he made me go with him to the river without telling my mother. Not heeding my screams and protests, clasping me tight to himself, he jumped from a boulder into the stream. Frightened at first, gasping for breath and swallowing water but still in his firm clasp, I felt myself gradually able to come up and go down into the water, to open my eyes in the water. Being tickled by the tiny fish, and elated that I was learning to swim at last, I slowly began to feel comfortable in the water. First neck, then mouth, then nose, then head; I plunged deeper and deeper only to be buoyed up again by the water. Then coming out of the cool water to lie down in the warm sand and dry under the sun. . . . The river in our village is probably all dried up now. As if poised to jump into the water, I stood there before Venkata, on tiptoe, and said, 'Hello there!'

'Can you believe the price of cucumbers these days, gentleman?'

I didn't budge. Staring into his eyes, I tried to laugh.

'Sir, what do you think I have under my arm? A fighting cock?' he said showing his toothless gums.

'Sure, Budan Saab. But how is it that your cock's comb is drooping like a Brahmin's empty sack of alms?'

'No. This is the cock that got beaten up by my cock in the fight.' He held his shopping bag to me as if he were holding the cock by its legs.

'What misfortune has brought thee, O Prince, toothless and dishevelled, clutching this cock under thine arm, thus wandering to this strange land on this day of the full moon?'

Recognizing my theatrical speech in the manner of the *Yakshagana* plays we used to frequent together, a baffled Venkata paced a few steps backward, and his buttock scraped the horn of an old cow that was chewing on a banana peel.

'Is it Ananthu?' he said, rubbing his buttock. Then turning back to the cow which was looking for more banana peels in the roadside gutter, he said: 'Pray, tell me, blessed cow, why did you cause me to fear that this Ananthu might be an *amaldar* or some such big officer? Or, are you my ever-haunting sorcerer playing one of your tricks on me?'

The cow had picked up the banana peel from the gutter and was now blissfully chewing it, contorting its mouth.

'How much *tondekaayi* shall I give you?' the cross-eyed Konkani shopkeeper asked me. I took the bag from Venkata and had it filled up with *tonde*, cucumber, *alasande* peas, potatoes and onions, and said to Venkata, 'Come on, let's go to your house.'

'Yes, yes. Come with me. I will give you such an oil massage bath that you will see the moonlight. We have got water ready in the bath-house, anyhow.' With the purposeful stride of one who is heading home after having purchased the provisions needed for a feast, Venkata walked briskly past the people in the street.

'Let me buy some Bhringamalaka oil then,' I said. We went up the steps to Prabhu's shop which smelled of tobacco leaves.

'Visiting your hometown after a long time, aren't you, Mr Murthy? Your brothers still buy on credit from us, just like in your father's time. Come in, come in. Shall I get you something to drink?' said Prabhu who sat there with a pencil tucked behind his ear and showed me a stool to sit on among the canisters of provisions.

'I come here for a visit now and then. But I come to the market-place very rarely. Is everything well with you?' I said. The sweet smell of the jaggery Prabhu was weighing had blended with the pungency of the tobacco leaves.

'How can things be well? There have been no rains. Customers who buy on credit don't pay me back. Last year my eldest son fell ill and died within three days. Not a paisa of profit can be made in this trade; but you go on doing it because that is what your father taught you to do. My sons were not lucky like you, to be able to go to England for study. They just settled down to the family business, trading in tobacco leaves and horse-gram. See that one? He is the second son. Over there is the fourth. The other two have opened a cloth shop. I married all my three daughters to lawyers. My eldest son's children are in high school now. How many children have you got now? Where do you live?' He talked on, placing the blocks of jaggery on the scale and all the time trying to keep the flies off. The conversation was familiar.

'We live in Mysore. I have two children—a boy and a girl. Have you got Bhringamalaka oil?'

'Oh! Is this for the oil massage bath of our Venkata Joysa? After all, isn't he the one who did the massage bath for K.T. Bhashyam when they were in jail together? So many cabinet ministers are known to him, all old-timers. There is hardly an important person in the whole of Karnataka who has not had himself massaged by Venkata Joysa. Yet, God only knows why he has not received his pension for the last two years. By the way, Joysre, why don't you have our Murthy put in a word for you? At least that way, if you get your pension we may get back some of the money you owe us. On the whole, like me, this Joysa here is down on his luck. To all appearances, he too has a son. What a scoundrel he has turned out to be! Dropped out of school! As if that isn't enough, he frequents coffee shops. Whatever you may say, our times were far better. Everything is upside down nowadays.'

Venkata grinned broadly and put down the shopping bag, took some snuff out of his pocket and tucked a pinch of it into his nostril. Taking the grimy bottle from the shop-boy he said, 'It's the B.V. Pandit brand oil, isn't it? Only that oil has the best cooling effect.'

'Yes of course, Joysre. The oil is quite fresh too. I am the only stale thing in this shop,' said Prabhu taking the money from me. 'You are the first customer in the whole day to pay cash. That is how bad things are for us.'

Venkata reached out for Prabhu's hand across the canisters and holding it in his own, he meditated.

'The moment I saw you, Prabhu, I thought to myself that you looked tired. What you need is an oil massage. It's all settled. I'll be back tomorrow and massage some oil on your head, all right?'

With his hand still in Venkata's, Prabhu heaved a sigh and said, 'Do you know, Mr Murthy, there isn't a single head in this town that hasn't received an oil rub at the hands of this Joysa? God only knows how such a good man got such a son. It seems the other day the boy beat up and robbed none other than the principal of the college.'

Venkata laughed and drew a line across his forehead as if to indicate the writing of fate there. Prabhu made a similar gesture in agreement with him and, wiping the jaggery off his hands, said, 'Do you think, Joysre, that he will be sent to jail?'

Venkata said, picking up the shopping bag and getting ready to leave, 'Whatever fate has written on his forehead will happen. I got him released on bail. Gave a fine oil-massage bath to the police inspector and one to the principal. Now I've got to give a massage to the judge. . . .'

Venkata's laughter made me uneasy. But Prabhu didn't seem to mind. Same old Venkata, always the laughing stock of the town! No shame whatever!

We were walking in the direction of Kerekoppa Village. The path was just a trail, unchanged in all these years. I began to feel a seething rage against Venkata. He has been like this always, an imbecile. Once, during the Quit India Movement, this genius got us into trouble. We were in high school then. One day, he woke us up in the middle of the night and said, 'Let's go and steal the mail box.' It was pitch dark on that night of the new moon. We carried the mail box in the darkness to the bank of the river and buried it in the sand. Next day there was a commotion all over the town. Putting on an air of innocence, we marched in the protest parade with everyone else, shouted slogans, hailed the national leaders, 'Victory to Mahatma Gandhi! Victory to Kamala Devi!' picketed in front of the toddy shop, laid ourselves down on the schoolground—all this under the leadership of Venkata. But he loved to babble. On the street, someone, an out-of-towner, stopped him, it seems, to inquire where he could get a good cup of coffee. The ever-helpful Venkata took him to Sheenappayya's coffee shop. What the fool didn't know was that the man was a secret agent of the C.I.D. 'What you boys are doing is hardly anything. Do you know what havoc the students in Shivamogga are causing?' the sneaky C.I.D. agent egged him on, as he sipped his steaming coffee. Venkata loosened his tongue, 'The Shivamogga students aren't the only ones, you know, who can cause havoc.' 'Come on. You boys here don't have the pluck to take on the Government,' teased the C.I.D. agent. Venkata then bragged to the stranger about our adventure of the previous night. The result: the police double-marched us along with Venkata to the river-bank.

What happened then? The entire town gathered on the

river-bank. The police handed us the spades and yelled, 'You widows' sons, start digging now!' After digging endlessly in that hot sun, we at last pulled the mail box out of the sand, and, in front of everyone, were made to carry it back to the post office ourselves. The police were not finished with us yet. Next, they took us in their truck and dumped us in the Sakre Bayalu forest. We dragged ourselves back eating wild berries or whatever else we could find on the way and trudged back to the town the following day, all fagged out.

Despite my rage, remembering those events made me laugh. Venkata joined me in the laughter, having put the bag down, clapping and dancing all the while. 'You are a good for nothing, stupid fool, you know,' I told him. Although he was older, he had become my classmate through having repeatedly failed his classes. Already at that time he had a wife—a veritable shrew. Sometimes, on his way to school, he had to bring her along to attend this or that auspicious ceremony at someone's house. Then, when they got to the market-place, he would walk fast in the street leaving her several paces behind as though she were a stranger to him, she all the while hopping to catch up with him. That is how we knew that he had a wife already when we were in the Lower Secondary School.

Once, when our arithmetic teacher was shouting abuse at him and thrashing him with a cane, Venkata tried to shield himself with a book, pleading, 'Please sir, I'm a married man! Don't hit me!' This made the teacher laugh so much that he took off his turban and started wiping the sweat off his face with his chalk-smeared hand. The grotesque look of the teacher's dark face, now all smeared with chalk powder, set us laughing. Then Venkata picked up the duster and started wiping the teacher's face with it. This made us laugh all the more. When the teacher turned to hit him again, he had crawled under the desk and was pleading with joined hands, 'I don't want my wife to see cane marks on my body; please don't hit me!' The teacher, who had rheumatism, couldn't bend down and so contented himself with kicking Venkata on the buttocks and shouting more abuse.

Even now, Venkata was making me laugh as though to prove that it was impossible for anyone to be angry with him. Still, thinking how he had allowed that son of his to grow up to be so irresponsible, I began to scold him harshly, 'You are an escapist, an imbecile, a spineless ninny!'

'All this raging and fuming, where does it get you? Come, I'll massage away all your rage.' Like a boy who has something to show you, he quickened his pace.

'Wait for me,' I said to him. I wanted to tell him: 'I have treated you with indifference. I didn't try to see you on my previous visits. Today I have run into you by chance and so you are being playful with me. This is a game, I know, which will come to an end sooner or later. I think this buffoonery has become a habit with you lately. I feel I am drying up. I don't fancy anything. A vague apprehension troubles me. No idea for writing comes to me. I mouth grandiloquent words, and the pliant heads before me nod appreciatively. When this drama is over, only emptiness is left. Why don't I see things? Do you see things or do you only pretend to see? This self-effacement of yours is a pose, isn't it? Or, have I perhaps become an empty vessel by trying to write about lofty matters rather than about you whom I have known intimately ever since childhood?'

'I smell *kedige* flowers,' Venkata said and, like the cannibal Rakshasa of mythology on detecting the presence of human beings, he started sniffing around with his nostrils dilated. All this while, I had said nothing of my thoughts to him. He put the bag down and disappeared into the *kedige* shrubbery saying, 'My daughter, Ganga, is very fond of wearing *kedige* flowers in her hair.' I didn't know that *kedige* was in season then. 'Damn these *kedige* flowers. Don't know where the devil they are hiding,' Venkata said, emerging empty-handed after sometime. 'Come, let's go.'

On the way we met a man who wore gold studs in his ears. He carried a bundle of clothes on his head. Spitting out saliva mixed with betel juice, he said, 'Ha! I just came past your house. Your wife stopped me and began to curse you profusely. She said you left home this morning to go to the market and hadn't returned. She called you all sorts of names. . . .'

Venkata helped the man lift the load off his head and asked, 'When you talked to her, was she in the backyard or the frontyard? Pray, tell me, O Learned One, in what quarter of our abode did my good wife receive thee?'

The man was amused by this theatricality. He spat out the rest of the betel juice, wiped his mouth with the edge of his dhoti and revealing his few reddened teeth, asked, 'Why? It was in the backyard.'

'Then it means she will have made the *palya* dish out of the *chogate-soppu* that grows in our backyard. My wife is a culinary wizard who can turn even cattle-feed into a savoury dish. We are grateful to the Learned One for the good tidings.'

The man, who had started on his way, stopped and turned round. 'But she has a foul mouth,' he said. 'By the way, Joysa, why is your son Subba so mean and ill-tempered? I try to make conversation with him and he tells me to mind my own business. I was about to tell the grumpy boy to go to hell, but not being one to meddle in others' affairs, I just kept quiet. People like you and me, trying to be helpful, show concern for one another; but that son of yours wants to be different. That's what happens to these boys who go to college.'

Balancing the load on his head with one hand and swinging the other, the celestial messenger departed. 'How right you are!' said Venkata to him and, joining me, started walking with his goose-step as if nothing had happened. What a chap! I marvelled. I was now convinced that Venkata had made a mess of all his affairs. Yet, look at the way he goes about unconcernedly! Is he a hardened wretch, or a perfect phony, or a shabby-looking saint? I wondered.

'How many children do you have now?' I asked.

'Four. Our first-born is our only male progeny. The daughters are all still unmarried. And so my wife, in addition to being the fierce Goddess Chamundi that she already was, has now turned into the fire-spitting Kali. In any case, I am a devotee of Kali, and so even her wrath is a blessing to me. Thus have I managed to remain blissful in this earthly existence.'

His theatrical speech was beginning to irritate me. Why should men like Venkata father children; live a life of humiliation at the hands of every passer-by? When Marx talked about the idiocy of the village life, no doubt he had men like Venkata in mind, I said to myself. Venkata appeared to me to typify all those who live a life of supreme passivity. If I had been among my friends in the city, I would probably have expressed my concern with a statement such as, 'Oh, will this country of ours ever change?' Here, with Venkata, I tried to urge my views as earnestly as I could. But would he listen to anyone?

'It hasn't rained at all. . . . It will be a miracle if the mango blossoms appear this season. Last year there wasn't a single pickling mango. . . . You see that tree over there? Sometimes hundreds of parrots come and settle on that tree. . . . The hill over there is called Peacock Hill. There is a cave there. Once my children are all married, I'll go and live in that cave. The view from that cave is simply breathtaking. I'll just authorize my wife to receive my pension, and then I'll go and live there.'

And so he went on and on while I was carrying on my own discourse with him: 'What is politics but a change in the way we live . . .? But change towards what? Towards the haves, or the have-nots? Why is passion essential for such a change . . .? At the basis of all politics, of all science, for that matter, is passion for changing the nature of things and of people into sharing your hopes and aspirations. It is at the basis of religious activities too, for religion is the politics of the everlasting. . . . Don't you wish your wife and children would also pursue what you have considered to be the right path? To wish for the status-quo is also politics. . . . Do you know why? Change is in the nature of things. Some try to prevent change for their own ends, but cannot do so for long. . . . All things expand, all things explode. Nothing remains the same. That is why we should constantly strive for an order that we think is right.'

And, like that, I went on talking.

'Everything is what it is because that's what one is born with.' So saying, Venkata put the bag down, turned his face up to the sky and brought his palms together as if to pray.

'I bow to heroes like you. But you must not mind an imbecile like this Venkata. Besides, when you heroes get your heads all heated up, you need people like me to give you a cooling massage,' he said and began tapping with his fingers on the imaginary head before him.

'Go to hell!' I said in disgust. Venkata saw that I was really angry.

'Look here, Ananthu. Far from changing the world, I can't even change the woman I married. Today I am alive. But tell me, is there any guarantee that tomorrow I'll still be living?'

We came to a spot where we had to cross a ford over a narrow makeshift bridge fashioned out of the trunks of three areca palms.

'After you. But be careful!' Venkata waited for me to cross first. I walked over the bridge gingerly and then waited for him on the other side of the ford. Satisfied that I had at last engaged him in my discourse, I said: 'We may die tomorrow or we may not. In any case, there will be others who live. . . .'

I insisted that he let me carry the bag now. We were walking along the paddy field.

'Do you know, Ananthu, that the grove we were in just before crossing the bridge is inhabited by a Panjurli spirit? The Panjurli is known for its short temper. Once, a long time ago, I was walking in the grove singing to myself. It was getting dark. Behind me, I heard the rustle of dry leaves. I turned around to see. Can you guess what it was? A tiger! I passed out. When I came to, I saw that I had wet my dhoti.'

'Why are you telling me this?'

'Oh, no particular reason. Look, Ananthu, I am a big coward. I don't know what to say when you talk like this, as though you were possessed by a Panjurli spirit. I tell my wife, 'This is the way I am. What can I do?' She may have a foul mouth, but she is a good person. If I say I have a stomach-ache or something, she will walk miles to bring this or that herb and brew a decoction for me. . . . I got scared when I saw that tiger. Do you know why? Because I don't know how to bring around a tiger and pacify it with an oil massage. If I knew, I would grab it by its whiskers and beginning with its forehead, I would gently massage. . . .'

Venkata started laughing hysterically. Remembering our schooldays when he used to get beatings, I too started laughing. But the suspicion that all his unsaid thoughts were contained in his laughter and that I was being ridiculed by his laughter made me uneasy.

'You idiot! Is it possible for anyone to live without any ego? Even the gentlest of beings needs to have an ego,' I said. Then, I began to feel that without destroying Venkata and his likes there is no progress, no electricity, no river dams, no penicillin, no pride, no honour, no passionate lovemaking, no satisfying a woman, no climax, no flying, no joy of life, no memory, no ecstasy, no bliss.

Absorbed in such thoughts, I looked at Venkata as he stood on the edge of the paddy field, barefoot and bubbling with bliss. I was confused. Was it out of pity for me that he was laughing? I wasn't sure.

'You say that your grown-up daughters are still unmarried. What if they go astray?' I asked. I was trying to hurt this Venkata who could be so kind to me.

'I would be so grateful to you if you could find husbands for them yourself. Where do I have the money for their dowry? They are precious gems, those girls. Why would they go astray? Still, if they do, it is their fate. Who am I to avert it?'

Faced with his disarming honesty, I was at a loss for words. What should I say to him? That he should go and make money? Somehow revolutionize society? Smiling, but without playfulness, Venkata said: 'Look, after all, I'm a priest by profession. My nature is to worship—worship whatever I see. If I come upon some heads, I worship. I worship the Panjurli ghosts and sundry spirits; I worship the school inspector, the police sub-inspector, the *amaldar*, now you, and Bhashyam in the old days. That is my way of worshipping anything and everything. What do you get by butting heads with your adversary? A swollen head. The Mother Goddess has looked after me so far. My wife Rukku makes cups out of banana leaves. I carry them on my head to the market and sell them. Soon, I'll be getting my pension back. The other day I gave our MLA a superb oil massage. I was telling him how in jail I used to make K.T. Bhashyam see the moonlight with my massage. . . . See how these trees and plants embody God within them? Likewise, we too should embody God within ourselves. But probably, there is still some residual bitterness in me. Or else, my son Subba wouldn't be so hotheaded.'

Venkata snatched the bag from my hand so that I could walk more freely, and he began to point out the birds of his liking to me.

'Look at those birds. They don't even care whether they are looked at by us. They want neither your social change nor my oil massage. They drop their excrement on the heads of even the fiercest spirits and then fly away. To live, they have to be neither imbeciles nor dare-devils. Don't you think so, Ananthu?'

I walked briskly, for I was getting hungry. Behind my back,

Venkata mimicked my gait, the way he used to mimic me when we were in school. Do I still hobble the way I used to? I wondered and felt awkward.

Here and there, villagers sat idly, looking anxious because the rains had not come. 'Joysre, when are the rains going to come?' someone would ask sluggishly, to whom Venkata would reply with mock seriousness, 'Just wait one more week.' 'There aren't even the leaves for you to make those cups. Are all your astrology and magic spells just mumbo jumbo then?' asked a young man in trousers with barely concealed sarcasm. 'Lately, we've been making cups from the *muttuga* leaves from the woods. We have to eke out a living somehow, don't we?' replied Venkata calmly. 'Lo, Chikka. It seems a cow belonging to your master had been missing. He came to me to have a charm made. Did the cow come home?' he enquired of a cowherd. 'Yes, it did,' said the boy who was playing with some pebbles, without looking up. I thought that this must be the daily routine of Venkata. It was the life of a simpleton, open for everyone to see, neither flourishing nor withering; he laughs and makes others laugh, dreams of living by himself in the cave on Peacock Hill, always gives in to others, gets abused by his wife. The king cobra which has the jewel in its hood also has venom in its fangs. No such fangs in this Venkata. No passion, no fury, no envy in him.

Venkata pointed out a huge tree to me, enormous in girth. 'There is something unusual about this tree. Look, how one of its limbs shaped like a hand is pointing to the ground. They say that it is because a treasure is buried under the ground,' he said. I laughed. 'A few greedy folks have even tried to dig up the treasure. But how can anyone get it? It belongs to a Jettiga spirit that inhabits the tree.' I was amazed by his intimate knowledge of his surroundings. He, this boyhood friend of mine, could expatiate on the legends concerning every square foot of this place. Nurtured by the myriad ghosts and spirits of the land, a philosophy of his own had evolved.

This is how I came to know about it: all the while as he led me expertly through the maze of those paths in the woods, he was narrating the legends that would somehow link those hidden paths we were treading to the mythological past. 'Once Mother Sita . . .,' and so he would begin an episode in the *Ramayana* when Rama and

Sita lived a life of hardship in the forest, and then he would show me a gummy leaf which, he said, Sita used for the wick of her oil lamp. The orchid on the tree in front of us was the flower Rama had brought for Sita to wear in her hair. The rock over there was the rock which Lakshmana pierced with his arrow to release a fountain of water. Pointing to a hollow formed in the rock, Venkata challenged me, 'Let me see you scoop up the water from that hollow with your palms.' I tried, but as I scooped, more water kept filling up the hollow. He asked me to drink the water. I did. The water tasted cool and sweet. 'This is the water with which Shri Rama bathed this *linga* idol here,' he told me, pointing to a protrusion on the rock and poured on it the water he scooped up from the hollow. Then, with his eyes closed and kneeling down like the bull at Shiva's temple, he muttered words to the following effect: 'Some people look upon the Supreme God as their mother, some as their father. Those for whom God is their mother have their eyes always on her breast, full and overflowing with milk. They suck at it and don't want to let it go. They don't want anyone else's breast, either. Those for whom God is their father, they look into the Lord's eyes and become intoxicated. They want to see everything, they want to drink up the whole world through their eyes and yet their thirst for 'seeing' remains unquenched. The child who is sucking at the breast sometimes falls asleep sucking; wakes up, and sucks again; I am the sucking type. You are the seeing type . . . Why did the sage Shankara, who set out to comprehend the universe through seeing, suddenly desire to taste it like a suckling baby? I wonder. You don't have to comprehend something in order to soak it up. The earthworm soaks it up; the tree soaks it up. They live and they flourish . . . maybe, if the Mother Goddess herself separates you from her breast and puts you down because you have drunk enough, you may perchance open your eyes and see, but it is all at the whim of the Mother Goddess. Sometimes she may even pull you away from one breast and set you to the other. It is a frightening moment, though! Passing from one breast to the other, from life to death, some fortunate souls may even glimpse her eyes, if they don't scream with fright. . . . All that grand heroism is not for me. It is as the fool that the likes of me serve this world. Now, you would like to suck at the breast, too. It is only natural. You too fall asleep while sucking. You too kick the mother while sucking. Besides, before you ride off on your heroic mission of making the world bend toward your path, don't you sometimes need cool nourishment from the Mother Goddess' milk, from my oil massage which I am going to give you . . .?'

Having spoken like the learned sage in the *Bhagavata* drama, Venkata was entranced by his own eloquence. He stood there and inhaled a pinch of snuff. 'After giving up beedi smoking, I took to this snuff,' he said. 'Wait till my wife sees you with me; her foul mouth will be sealed up instantly.' Gloating over the prospect, he scampered on. Because of his knock-knees, he walked rather clumsily.

*

In front of us there was a house, an unwhitewashed, unswept, dilapidated house. 'This is Sheshanna's house. He's very ill. Let's go in and take a look at him,' Venkata said, and, leaving the hand bag by the front door, led me inside to a dark veranda. 'This is Ananthu, Achar's son. He is a professor in Mysore. You know him, don't you?' he said. Adjusting my eyes to the darkness and still musing over Venkata's words, I said to myself: look at this Venkata, he is a philosopher too. If I try to answer him, I'll have to use words and phrases in English, or else, translate them into expressions unfamiliar to him. Somewhat like these: the frivolous insensitivity to suffering . . . the stoic resignation of a coward . . . inauthentic being . . . escapism . . . complacency born out of superstition . . . innocence of the village idiot . . . and so on. . . .

If he read what I have written about him, he would read it only as he knows himself to be. Simpleton that he is, he is untouched by irony. The constant whirling of the world, the flux and the changes have no meaning to one who has no desire of his own. Before such a non-political being, all my knowledge is futile. He is the direct antithesis of Kissinger. Even Gandhi desired change and so, was involved. . . . Wait a minute! This Venkata, who came to me as a story, is developing into an essay! I am finding myself confronted by that which to me in the beginning was only a subject for writing!

'This is Sheshanna. His son works in Bombay, where they

make atom bombs. Smart, just like you. My son also wants to become like him. Has married a white woman. She visited here. In a sari, and with *kumkum* on her forehead, she looks like the Mother Goddess, Kali. She asked her father-in-law to go and live with them. But how can this man go? He cannot live without his potato and onion *huli*. Beides, he likes to lord it over the family. Why would a son who is educated put up with it?' Venkata chattered on as he chopped the betel nut into fine pieces.

Sheshanna started coughing. He coughed as though he was going to run out of breath. Venkata lifted him, sat him up against himself, and, patting his back, held a bowl to his mouth. I thought his last moment had come. With his head thrown back and coughing incessantly, he was gasping for breath. Propping his head up, Venkata coaxed him to spit. Sheshanna must have spat blood. Venkata laid him down on the bed and went to the backyard to empty the bowl. 'I'll make you some coffee,' he said when he came back and went into the kitchen. Sheshanna was panting heavily with his mouth wide open, his eyes fluttering. In the dim light that came through a glass tile in the roof, I sat there crouching, counting the gourds that hung from the ceiling beams. On a rickety cot in the corner, covered in a thin blanket, Sheshanna lay like a corpse. He must have been in the advanced stages of tuberculosis. Most probably Venkata himself was nursing him. That was how Venkata had always been, at the service of others. On our way back from school, if you looked in his schoolbag, you would find medicine bottles for all sorts of people, vials in which to bring snuff for the women who had become secret snuff users, ribbons for young girls, double-edged licing combs, silk threads for the Anantha-worship, decoration tinsels for the Gouri festival, sugar candies from the Mussulman's sweetshop for the sundry children—anything and everything except schoolbooks. Along with his own umbrella, he would be carrying two more tattered ones for repair. His clothes showing patches, a basil leaf in his tuft of hair, he sauntered along the market street as though he owned the place. He would sometimes bring us sour plums.

Venkata brought hot coffee from inside and helped Sheshanna drink it. 'God knows when my life is going to come to an end,' he said and slurped his coffee as Venkata blew on it and held the cup to his lips.

'Nonsense! You are not going to die so soon, take it from me. Suppose the Lord of Death were to come to your doorstep riding on his water buffalo, you are the kind who is quite likely to ask him to wait until you have finished eating your delicious potato and onion *huli*. And if by chance he tasted it, then instead of taking you away with him he would let you stay right here on earth, so there would be a place on earth where he could go when he is in the mood for a good, tasty curry. However, it would be unlike the God of Death to return from his rounds empty-handed. So, not wishing to waste a trip, he would ask you to show him someone else to take your place to go with him. You would then send him to this buffoon Venkata who, though younger than you, having played out his buffoonery, is ready to go. Then, if the Lord of Death gets scared away by my wife's sharp tongue, I live. If not, I go.'

Seshanna's face perked up a little. Venkata laid his head on the pillow and got up to leave. 'I'll send you rice gruel mixed with lentil water; my daughter will bring it to you,' he said and motioned me to get up.

'Your friend might know my son, Dr Subramanya Shastri. He studied in London and is now an engineer in Bombay, at the place where they make atom bombs. They say he gets three thousand rupees monthly. Lives in a spacious bungalow,' said Sheshanna, trying to sit up. Venkata made him lie down and told him to go to sleep. Taking leave of him, I came out of the house.

Keeping me a few paces ahead of him, Venkata opened the fence-gate. 'Come and see whom I have brought with me,' he called out to his wife, flaunting me as his shield against her. On seeing me, Rukku, who came out fuming, cooled down like a burning log being doused. Wiping her wet hands with the edge of her *saree*, she now beamed at me. 'Ananthu here insisted on bringing these for you. He wouldn't listen to me,' Venkata said, handing her the bag filled with vegetables. The wrinkles on her face etched by a thousand hardships now eased in a smile of gratitude.

A broad stripe of *kumkum* across her forehead, a champak flower tucked in her greying hair, eyes reddened by the kitchen smoke, Rukku looked mere skin and bone. Next, Shakuntala, Gouri and Ganga appeared. The older girls, who had come of age, wore sarees, and had their hair braided neatly. Glass bangles, plain ear studs, fresh fragrant champak in their hair—that was all their adornment. One girl bashfully brought warm water for me to wash with; the other brought a small towel. The youngest, who wore a skirt with patches on it, peeked at me from behind her mother. She had in her hand a garland of jasmine flowers which she had been stringing. Outside, while washing my feet, I looked around: there were flowers which I hadn't seen in years. Many kinds of jasmines, roses, chrysanthemums, shoe-flowers, *tumbe, parijata,* champak, shell-flower, the peacock's pride—it was a lush and water-soaked garden. The water in the well was still plentiful even though the rains hadn't come.

The house, too, was very orderly. The earthen floor had been polished to a shiny dark colour. On it were *rangoli* patterns made of white flour. Whitewashed walls; gourds hanging from the ceiling beams. An almanac hung by a nail in the wall. Venkata removed his shirt and hung it on another nail. In a corner was a neat pile of rolled-up mattresses. From the upper sill of the door hung a piece latticework made of pieces of glass bangles and a decoration in cotton, probably from the last Gouri festival. The copper pitcher I was given for washing my feet was brightly polished. Shakuntala brought me a brass cup filled with a cool drink made out of a mixture of rice water, milk, jaggery and cardamom seeds. 'I have two children too,' I said. 'Is everyone well at home?' Rukku enquired. She and Venkata started arguing excitedly as they paced back and forth to the kitchen. He wanted to give me his oil massage and hot bath right then. She argued that I should bathe and eat first and later at night should get my massage and hot bath. She won in the end. Venkata followed me to the bath-house.

'Because you have come, I didn't get my usual dressing-down,' he said. I laughed and started pouring hot water on myself. In the room there was a granite tub for the hot bath after the oil massage. Next to it were cauldrons for hot water, a pot filled with cooling *matti* leaves, and canisters of soap-nut powder. Looking at Venkata's paraphernalia, I became somewhat apprehensive about the evening.

'Why do you make your wife angry?' I asked.

'Why would I make her angry? She gets angry. It is the weapon that the Mother Goddess has granted her in order to protect me. You see, somehow this idiot has to be kept under control, the children have to be attended to, firewood in the house has to be kept dry. If there was no nagging at home, I would probably just go on chattering with whomever I run into and forget to come home. She has to be abusive to scare off all those who take this gullible fool for a ride,' spoke Venkata as he kept pushing the burning logs into the kiln.

'Where is your son? I don't see him,' I asked.

'He spends most of the time playing cards with his cronies. None of these weapons of mine works on him. If he sees me he flies into a rage.'

The futility of your philosophy is confronting you in the person of your son, I wanted to tell him, but didn't. Instead I looked at him in an accusing way. He went on talking as if none of it made any sense to him: 'He is infuriated that his father doesn't command any respect. But how can I change what I am? The principal of his college didn't allow him to sit for the examinations because he didn't attend classes regularly. Do you know what he did? At night, he attacked the principal. They say he even robbed him of his money. He pesters me to give him money to start a flour mill in the town. I am down and out. Where am I supposed to come up with the money he wants?'

'You poor wretch! You don't understand evil at all, do you? You are like the lotus flower that blossoms only in stagnant water! I don't think I can put up with you even for two days. Stoic that you are, the changing times are not for you. You will go on living like this, scratching when it itches, wallowing in complacency, forever playing the fool.' I held myself back from speaking out these thoughts and, feeling affection and disgust for Venkata, I finished my bath. After me, Venkata bathed ritualistically, chanting the prayer hymns. The water he poured on himself was made to flow out on a bed of *keswu* leaves that grew profusely. Seeing me eye the *keswu* leaves, he said, 'I'll ask her to make the *patrode* dish from these leaves for the evening.'

For my lunch, Shakuntala had placed a floorboard for me to sit on and, in front of it, the end part of a flame-dried banana leaf, having circled it with a *rangoli* decoration on the floor. On the leaf were a variety of mouth-watering pickles, *happalas* made from jackfruit, pungent fries the names of which I was too shy to ask, and rice *payasa* in the corner.

'Not much of a lunch; everything was done in a hurry,' said Rukku apologetically and served me dish after dish. There were two kinds of *tumbulis* to go with the rice. There was, just as Venkata guessed, *palya* made out of chogate leaves; diluted butter-milk garnished with fresh ginger and coriander; the *saru* made of water drained from boiling rice and mixed with sour butter-milk and then garnished with spices—I had forgotten its name and hadn't had it since childhood. Venkata ate everything with blissful relish. The meal was so savoury and light and yet quite filling.

Shakuntala and Gouri, competing with each other, had prepared a bed for me. Just as I was laying myself down for a nap, I heard Rukku calling out, 'Ay, Subba, Subba, come and eat.' Half out of anxiety, half in helpless anger, she appealed to her husband, 'For God's sake, ask Subba to come to eat.'

I came out with Venkata, but saw only the back of a person in shirt and pants, with shoulder-length hair in the style of the hippies. He was walking away briskly without looking back. His gait was just like his father's. But he was taller than his father and lankier. Venkata, shirtless and just in his dhoti, ran after him. Subba stopped, turned round and shaking his hands menacingly, shouted some insult at his father. His body contorted, Venkata cringed and pleaded with him. Subba looked around suddenly and picked up a stone. Venkata began to back off shielding his face with his hands, still pleading. Subba then walked away briskly. I felt uneasy looking at Rukku who stood there helplessly in anguish for her son. Venkata came back, his face downcast. 'Subba is all agitated. He was about to pounce on me like a tiger!' he said quivering in mock fear.

'Can't you stop your clowning at least now? What kind of a father are you who couldn't give his son a slap or two and bring him back?' said Rukku and went inside wiping her eyes. Venkata followed her into the house saying, 'You go and eat. Set the things aside for Subba. When he feels hungry he will come home on his own.' I went and lay down on the bed. The little girl, Ganga, was playing with cowrie-shells by herself.

Rukku was saying to her husband all that I wanted to say to him myself, only more harshly: 'Just because you don't mind rotting here in this place, it doesn't mean that your son, who is of this generation, would also like to rot here! Some father you are, a worthless nobody in the eyes of the people! You just settle down wherever you go and grin stupidly at people. What should the children look up to you for? Why should people like you have a family at all? God knows how many years it has been since your pension stopped coming. I have to manage everything myself—make banana leaf cups, keep the house in order, attend to the children, I must prepare the special food freshly, three times a day, for that stingy Sheshanna. I send him soft-cooked rice and he says, "Couldn't she have sent some mango pickle? Your mother is mighty close-fisted." As if it is not enough that I break my back here for my own household, I get criticism from this man. None of us, not even the children, have stepped out of this wretched place even for a day. A country fair, or a cinema, or another town—what have we seen, tell me? That poor boy, Subba. I make his favourite *payasa* of rice and black gram, but he roams in the hot sun on an empty stomach like a mad dog. He has got so wicked as to strike his own father. I know, someone who doesn't like us has put an evil spell on him. You are so simple-minded that you don't understand evil things at all. . . .' As the litany of abuse kept pouring down on him, I must have fallen asleep.

I don't know how long I slept. When I opened my eyes I sensed that Venkata was pacing about me with the bottle of Bhringamalka oil in his hand. I sat up and looked at him enquiringly. With a mouth full of betel juice, he smiled and said, 'Let's go.' I got up and followed him to the bath-house. It was getting dark. He made me undress completely and tie a piece of cloth over my groin. A roaring fire was heating up the water. There were other cauldrons filled with cold water. He shut the bath-house door and made me sit on the wooden board. He was wearing a towel around his waist and had tucked it between his legs above the knees as if he was about to wade into a pond. Dipping the sacred grass in the oil and touching my forehead and the top of my head with it, he muttered the ritual chants. He spat out the betel-mixed saliva and, beginning with the feet, he applied oil all over my body. Then he sat me on a stool and placed my feet in a bowl of castor oil. 'The coolness of the oil will gradually climb up until it is absorbed by your brain,' he explained. In his cupped palms he scooped up the Bhringamalaka oil and poured it on my head. Chanting the names of the Mother Goddess, he rapped on my head with both hands as though he were beating a drum. 'I am now talking to your head. Doesn't it sound like a *mrudanga*?' he asked, varying the rhythm and the beat. 'Yes,' I said timidly. All that worship-like attention was making me uncomfortable. From the way he was beating the drum on my head, I suspected that he could even be dancing at my back. 'From your head this rhythm will flow to your navel,' he said. 'The sound will raise the six coils of your Kundalini. Though I don't know much about such things, I know that it works,' he said breathing rapidly. I was now certain that he was dancing. I thought of a *ghatam* player performing in a music concert.

The ritual that followed the drum-playing consisted of many rhythmic actions which were accompanied by a running commentary by Venkata in his soft, quivering voice. My backside had become warm because of the fire. He was circumambulating my head as if he were worshipping it. Tickling, pinching, plucking, pressing, patting, pulling, pushing and scratching, his agile fingers worked all around my head. 'Now your head will talk to me on its own,' he said wiping the sweat from his face and got ready for the second of the ritual oil massages and the raising of the Kundalini. As I wondered whether the fingers he had in his hand were twenty or hundred, the voice of his running commentary was assuming the tone of an incantation, rhythmically rising and falling according to the need, thus:

Here we go, Ananthu, Ananthu, entering the woods entering the woods. . . . In the woods there is a tree, a tree. . . . On the tree, a parrot, a parrot, a green parrot, a green parrot in the green leaves. In the hooked bill of the green parrot . . . a red fruit, a red, red fruit in the hooked bill of the green parrot. . . .

Down there, a cool bower . . . a cool, cool, cool, bower . . . the fragrant bower, fragrant with the yellow *kedige* . . . . Watch, watch . . . watch how it's bursting. . . . Watch the rough, long, thorny-edged, green leaf. . . . Inside the green leaf, soft yellow . . . smooth yellow, fragrant yellow, powdery yellow, slippery yellow, slinky yellow. . . . Walk on, walk softly, softly walk. . . . Watch here is *basaree,* here jackfruit tree. . . . This is *nandi.* . . . This is *muttuga.* . . . This is mango. . . . This is *ranja.* . . . This is banyan. . . . Look at the roots that grow downwards from its branches to reach the ground. . . . Look at the nail at the tip of the root, the roots that are the matted hair of the rishi. . . .

The blue sky above. . . . The wide open space below. . . . Walk on. . . .

Look at the little sapling. . . . On the sapling, a leaf . . . . On the leaf something springs . . . springs suddenly. . . .

Remember that day on our way to school, how it sprang, the grasshopper? You dropped the books and stood there watching transfixed . . . watching . . . watching the sun's mount . . . the galloping stallion. You watched how the sun rode on its humped back. . . . The mighty sun, sitting lightly on it, sitting invisibly on it, shimmering in a corner.

Look where the sun shimmers. . . . Shimmers in its feelers. . . . Shimmers in its green peak. . . . Shimmers in the pupil of its eye. . . . Shimmers from the cloud's edge . . . tumbles, slips, breaks into pieces . . . forms shadows, forms colours . . . sets, rises, burns. . . .

See the wide open space, vast space. . . . Above, the burning sun. Carrying him lightly on its back and hopping, all along in the open field, is the sun's mount. . . . See its saddleless swagger . . . its crooked legs . . . its stiff tail . . . its feelers groping for the world . . . it is hopping from leaf to leaf. . . . See the whole of it. . . . See the parts of it. . . . The eyes green . . . a heap of green . . . frothing green. . . . Listen. . . . Listen to the stallion of the sun . . .

I am no beast. You are no man. So, let one be the other.

Brother Ananthu. . . . Hop on, Ananthu. . . . Carry the sun on your back . . .

Be gone, gone . . . the fury gone . . . the frowning gone . . . the ego gone. . . . Greed for the gold, bragging of the birth all gone . . .

Be gone, evil spell. . . . Wicked spell. . . . Father's
spell. . . . Mother's spell. . . . Priest's spell. . . . Layman's
spell . . . . Prostitute's spell . . . . Paramour's
spell. . . . Spell of death . . . spell of vulva . . . spell of the
street . . . spell of the books. . . . All spells, be gone.

The stallion of the sun is all that is left. You are the
stallion. . . . You are the stallion of the sun. . . .

In this manner words poured forth in rhythmic
accompaniment to the dance of his thousand fingers on my head.
Venkata wiped off the oil flowing down to my eyes. He asked
eagerly: 'Ananthu, are you beginning to see the moonlight yet?'

I said, 'Yes,' not wishing to disappoint him. He was drenched
in perspiration. Sitting still, naked before him, I became
self-conscious.

'This time, you only got a glimpse. Wait till I give you my
next oil massage; you will see the real moonlight,' he said inhaling
the snuff.

I was wrong. This simpleton Venkata, too, is a scheming
politician. What a manipulator! He was trying to change my very
'being'.

He made me sit in the tub filled with hot water and told me
to rub myself under the armpits and between the legs. He poured
the cool *matti* essence on my head and vigorously rubbed my head
with soap-nut powder. Scooping up water in a pitcher, he poured
it on me with force. The steam and the boiling water made my
body flaming red. I was too weak to dry myself. He dried me, gave
me a cool drink made of jaggery, smeared my forehead with some
soot from the bottom of the boiler. Then bringing me into the
house, made me lie down on the bed, covered me with all the
blankets that were in the house and said, 'You have to sweat it out.'
In a while I was all soaked as if I had taken the bath once again.
He dried me again and laid me on the grass mat. He brought me
steaming coffee. After drinking it I felt drowsy. In the kitchen
Rukku was crying and preparing *patrode*.

When I woke up, I heard Venkata pleading with his wife,
'Please make some rice gruel for Sheshanna. I'll take and feed it
to him myself.' 'They say his son sends him five hundred rupees

every month. But he doesn't pay you a single paisa. You don't care about your own son, yet you expect me to care about that miser. What is it to me whether he lives or dies?" Rukku screamed. Still, Venkata got Shakuntala to make some rice gruel and took it to Sheshanna's house.

I had sat up in the bed now. Rukku came and stood before me and started to cry. According to her, Subba was under the influence of inauspicious stars. He wanted to go to Bangalore or Mysore to become a mechanic. Why shouldn't he also prosper like Sheshanna's son? He didn't lack brains. At least, as a favour to my childhood friend, I should take his son with me to Mysore and set him up there in some job.

I was afraid. If I took him home with me, my wife would not put up with his antics. Still I promised Rukku that I would do something for him. I'll get him a room on rent somewhere, I told myself. My assurance made Rukku so happy that it brightened up the whole house. When Venkata returned, he saw the changed mood of his household, and he too became exuberant. But he didn't know of the promise I had made his wife. As if he were enacting a scene from a comic drama, he acted out a past instance of Sheshanna's stinginess, without showing the least bitterness for him: Venkata had just then bought some medicine for him. Again and again, Sheshanna counted the change Venkata had brought back. (Seeing Venkata mimic Sheshanna's cough and count the coins with shaky hands, even Rukku laughed.) When Sheshanna started counting once again, Venkata asked him, 'Anything wrong?' 'This quarter seems all worn off,' said Sheshanna. 'It's a good coin. It'll still pass,' said Venkata. 'But why take a chance? Go back and pass this off, and bring me another quarter, will you?' (Venkata begged in a illness-stricken voice, just like Sheshanna's.) 'Do you want me to go right now?' asked Venkata, having just walked three miles from the town. 'Is there anything else you want done in the town that cannot wait till another day?' Sheshanna's ashen face showed supreme contentment. 'I knew that he wouldn't be able to sleep. So I gave him a different quarter I had with me,' said Venkata and took out from his pocket the worn quarter he had been unable to pass off. 'When he dies, throw it on his corpse,' Rukku said angrily, and got up and went inside to get the supper ready.

Since childhood, I was very fond of *patrode*. But now something had happened which prevented me from eating Rukku's *patrode*. I couldn't help noticing that Rukku was crying uncontrollably while Shakuntala and Venkata were trying unsuccessfully to console her. Soon I learned what had happened: she wanted to serve me the *kheeru* in the silver cup. So, she went to look for it in the brass trunk in which she kept all the things she had brought with her as dowry when she got married. When she opened the trunk, what did she find? The *gorochana* dye kept for her future grandchildren, some nutmeg, dried ginger, *kasturi* pills, a *rudrakshi* berry, dried shell of pomegranate, a piece of sandalwood, soap-nut for washing jewellery—everything else was gone. All those pieces of jewellery which, despite poverty, had been saved from being pawned away because Rukku had the foresight to put them away for the girls when they would get married—earrings, ear chains, a four-stranded necklace, four bracelets, a waist-band, an ornament of floral design for the braid, a nose ring, a pair of anklets, a coral chain, two silver bowls, three silver cups, a silver cup used for worship, a silver pitcher, a silver spoon, silver boxes for *kumkum* and turmeric. Everything that had been put away, wrapped in a piece of an old silk saree after the Gouri festival, had now vanished.

Venkata had been pressing me to eat the *patrode* pretending that nothing had happened, when Ganga, the youngest girl, came running and said anxiously: 'Mother is crying. Subba has stolen all the jewellery. Everything was there when Mother opened the trunk on Friday to get the pomegranate shell to make medicine for your stomach-ache. You remember, the day before yesterday, Mother went to the river to wash clothes and Shaku and Gouri also went with her? That same day Subba came to me and handing me a wet strip of banana fibre, told me: "Go, string some jasmine flowers; I'll sell them for you in the town and bring you some money." I went to the backyard wondering why Brother was not nice to me that day. When I got back, he was doing something in the room. I told myself that he must have shut himself in the room to smoke a beedi.'

Neither Venkata, nor Shaku, nor Gouri said anything. Shaku went inside to comfort her mother. 'We will find it. Where will it go? He must have pawned it. You eat,' Venkata said urging *patrode* on me. He finished eating quickly. I went through the motions of eating. I went out of the house and sat down on the front steps. Thinking 'what hardships for these innocent creatures!' I looked around me for any sign of Subba. From where I was sitting, I could see one or two houses in the distance, a temple and a dirt-track made by the walking of people, another path leading to town. Further on, a green hill. The air was permeated with the fragrance of yellow-stemmed *parijata*. All over the frontyard of the house were flowering plants. The moonlight I had failed to see in Venkata's massage had now filled the flower garden. I could hear Rukku crying and whimpering inside: 'Oh! How am I going to see my daughters married? Instead of what he did, why did he not stab his own mother's womb?'

Venkata came out and stood near me, and said, 'Ah, moonlight!' Probably he was seeking me out to wait for his wife's sorrow to subside. Maybe he felt uneasy thinking that I might be distressed. It pained me to see my friend so uncharacteristically quiet. 'Come and sit,' I said. 'Nice fragrance, isn't it?' he said. I smiled and motioned to him to keep quiet. I am not good at comforting others. Still, I went inside to urge Rukku to eat. She went on weeping. I came out of the house again. 'You know, our Ganga is very fond of this garden,' Venkata said, pacing to and fro in the garden.

Far into the night, nobody seemed able to sleep. It seemed to me unfair that of all the people in the world this innocuous Venkata should be punished with a son like Subba. Who knows what would have become of me, if I too had remained rotting in this village? Because I dared to defy my father and reject the family's traditions, I was able to grow and become what I am today. But was it inevitable in this family too? Venkata seemed cowed by his son. His clowning, his massaging, his altruism—nothing seemed to be of any use here. This very moon, this shrub, this tree, these birds have nurtured a nature like Venkata's as well as inexplicable violence like Subba's. Can Venkata's nature stomach it? Or, will it give in? If so, one can only feel pity and discomfiture at the clowning of an escapist. All the same, I couldn't just brush aside my childhood friend who had just begun to resuscitate my waning love for humankind. The image of Venkata petrified and cringing before his menacing son was still troubling me. With a stone in his raised hand, Subba had seemed like a barbaric caveman whose indomitable brute strength was about to explode. This barbaric defiance and denial seemed the very source and vital energy for the creation of nuclear weapons and poisonous gas. It was born, of course, out of the rejection of Venkata's narrow and insipid world. I know it, for I, too, defied my parents. In a state like Venkata's, one can only blossom like the *parijata* and then wither away. There is no movement in that state.

My imagination had probably exaggerated it when, before falling asleep, I thought of Subba as the image of movement. 'What is so heroic about stealing?' I later tried to temper my revolutionary thoughts. But I was still troubled by what I saw afterwards. Just before daybreak, when everyone else was asleep and outside, one could clearly see everything dew-drenched under the starlit sky.

I thought that I heard a sound coming from the garden. I got up and went out to see. It was the sound of a tree being cut down. 'Who's there?' I called out and was about to go down the front steps when Subba shouted, brandishing a scythe at me, 'If you come near, I'll cut you to pieces.' I stood still. With his hair dishevelled, teeth gritted, cutting down the *parijata* tree in the morning twilight, he seemed a *rakshas* to me. He had already cut the flowering plants and shrubs down to the ground. Only the rugged and knotty *parijata* tree had still withstood the sweeping strokes of the scythe. Venkata, who had got up after me, ran toward Subba. Subba raised the scythe and would have brought it down upon his father had Venkata not ducked in time and ran back calling out 'Mother Goddess!' I tried to restrain Rukku who squirmed in my clasp and shouted to her son, 'Come, cut me up! Kill me! I gave birth to poison and I'll die by it!' Freeing herself, she ran and stood before Subba while her daughters tried to stop her. 'Don't you dare me! I'll chop your head off!' said Subba raising the scythe. We all stood there, eyes closed, stupefied. When I opened my eyes fearing the worst, Subba had jerked out the hand that held the scythe from his mother's grip, and, shouting curses, was walking away past the fence-gate. He walked briskly towards the town and was soon out of sight. Rukku still stood with eyes closed as if she expected the scythe to fall on her at any moment.

Venkata dragged her by the hand into the house. Seeing the garden all razed to the ground, Ganga began to cry and, looking at her, her elder sisters cried too. I sat down on the mound of earth, my senses all numbed. No comforting words were left in me. But I, who thought that all that had happened had left Venkata devastated, was in for a surprise in the morning.

It is astonishing how, no matter who dies or what the calamity is, life's routines go on. Despite the funereal air in Venkata's household that morning, Shakuntala made coffee. I cleaned my teeth with ashes of rice husk. Having had his early morning bath, Venkata was making the sandal paste for worship at the riverside temple. Only Rukku had taken to bed. Gouri hurriedly milked the cows, for the cowherd boy was already there to take them for grazing. I sensed that something inside Venkata had died, and not being able to look him in the eye, I came out and sat on the front steps but couldn't bear the sight of the ruined garden and so went around to the backyard and stood there under the pomegranate tree.

Near the fence stood Venkata in his bandy-legged posture, with no clothes on except his loincloth. That was Venkata there by the backyard fence! 'What is he doing there, standing so engrossed?' I wondered. He couldn't have gone out to evacuate, because I didn't see his sacred thread over his ear. Besides he had already finished his morning ablutions and done his morning prayers. I watched him, standing there by the hedge, motionless as a temple idol, almost naked, engrossed. The green fence-hedge facing him was tall, so he couldn't be seeing anything beyond it. I walked towards him softly, noiselessly, and stood behind him. Still, Venkata didn't know I was there. Curious to find out what he was looking at, I followed the direction of his gaze, peering at the hedge and scanning its leaves and flowers and everything else that came in the range of my vision. What came in sight was a grasshopper. For a moment, it was amusing to watch my friend, Simpleton Venkata, looking fascinatedly at this humpbacked, bent-legged, gaunt, green triangular insect, but only for a moment. Pressing down its bent legs, the grasshopper sprang and hopped away. The moment it sprang, Venkata's half-shaved head shook as if he just came out of a trance which I was glad to notice. Turning around and seeing me there behind him, he beamed an innocent smile and said, 'Stallion of the Sun!' I looked into his fascinated eyes and my mouth fell open.

'Stallion of the Sun,' I said.

— *Translated by Narayan Hegde*

Orphans

Raghavendra Khasaneesa

The stream had just enough water to cover a man's foot, no more. It was flowing down a slope to join the river. So the current was fast. But the driver couldn't have known how muddy it was and how it would mire the wheels of the bus in the shallow water. He started the engine again and again at full speed, revved it, and turned the steering wheel over and over. But the bus didn't budge. It would neither go forward nor backward. Meanwhile the water level was rising. In despair, the driver angrily turned the steering wheel a full circle and let go of it. The bus suddenly jumped forward and stopped dead.

Sister let out a scream. Her head had hit the bar behind her seat. Water had rushed in through the half-open door. People standing inside had lost their balance and fallen over one another. Sister didn't understand any of this confusion. Through the window she could see big rocks some distance away. Even as she looked, the water seemed to rise and swirl around the bus. She covered her face and screamed again.

Father, who was sitting behind Sister, dozing all this time, was suddenly jolted by the way the bus came to a dead stop. He woke up, looked around, and fell asleep again. When Sister screamed a second time, he sat up, bolt upright. It began to dawn on him that some disaster was imminent.

Mother was not particularly afraid. She was sitting by Sister's side and trying to hold her down by the shoulder. A chill ran through her as if someone had poured ice-cold water into her bowels. She thought that Sister's madness was coming back. Why else would she let out such terrible screams?

Brother, who had moved deliberately to the front seat to escape the rest of his family, didn't hear his sister's screams. The woman in the next seat had been thrown against him by the jolting of the bus. The heavy scent of the jasmine in her hair had overwhelmed him and wiped out the accident. It was some time since a woman's body had dashed against his, like this, with force. Touch fused with smell and it seemed to him that her touch itself was heavy with the scent of jasmine. The next minute he feared that his mother might be staring at him from behind. Helplessly, he moved away from the woman and sat up.

The bus stood stock-still. The driver had put a beedi between his lips, struck a match, lifted his face upward and exhaled a puff of smoke. The bus conductor, who was standing at the front door, looked around at everyone and smiled as if such accidents were nothing unusual, mere routine.

'What, do you mean to dump the bus in the water and offer us all up as a sacrifice this morning?' asked the old widow who was sitting nearby, turning to the driver and glancing at the conductor. She was hugging a bundle close to her, as if it were a baby or something. She looked around to see if anyone approved of her complaining. But everyone was silent. So she continued: 'I've made pilgrimages from Kashi to Rameswaram. I've gone up the hills of Tirupati on a bus. I even went to Badri in the Himalayas in a bus. But I haven't met with this kind of accident anywhere else. This is the way private bus companies are run. This is their fate. They employ scoundrels who are really fit to be *jutka* drivers. Good-for-nothings!' Having said what she did, she took out a rosary and began to mumble and count, as if to justify herself. The conductor didn't even wait for her to finish her speech, let alone answer her. He had moved away. A dark-skinned merchant had begun to shout at the driver from the seat behind him.

As a last resort, the conductor got down and tried to get the passengers to push the bus towards the bank. The wheels were raised and pulled out of the mire. The muddy water around the tyres was divided in two and beaten into foam. Sister stared at the water and the foam on it. It seemed to her as if the bus was floating on the water and spinning like a top in a whirlpool.

It took a long time for them all to bring the bus to the bank, find the missing conductor, and climb back into their seats. The bus moved fast this time.

The widow was rapt in telling her beads. The woman next to the widow looked intently at her and asked her with great interest:

'You have made so many pilgrimages. You have earned much merit. Are you also going to Mantralaya now?'

The woman's face was lustreless. A big vermilion mark on her forehead. Maybe she was a very sick woman: her body seemed dry and wasted; the veins on her hands were standing out; her eyes were sunken and there were dark lines under them. Right next to her, holding on to her, sat two weakling boys.

The widow said: 'I haven't gone home in two years. I've been on pilgrimages all this time. Still there are so many holy places to go and see. How about you . . .?' Her words were suddenly drowned by the horn that the driver blew. He was trying to shoo away the bullock-cart that was in his way, occupying the entire road. When the sound of the horn stopped, the woman was telling the widow: '. . . I've seen so many doctors, tried special diets and medicines, offered vows to so many gods. But nothing has helped. Some good people told me to come here to Mantralaya and make offerings to the Lord. So I am going there. What can I lose? I've no fears. These boys are so young. Who'll take care of them when I'm gone?' The mother looked at her boys and they looked back into her eyes as if ready to obey her every wish.

'Have faith. The Lord is great and powerful. All things will be well. I've myself seen it happen many times,' said someone from behind. The woman turned around to see who spoke. It was a middle-aged married woman. Her chin and her cheeks were covered with the yellow of turmeric. The jewel on her small nose seemed rather large.

The sick woman with the children smiled at her and the middle-aged married woman opened a conversation:

'Mantralaya is a great centre for pilgrimage, a place where people earn merit. O, what great miracles have happened there! There's a boy in the shrine; he's the one who brings the lamp offering and the camphor to the devotees after it has been offered to the Lord. When you go there, you'll surely see him. Four years ago when he came here he couldn't move his tongue. Born deaf-mute. But now, after serving the Lord, he has begun to stammer and speak slowly. Not once, not twice, I've seen this kind of thing happen many times. A month ago, a woman brought her husband who had gone crazy. Everyday, at puja time he would stand before the Lord's image and weep, tears streaming down his

face. One day, I don't know what occurred to him. He went to the
river at night. He must have gone there to drown himself. As he
was getting into the water, he heard someone calling him. He
turned around and saw a holy figure swathed in light. The figure
said, 'You've had your bath. You're clean now. Get up and come
out.' Then he held out something and said, 'Here, take this
sandalwood paste, wear the sandal mark on your forehead. Go to
the Maruti temple, offer your devotions, get His blessing and go
home.' Like a man under a spell, the man came out of the water,
received the sandal paste and walked towards the temple. He
didn't think very much about it at the time. He thought it was some
holy guru, some *acharya*. But after walking a few steps he turned
around. There was no one there. Even that didn't particularly
strike him as odd. In the middle of the night, he walked straight
into the enclosure of the temple, offered his devotions to Maruti
the Monkey God, and then went to see the *vrindavana* of the Lord.
Near the threshold he fell and fainted. It was morning when he
woke up. The priests of the *math* were standing all around him,
aghast because every night at ten o'clock they lock up all the doors
of the temple. There is no way anybody can get in. The doors were
still locked just as they had left them. When they asked him how
he got there, he was in no state to answer their questions. For the
next three or four days, he searched restlessly for the holy figure
he had seen that night. How would he find the vanished figure?
The Master had come personally and given him back his life as a
boon and he was gone. The man was utterly changed—he has now
given up everything and has become a servant of the Lord.'

By this time, they were near Mantralaya. Through the
windows of the bus, they could see the Tungabhadra river flowing
quietly, in several strands. The whitewashed big walls of the *math*
seemed to move and approach them.

The ailing woman's face brightened up a little. She said, her
voice trembling, 'Then I too may get better. Who are you, good
lady? You've seen all this with your own eyes. Have you also come
to offer services to the Master?'

The middle-aged married woman laughed for no reason at
all. Then she picked up her satchel from the floor of the bus and
said, 'I'm not an outsider. I belong to this place. My husband is a
priest who performs Vedic rituals here. This is probably your first

time here. There, we've reached Mantralaya. There. But don't get down here. Go to the *choultry* and find a place to stay there. If you go anywhere else, it will cost you money.' Just then the bus suddenly turned. The married woman who was about to get up fell back in her seat. 'I'll take leave now. I'll see you tomorrow near the river. If you're giving ritual gifts, don't give them to anyone else. My name is Kalavati. Everyone calls me Kallavva. If anyone asks you to whom you're giving your ritual gifts, say you're giving it all to Kallavva.' Giving the visitor no choice, Kallavva had bound her to a promise.

Outside the bus, at a distance, the water of the river shone and flashed, like a broken mirror held up by little boys. The weary faces of the travellers, tired out by the journey, crowded at the windows longing to see the sights of the outside world.

When the bus reached the bus station, Brother had strayed far away, following the scent of jasmine, lost in some forest of memory and fantasy. Sister remembered the waters bubbling and foaming under the wheels of the bus and she was shaking with fear. Mother was holding her tight and sat there with an empty heart. Father was still groggy, half-asleep.

*

Though dawn was still an hour away, crowds of people had gathered at the river-bank. Their ritual baths would be over soon as the temple services began before dawn.

The foursome—Father, Mother, Brother and Sister—walked carefully on the boulders and reached the water's edge. Father was really angry. Where was it written that one should take a dip in this ice-cold water and stand before the God at dawn? Wouldn't it do if one took a bath after the sun was up and then went to the temple? As soon as he woke up, he had told Brother quite firmly, 'You folks go ahead. I'll come later.' Mother had heard this. When Father looked at her face, he knew she didn't like it. She was muttering, 'He's always like this. He thinks he's doing all this because of me. Our sick daughter should get well, that's why we're here . . .' But Sister came running at that moment and the words stopped half-way.

Someone said, 'Sir, don't go that way. The current is strong there. Here, come this way. And look, don't swim there either. Lots of rocks lie under that water everywhere.' Father couldn't tell who was shouting these warnings. Neither could he tell to whom these remarks were addressed. There was quite a crowd in the river.The noise level was high. One couldn't hear anything anyone said. He sat down on a boulder till Mother finished giving Sister a bath and came out of the water. A voice said, 'Please move aside and sit a little to one side of the path. Women and children walk this way. If you sit like that in the middle of the road where women, especially orthodox widows, walk after their ritual bath, where would they go?' Father turned around to see who it was. The same hunchbacked woman. She was still walking bent double, her back curved like a bow. No change in her after all these years. She had just become thinner and darker, that's all. She had a small brass vessel in her hand. The metal was dented and worn out in places. Maybe the same vessel that was in her hand twelve years ago . . . at that time Mother had quarrelled with him and left for her birthplace; so he had come here to Mantralaya with the two children. Brother was still in high school and his sister had just left school. Father had come here then mainly because he had a free railway pass. And because the children happened to have holidays right then. He hadn't come to the holy place to petition the God that his wife should return to him—no, not by any means. Her character was like that. He hadn't refused her anything at anytime. Still she had got together a hundred rupees by stealth. When she left town, she had secretly tied it in a knot of her saree and transferred it to her suitcase. He had noticed that. He had said that it was not a good thing for a woman to hide money from her husband and carry it out of the house. She didn't like that. She was angered by his remark and that's why she had left for her birthplace. . . .

Then he had come to Mantralaya.

That hunchbacked woman has been here from that time. When Sister had seen her then, she had taken fright and stood at a distance. Her fear had been mixed with disgust. Brother had noticed the brass pot in her hand and had named her, 'The Hunchback with the Pot.'

Sister remembered nothing of all that now.

But did Brother also forget?

Father wanted to remind Brother of the previous visit and turned around to find him. But where was Brother? A blue sky on one side. On the other, black rocks strewn about. Brother was nowhere to be seen. Behind a boulder in the distance, women were taking baths. They had spread their clothes to dry on the boulder.

Father looked around again and again. But Brother was nowhere. He felt great compassion for Brother. He felt like asking him to come sit next to him and caress his back tenderly. When he was Brother's age, he hadn't even been married. But Brother had lost his wife. So young, he had become a widower.

Father remembered Brother's wife. He remembered the old station where they lived. He remembered the railway tracks. Only yesterday, it seemed, she was a girl who had grown up under his care, right before his eyes. She had become a wife. Now she was a mere story, a memory. She had died so young, a child who hadn't even heard of death. The day she died, it felt as if she would have got up and walked straight home, rubbing her eyes, if only someone had touched her and woken her up.

Gradually Father began to realize that his head was getting hot under the sun's rays. He picked up his wet dhoti from the ground and put it on his head.

Big black rocks lay all around like chunks of iron. The way from the river to the *math* passed right over the rocks. At the end of the path there was a high wall, looking quite splendid. If you cross the wall, you get to the *math*. The wall was whitewashed with lime and on it were long vertical stripes painted with red earth.

Mother had finished bathing Sister and was walking towards the riverbank in wet clothes. She was a little embarrassed to get up from the water and walk to the bank. Wet clothes clung to her body. She was a respectable woman. So she felt even more embarrassed than others. But Sister walked unawares. Like a little boy running from his bath, she was running, without a thought.

The noise around the river was dying down. People were making haste to go the *math*. The clothes spread over the rocks to dry were vanishing one by one.

A *komata* woman sitting near the water washing her clothes said, 'Come up slowly. The rocks are covered with moss and you may slip. Two days ago, when I said that to a lady, do you know, she got terribly angry with me? What wrong did I do by saying that? But in the end it happened just as I said; as she walked out in a rage, she slipped on the moss and broke her leg.'

Mother also got annoyed with her. She felt like telling her to mind her own business. But she held her tongue. What was the point of picking a quarrel with someone at daybreak? She took little steps carefully and she helped Sister get on to the bank, and sighed deeply.

Sister seemed very calm ever since she'd reached here. Her face was sad. Lost in some fantasy of her own, she looked as if she was drugged. But what a ruckus she made when they were all living near the railway station! If she so much as heard the noise of a train, she would run here and there towards the railway lines. Everyone had to run behind her and hold her down. Even if there was no danger of a train coming that way, there was a disused well on the other side of the railway lines, right down the slope.

Mother looked around as she began to drape her body in her saree. She was looking to see if anyone was watching her. Just then a stiff wind blew in her direction and filled the saree-end she held in her hand. The saree grew full and fluttered like a ship's sail. Mother was flustered. She gathered her saree in a bunch and held it close and tight. If anyone was sitting where Sister was sitting, they would have had a good look at her calves, firm and fair-skinned and fleshy.

At a distance, Father was talking to a couple of people. He was moving his hands and obviously explaining something. She could not see anyone's face clearly. Mother remembered something. She looked around in panic. Sister, where was she? She was sitting right here a minute ago. Where had she gone?

Father didn't remember having seen that gentleman anywhere before this. The man was short and dark, maybe over fifty-five. When he laughed, his youthful teeth flashed. Maybe they were not even his real teeth. And the gentleman who was with him seemed to be an utter stranger. The dark-skinned old man said, 'I couldn't recognize you at all. You have changed so much!' Father was rather baffled by this man's talk. Saying he couldn't recognize him, the man recognized him and talked to him. He hadn't changed, had he? A whole lifetime had passed by, but he was the same man he always was. Not a change. Maybe he would change at least from then on.

When Father was silent, the old man raised his voice and said, 'When you were a goods clerk in the Sholapur Station, I was a signal man there. That must be thirty years ago. I retired recently as station master at Takari. You've really lost weight, I must say.'

'O, I'm getting old. Who can stay the same, tell me? Now I remember you. You haven't stayed the same either.'

Father didn't really recognize the old man. He didn't have a clue. He was being polite, that's all.

The old man continued, 'Have you come here alone, or with . . .?'

'The whole family is here. My daughter is not well. So we've come here to offer prayers.'

'Why, what's the matter?'

'O nothing much. Now and then she seems to forget herself.'

Mother meanwhile had caught up with Sister who had moved towards the water. She was restlessly waiting for Father to join her.

'Well, then. Let's get together later. Will you be here till the festival or will you leave just after you've made your offerings?'

'We must see what the Lord wills. I've thought of staying on. I hope it will work out.'

They could hear the peal of bells and gongs from the *math*. The river-bank was filled with smells of turmeric, vermilion and sandal paste. When Father left them, the dark old man said to his companion, 'He is a rich man. He has lakhs of rupees. He retired as goods-master, made a lot of money. But what's the use of mere money? His wife is an ogress. They never got along. Against her husband's wishes, she got their son married to a girl from among her own kin. And she didn't even treat that girl very well. So the girl couldn't bear the ill-treatment and killed herself. She fell under the wheels of a running train. Not very long ago. Three months later, his daughter went mad. People say that she is possessed by the dead daughter-in-law. All this talk about her being forgetful is hogwash. The girl is off her rocker, stark mad, I tell you.'

Father had the wet dhoti on his head. Mother had tied her saree rather high over her calves, taking it between her legs, tucked at the back in the customary way. Sister was running, taking long strides like an athelete. She was spreading her wet hair wide over her shoulders.

They could hear the sound of bells and gongs from the *math*.

*

From where Father sat, he could see the white northern wall. There was a small window-like door in the wall. People were coming in through the door, one by one, after bathing in the river. Right outside the door stood a big neem tree. Father had heard, when he was a child, that demons who were once Brahmins lived in the tree. A branch of the tree had cracked the wall and jutted through it. Father sat there, staring at the branch. One night, a devotee passed through that door when a Brahmin demon attacked him. But the devotee, scared though he was, took courage and chanted a hymn to the Lord, and the demon left him alone.

Right in front of him, he could see Mother and Sister. They were circumambulating the temple. Sister's brow was covered with sand. Her eyelids were wet. Mother was panting, out of breath. When he looked at them, Father felt strange feelings go through him. It was as if they were complete strangers, two drops in the sea of people. Who were they? If they hadn't all been together all these years, would there be any relation between him and them? Could he say that? Why were they together all these years and how did it come about? Father had no answers to these questions.

The public noon meal at the *math* was usually late. As the mealtime approached, the crowd grew. Father was already hungry. He couldn't bear hunger, he never could. When he was hungry, his brain got addled. He couldn't think. When his daughter-in-law died, the same thing had happened to him. On that day, supervisors had come to inspect his station. Obviously someone had sent in a complaint. He had had to gobble his meal in a hurry and run to the goods shed. By suppertime, things had happened. Nobody could have imagined how a terrifying death would swoop down and carry away Daughter-in-law so easily, suddenly. She was sitting at the knife-stand slicing potatoes. Mother had scolded her for being careless; she had let the milk on the stove boil over. Daughter-in-law had suddenly got up and left the house. She never returned. She ran and ran, and before his very eyes, she had merged and disappeared in a rattle and thunder of the evening express train. By the time the confusion had died down and he returned home, it was four in the morning. He had been hungry like this on that day.

He marvelled at Brother. He didn't know when he had turned religious and become a devotee of the Lord. Did his wife's death do this to him? Brother was now circumambulating the temple. His eyes were closed. He was full of devotion. What was he praying for, what desire was he trying to fulfil through prayer?

Brother was a bit bored with his many circumambulations. His legs were aching. If his wife were around, she might have scolded him: 'When you're in town, you don't mind roaming all over town. Your legs don't ache then. But when it comes to going round the temple, they hurt, don't they? You shouldn't stint in the service of the Lord.' When he remembered that, he felt he should continue walking round the temple. But, as for him, he didn't have any faith in God. He never did. Then why was he now going round and round the temple? To please her? When she was alive, it had never occurred to him to try and please her. Why now, what can give her any pleasure now? When she was alive he didn't manage to satisfy even a little wish of hers. In the early days of their marriage, she had wanted very much to visit this very place, this Mantralaya. But Mother squashed that plan. She had said: 'Why go now, she is so young, where's the hurry? She will certainly go there some day. We've spent such a lot on the wedding. Why do you want to spend some more now?' So that wish had remained a wish. She'd never laid eyes on Mantralaya. Now, hardly six months after her death, here they were, all of them, visiting Mantralaya.

As he walked, his feet got tangled in his dhoti. He stumbled and was about to fall. But he held on to the wall next to him and avoided the fall. At some distance, Mother was talking to someone. She had stopped her circumambulation half-way and she was explaining something, moving her hands. He knew very well what she was saying. She went about telling everyone that her daughter-in-law had had a bad death, that she had become a ghost and possessed Sister. She cried loudly before everyone and said, 'I did so much for my daughter-in-law. But she has gone and given me a bad name, even in death.'

Everyone in the family was unhappy about Mother's

temperament. Brother had long known, ever since he came of age, that Father had long ago given up all hope of happiness in his marriage. Mother's behaviour was always strange. She suspected something or other if Father ate well at dinner; she also suspected something if he didn't eat well. If Father forgot himself somewhere and spoke smilingly to any woman, that would be the end. You couldn't really watch the *avatara* that Mother took then. Brother had begun to understand these things, bit by bit, as he grew up. If anything was said against her any time, she would scratch everything up. Fits of anger, sullen moods, words of bitterness. It was a mess. When he was small, she had fought with Father over some small thing and had walked away. She had sat all day outside the Monkey God's temple and come back in the evening. At another time, she had threatened to throw herself down the well. She had sat on the bund around the well all day and returned home in the evening.

Talk of death was an everyday event with Mother. It was always on her lips. Anytime she was angry, she threatened to kill herself. She walked out and returned when she had cooled off.

Brother's legs were really aching now. He felt weak. He was bored with his circumambulations. The ground under him was hot under the afternoon sun. He realized that he was also thirsty. He walked towards the platform where he had left a pot full of water from the river.

From where he sat, he could see the *vrindavana* of the Lord. Just under it, leaning against a pillar, sat an old man. He was wearing a bright red silk dhoti. It looked as if half his body was paralysed. The woman sitting next to him, holding him, must be his wife. Next to them, two girls were busy making a garland out of jasmines. One of them had no vermilion on her bare brow, only a green tattoo mark. She was wearing no ornaments of any kind. She was wrapped in a clean white saree. Must be a widow. The other girl had a mark of vermilion on her brow. She was not married yet. Brother didn't particularly pay attention to her.

He was looking intently at the young woman with the bare forehead with the green mark. After quite some time, he realized why he liked looking at her. From one side, she looked exactly like his wife. He had been staring at her for quite some time. Her smile was really like his wife's. When she noticed that he was staring at her, he turned away. Brother was startled by his own behaviour, looked this way and that, and then tried to focus his gaze on the peepul tree nearby.

A shiver ran through him. Her stare seemed to express nothing. Brother was afraid. He wondered why he was so afraid of Mother. What was wrong with his looking at that woman? Didn't Mother ever look at any man? But . . . why do all of them get so scared of Mother? Father was scared. Sister was wilting under the heat of Mother's terrifying gaze; she was withering, slowly fading away. He too was terrified. The one person who didn't flinch before Mother didn't last very long. Brother thought of his wife and felt proud of her. She was sick of the trouble that Mother gave. She wept. She suffered it all without a sound all her married life. But she never once was afraid. In the early days of their marriage, they had told Mother they were visiting a friend, but they had gone to see a circus together. Mother somehow found out about it the very next day. She was beside herself with fury. She screamed at them. She accused them of lying to her. She said they had done that just to avoid taking Sister with them. And wilfully she had sent Sister to the circus that very day with a neighbour's daughter. In spite of all this ruckus, his wife didn't utter a word, she kept her peace and went about her business. Another time, they had gone out without telling Mother and they had had their picture taken. Mother was wild. She howled in rage. It got worse and worse, till Mother threatened to throw herself down the well and kill herself. Daughter-in-law faced her this time with an anger that matched hers. She had said boldly, 'Why don't you do as you say and just throw yourself down the well? Let's see how strong you are. Do people who really mean it ever tell the whole town they are going to die before they die? Do they call the town-crier and announce it with drums?'

As if to prove her point, Daughter-in-law had died without a word to anyone. Did she run out like that just to make good her words? In Mother's hands, death was a mockery, a cheap commodity. Talking and thinking of death all her days, she didn't even get to live well. Life was no pleasure to her and she didn't earn the peace of death either. This Mother who chattered about death every day of her life would beg for life on the day of her death.

Brother counted. How long did it take to run from their house to the railway lines? How did it happen that her running time coincided with the coming of the train that day? When Mother scolded her, maybe her eyes filled with tears. Did the tears blind her eyes, make her lose her way? He himself had stumbled many times on the signal wires near the railway lines, and that too, in broad daylight, hadn't he? Why didn't that wire cut her speed that day and stop her? She was always afraid of the dark. How did she get the courage to run out alone that day? None of the questions had any answers. Everything had just happened. It was all over.

Memories of his wife troubled Brother. But he shed no tears. Tears had dried up in him, turned to ash in the funeral fires. Father, Mother, Sister and himself—they were not close, they were not knit in a relationship. Somehow, without any choice, they were all together, dependent on one another, living together. He remembered the circus, the way the acrobats flew from trapeze to trapeze in space. Like them, they too had to rely on one another, have faith in one another, for dear life. One person's life depended on another's, everyone's seemed to depend on just one person. His wife had tried to ignore this subtle principle. She had tried to shake free. She had lost her hold and had fallen to her death. Now was it Sister's turn, was she hanging by a thread? If she let go, all of them would crash to the ground one by one. But Sister didn't know a thing. She didn't know that she held everyone's life-thread in her hand. When was she capable of reasoning? If tomorrow she got well and got back to normal, everyone would go their own ways. Father would probably not stay home very long. And he himself, what was there to keep him in that house? This family's honour depended on her not getting well. If she got any better, this family would go to pieces. Everyone would fall apart.

The heat of the sun was unbearable. Sweat was pouring from his body. He was weak from hunger and felt drowsy. But he wasn't really sleepy. He was sitting next to a wall and he leaned his head against it. A couple of people who were sitting near him were talking among themselves.

'Say what you will, the *math* is not as it used to be. Its glory is gone. Its prestige is not what it used to be.'

'What are you saying? The guru's power is felt everywhere. Pilgrims from different provinces, speaking so many different languages, are crowding this place more than ever.'

'I'm not talking about the guru or the Lord. I'm talking about the prestige of the *math*. When the late guru was here, you probably never visited this place. O, the banquets he gave the pilgrims! For months you could have eaten meals here, and no one would have said a word. No one had the courage. But now, if you eat here for four days in a row, even the fellows who serve food stare at you. And the taste, the flavour of the food in those days, I can't tell you how good it was. In our part of the country, the vegetable curry of this place was a byword. If you ate it in the morning, you would still feel the aroma of the spices all day till evening. The *math* has fallen from those high standards. It is poorly administered. Look at the curry. It's no good any more, not as it used to be.'

'What has the taste of the curry got to do with the power of the Lord? What are you talking about?'

'You didn't get me right. People measure the quality of a temple by the food they serve. You know that, in the Krishna temple at Udipi, they feed the pilgrims two great meals every day. What lucky people! The age of Kali, the age of iron, is here, that's all. The great meals at temples have been cut everywhere.'

The sound of the lamp offering woke everyone up from their stupor. Brother stood up. He saw Father in the distance hurry up and join a crowd of people. The sound of the priests' chanting of mantras reverberated in the temple. Hundreds of lamps were being waved before the God. The brilliance of that light seemed to blind and mist his eyes and Brother's body suddenly broke out in sweat as he felt the glow of that heat. When his wife's body was being cremated, he had stood in front of that fire. And when the wind blew the heat towards him, he had felt the same kind of sweat pouring from him. The wicks of the offered lamps were burning and he could smell them getting charred. During a ritual, when they threw ghee or rice into the sacred fire, it smelt no different. Brother watched with unblinking eyes the circular motion of the lamps waved before the Lord. The gongs were loud and harsh.

The crowd of devotees rushed forward to get a better look at the Lord and the offerings. Brother stood there, stock-still.

*

During the time of the lamp-offering, Mother was caught in a crowd of women. Lots of bustle and noise. In that confusion, someone stepped on someone else's foot. Abruptly, a woman of the merchant caste jumped and touched her. It was a polluting touch. She had just bathed and purified herself and just when the holy hour was approaching and she about to receive the holy water, she was polluted—what a nuisance! Heads were dashing against each other. Mother lifted her head as if she would break her neck by stretching it. But she couldn't get even a glimpse of the Lord. Heads of black hair mobbed her eyes and darkened her vision. She could hear the bells. She could see at a distance, and dimly, the movement of lamps. But she couldn't see the *vrindavana* at all.

In all this confusion, Sister had shaken off Mother's grip and come out of the crowd. She sat under the neem tree, scattering the dry leaves that lay around. The sun was heating up the sky. Not a trace of clouds in that sky. Sister was looking at the sky. Right in front of her, a road led through the hot rocks and stones straight towards the river. In that windless afternoon, the water of the river was getting hotter. It was steaming. Sister suddenly rose to her feet. She picked up the banana peels that were drying nearby and tried to feed them to the dog lying in the shade. The dog sniffed at them, sneezed, and walked away. Then it occurred to Sister that she too was hungry. She thought about raising the banana peel to her lips and eating it herself, but half-way through that thought she forgot all about it.

Sister didn't remember anything these days. She felt as if she was wandering through two different worlds at the same time. One minute the world around seemed dull, another minute it looked strange. Now and then she had the terrifying fantasy that she was floating in another world, reaching the very tip of it, getting stuck there, kicking her heels, being frantic. But she was still in this world. Like stars swinging in the dark, darkness would spread before her eyes and in it particles of light would take on different shapes and suddenly line up in rows, wave about, float and disappear. A thousand events, a thousand faces would stumble and scramble, fall and rise in absurd ways, and throw her into confusion. She never knew why these things happened and when. Reasoning was not in her control. Helplessly, like little children watching a movie, she would sit and watch whatever appeared before her eyes, whatever formed and vanished on the screen of her mind.

When Sister-in-law died they all cried—Father, Mother and Brother. When she remembered it, she felt like laughing. That was the first time she had experienced the strange sight of adults crying aloud. Mother cried in gasps, without giving it voice. Father's voice wasn't at all suitable for crying. And his face got terribly twisted when he cried. She wanted to go near him and ask him not to cry. But she didn't have the courage to go anywhere near the scattered bits and pieces of Sister-in-law's body. The big wheel of the engine that had cut her into pieces glinted in the light of the railway guard's lamp. In her last helpless moment, Sister-in-law must have tried to hug that wheel.

The big wheel that had glided in space on the wire, appeared before her eyes. She remembered the circus. That woman who rode the one-wheeled cycle on the wire—if she had lost her balance even a tiny little bit she would have slipped from the wire and toppled down. In the many-coloured lights, horses were running in circles, without any enthusiasm, yet without any boredom. They were moving to the music of the band. And she was not scared when she saw the lion. The beast was angered by their teasing, playful torture. But he cowered under the strokes of the whip. He had been moving towards his cage and then he had turned around to face the spectators. It was only then that she had been afraid. She had shivered.

All sorts of events crowded in on her. Like children standing in a circle and inviting her to catch them, in a game of tag, they invited her from all four sides. The *math* was left behind, far away. She had begun to follow the events in her mind like a girl following the magician who had cast a spell on her, who had thrown magic powder in her eyes. Following them, she had walked and come close to the river. The rocks and stones were hot like a frying pan. Her feet burned and she pranced up and down, and it made her laugh. But then she couldn't bear the way her feet burned. So she raised her voice and cried aloud like a baby. She didn't know which way to go. The river stood in her way. Behind her stood the big walls of the *math*. They looked like the walls of a prison. They blocked her way back. In that stillness, the scattered cruel-looking stones seemed to gather in a circle around her and she felt cornered. She screamed and ran towards the water. Behind her four rocks waited, their arms locked, surrounding her. To escape them, she would have to go into the water. She was terrified. Holding her head in both her hands, she lifted her face to the sky and shrieked.

The pilgrims had received the holy water and the offerings in the *math*. They were getting ready for the midday meal. Women and children were scrambling to reserve a banana leaf for themselves. The *math* was filled with the smells of vegetable curry. They had arranged rows and rows of banana leaves where the pilgrims would take their seats and enjoy their meal. Various dishes had already been served on the leaves—rice, sweet, porridge, vegetable curry and cooked pumpkin.

Father and Brother were sitting in the men's row. Father had already smeared the sandal paste on his body. The guru had only to say in Sankrit, 'May it all be offered to Krishna!' and the meal would begin. Father raised his head to put a dot of ritual rice and sandal paste on his forehead when right in front of him stood Mother. Her face was white and bloodless. She couldn't speak. She was panting. She held her breath and said faintly, 'Sister is nowhere in the *math*. She's disappeared.'

Father got up from his meal. Brother and Mother followed him. They ran towards the river. Sister was lying among the rocks. She had beaten her head against the rocks and lost consciousness.

The sun was fierce.

Even the wind had lost its breath.

But Sister was still breathing.

*

'Don't let go of my hand. Hold on to me. Don't you lose me in the crowd,' said Mother, tightening the grip on Sister's hand. Sister was looking at the festival crowd, her eyes big in wonderment. In the field in front of the *math*, there was a row of shops. Even though she didn't need to buy anything, she wanted to go and look at the shops. She was in good spirits that day. She was not sad any more, her body was brimming with energy. Father and Brother were walking behind them. Father felt the novelty of the way they were going together. He was even a bit embarrassed. It was rather rare for them to walk like that, as a whole family, their bodies touching each other. For a second, he felt happy about it, felt content. If we had only got together like this in life, how good it could have been, he thought as in a dream, and walked on. Brother was falling behind the crowd. Father waited for him to catch up, held his hand and then walked forward. But he was feeling weak. He began to be convinced that he didn't have the strength to withstand the crowd and keep his balance. Mother's face was shrunk, maybe in disgust. She didn't like nor understand why people in the crowd suddenly jumped on her and pushed her around. Holding on to Sister, she shrank away from people as she walked. Yet people dashed against her.

The sky was overcast. The road on the river's edge was covered with the used banana leaves on which thousands of people had eaten their meals. There was no one to pick them up and throw them away. People were massed in a crowd in the outer yard of the *math*. They were waiting to get a glimpse of the festival chariot.

All four of them pushed and elbowed their way through the crowd and somehow reached the main door of the temple. Brother was disgusted. Two days of these crowds were more than he could take. He felt like gagging when the sweat smells and body odours of people assailed him. He looked around from the steps near the big temple door. He could see only heads, hundreds of heads. He wished intensely he could shake them all off and escape outside, leaving them all behind. But as he went forward the frontyard of the temple got narrower. If they moved forward like that, he might be caught in the milling crowd. He was afraid he would get crushed. When he turned around, he could see the row of shops. People were leaving the shops and joining the congregation. Brother had no interest in this festival. He was reminded of his wife. She was forever enthusiastic about festivals and holidays. Once she got enthusiastic, she would heed nothing else. Once when they had gone together to the temple of Venkatesha, she had lost a diamond earring in the crowd. It didn't take long for it to come to Mother's notice. As a result, all the jewellery on her body was taken away piece by piece. Only the ring on her finger remained till the end. The day she died, Mother had held her daughter-in-law's hand and howled. Daughter-in-law had worn the ring meant for her little finger on the middle one. It was too tight and it wouldn't come off. Mother's ruses to get it off didn't work. So she had to pull off the ring from the dead finger by sheer force, right in front of everyone.

A beam of sunlight had somehow escaped through the cloud-cover of the sky. The light of that beam fell on the beautifully adorned chariot and made it glitter. Ceremonial torches were burning high in front of the chariot. Green wreaths had been added to the red parasol of the God in procession.

Hundreds of assembled voices made the earth shudder with their cries of victory for the God. People were vying for the privilege of pulling the chariot. It would bring them merit in this and the next world. They didn't care who fell or rose before them as they scrambled, pushed and shoved for a place near the chariot. Again there was a huge shout of victory for the God.

By this time, Brother had released his hand from Father's. The crowd was restless. In the press of that moving crowd, Brother and Father were separated and they were now far from one another. Mother and Sister had merged in that seething crowd sometime ago. Father began helplessly to look for Brother. But the sea of people had lifted Brother on a wave and thrown him far away. Father panicked. He felt he had lost his legs. Losing control, he surrendered to the current of the crowd and stood in it in despair. Brother may not come looking for me, I don't know how to get out of this maze, he thought. Would Brother know the way out of this? He forgot to ask Brother when they were close together. Where did they all go and melt in the crowd? Sister's delirium was a bit worse that day. If she shook off Mother's hand and got away, there was no hope of finding her again. What if she ran back to the river as she had earlier?

The big temple drum was being beaten. Its huge sound reverberated everywhere. The chariot had moved forward. Brother wanted to struggle against the crowd and get out. But coming out was impossible. He knew it. Mother and Sister were caught in the whirlpool. When he reached the middle of the flood, Father had given up and left it all to God. How could he leave them all in this plight and get out? Would that be right? He worried about it. The beat of people's feet became more powerful. He decided that no one can save anyone else from this flood. So he left them all behind and got out of the crowd.

The clouds were dense. A hurricane had arrived whirling from somewhere, carrying the dust of the fields and throwing it all on the *math*. People were pulling the chariot of the God with all their might. It was moving fast. Others were troubled, rubbing the dust from their eyes, trying to disperse and find a way out.

As the chariot came closer, Mother dragged Sister with her and rushed towards it. Beads of sweat stood out on Sister's brow. Her eyes seemed to be under a spell, her stare fixed on the chariot. Her body was shaking like a leaf. In a trance, stricken with fear, she was oblivious to everything around. She was staring at the chariot. The clockwise procession of the chariot was coming to an end. Everyone was bending low and saluting it from wherever they stood. The idols on the chariot, with all their ornaments, were shaking in the pull and push of the wheels.

Sister suddenly shrieked, with her hand pointing towards the chariot. '*Ayyo*, fire, fire! Mother, the chariot is on fire! Look, look, the chariot is burning! Mother, fire! There!' Sister pulled away her hand from Mother's and rushed towards the chariot. The muscles in her legs seemed to crack and lose life. She felt that she, too, was like the chariot, burning with a single flame that was enveloping her, all over. The earth on which she stood was circling, whirling all around her. She couldn't find her balance. She fell and rose and tried to move forward. The chariot was in flames in front of her. The light dazzled her eyes. In that heat and glow, her body was melting and becoming nothing; turning into steam, into thin air. Mindlessly, she pushed herself through the throng blocking her way and ran towards the chariot.

Mother stood there not knowing what to do. The women near her scolded her. Shouldn't the mother hold on to her mad daughter instead of letting her run wild, say ugly things, pollute the holy chariot of the God with her touch? Why would she bring a mad girl to the temple? Even the guru of the *math* was upset by this event. What awful inauspicious words at the holy hour of chariot festival? What did it matter if she was crazy? How could she cry that the chariot was on fire at this holy time? But even as he shouted, 'Stop that mad woman!' Sister had reached the chariot and had hugged that great wheel.

Dust all round. No one could see anyone's face. Rain was pouring down in torrents as if the sky was torn in pieces. People were running everywhere, scattered. In a few moments the chariot would have reached its journey's end. Sister was holding tightly on to the wheel and seemed to have lost her senses. Tears were streaming from her eyes. The remaining crowd shouted cries of victory to the God. They got ready once again to pull the chariot through its last lap.

Mother searched for Sister. If she could have found Brother or Father she would have been enormously comforted. But they were all somewhere else. How should she look for anyone in this confusion? If Sister got caught under the chariot wheel, she would be crushed to pulp, cut to pieces. In this torrent of rain and in this dust, she could see nothing.

Father stood firm holding on to the compound wall. Rain was beating down on him. But he didn't mean to move from his place. He leaned his head against the wall, lifted his face and looked at the sky against the wall. The great wall seemed to narrow down as it grew taller. It seemed to become sharper and seemed like a dagger stuck in the sky. The rainwater was running down the wall, mixed with the red clay of the stripes, and it oozed down like blood. The whole wall was wet and smelled of damp earth. Father began to lick the wall with his tongue again and again.

He was hungry. His throat was parched. Water was pouring on his head like a waterfall. Beyond the wall, hundreds of banana leaves on which people had eaten lay strewn all over. Fatigue, or disgust, was shutting his eyes. Slowly, he slid down the wall he was leaning against, and fell to the ground.

The hands of the people who were drawing the chariot were slipping. The chariot that had started moving was stuck, as if in a mire. Everyone shouted victory cries and tried once again. The rain was now beating hard directly on their faces. It hit their eyes. Like men born blind, they pulled the chariot straight with all their will. Like beasts of burden, they were straining every muscle. But the chariot did not budge an inch. Something must be stuck under the wheel. Or else, the wheel must be mired in the mud.

Mother's body was a wet mass. She looked around for a long time. She couldn't see Sister anywhere. The chariot was stuck in its path, unable to move. The endless rain must have filled the river to the brim. Mother ran towards the river.

Her wet clothes were sticking to her everywhere. In that

deserted road maybe no one noticed it. She wanted to walk fast, but her feet slipped at every step. The rainwater was streaming along the road towards the river. The banana leaves were a mess all around. The leaf-cups were floating on the rainwater and moving towards the river.

Mother was running towards the river, stepping on unclean things, left-overs, pieces of food.

— *Translated by A. K. Ramanujan*

Rama Rides to the Fair

K. Sadashiva

'Parvathi, did you hear, make some coffee fast. Maybe Abu Byari will come to the fair. He doesn't worry about repayment, but talks baskets-full. I did say I didn't want to have anything to do with the Byaris and Parbus. But that Achutayya wouldn't hear of it. He got me to give Byari the loan, playing the middleman. Now, this very same Achutayya. . . .'

Rama jumped up and down the minute he heard Grandfather mention 'fair'. That's when his pleading began. He hung on to the *pallu* of Parvathi's saree and followed her everywhere. He said 'Mother, Mother,' endearingly, a few times, craning his neck. She was a little irritated as she got the stove burning and set the coffee pot on it. She said: 'What's it, my son? You have begun your music this early in the morning.'

Parvathi's mother, Kalyani, spoke breathlessly from the inner room, 'Parvathi, what does the boy want? Why are you scolding him? Today is fair day, isn't it? Why don't you send him? Shenoi's children are going there to set up shop anyway. Rama can go with them. My husband is going there too. He won't say no to bringing the boy back with him.'

Rama was delighted. He leapt over to Grandmother's room. Parvathi heard her mother comforting him, 'It's all right, son. Quiet down. I'll tell Parvathi to bathe you and send you to the fair.' Rama ran from there to his mother's feet and murmured, 'Mother, Mother.' She spoke angrily, 'Okay! okay! my son. Please let me make some coffee first. Otherwise my Appayya will get upset.' Rama ran over to the bedroom. He pushed the footstool to the wall; standing on it, craning his limbs and neck, he tried to pull down his clothes from the swing's seat. The footstool slipped and he fell flat on his back. A whole bunch of clothes came down on him and he screamed. His cries brought Parvathi and Manjayya running to him. Kalyani asked, 'What happened to the boy?' four times, from her sick bed in her feeble voice. Parvathi picked up Rama, cursing all the while, 'Why doesn't death take me away? I can't control this boy.' She spanked him. But he was encouraged when his grandfather admonished Parvathi: 'Parvathi, why do you thrash him so? He's only a child. What does he know?' Rama blew his sad trumpet even louder. From the inner room Kalyani repeated herself, 'What happened? What happened . . .?' Manjayya tried to silence her, 'Nothing has happened. Why don't you lie down quietly?'

Rama went through the formality of a bath. Then began his litany about being hungry. Lucky that she had some left-over fruit dish from yesterday, thought Parvathi. She gave her son some of it. Where did he have the time to finish it? While some of it went into his stomach, the rest of it rested on his face. He received the usual rebuke from his mother.

Sunday was the only day off for the school on the hill. And so, that Seethu with the crooked face would not be coming to take Rama to school. Besides the weekly fair was on the same day at the market-place. A trip to the fair was far more enjoyable than sitting on a stool at school and practising the alphabet.

Manjappa drank his coffee, put on his sandals, crossed the yard and reached the street.

Parvathi changed Rama's clothes, smartened him up. Rama remembered something, broke away from his mother and ran to Grandma's room. Grandma could be heard asking, 'What is it, my child? Why are you rummaging under my pillow?' Parvathi shouted, 'I have to feed the cow grain-water. Are you going or staying? Why don't you leave for your weekly fair or whatever?' Rama came out with a broad gleeful face. His short pant's pocket was bloated like a frog that had just eaten a smaller frog.

Parvathi put her hand in his pocket and wondered, 'What on earth do you have there?' She smiled. A couple of marbles. Grandpa's empty snuff box, a few pieces of slate pencils rattling in it. A tin whistle. 'Where did you get this?' she asked. He answered, 'Appu gave it to me.' 'Yes, yes, Appu gave it, did he? You must have stolen it.'

'No, Mother! He did give it to me.' He blew it once before pocketing it. 'Who the hell knows?' Parvathi grumbled and started smoothing his hair. Before she was done, Appu from the Shenoy's came to the door. 'You are taking him to the fair, aren't you?' she asked. 'That's why I came,' said Appu.

The two got up to go. Parvathi took a few coins from the pouch she had made from her saree folds at the waist, and gave them each two coins. 'Don't get him any fried stuff.' Appu said yes and took Rama's hand in his, and the two walked out to the veranda.

Finally, at about ten in the morning, Rama launched his excursion to the fair with Appu, his older companion. Rubber pump shoes, that Manjappa's sister, Kaveri, had recently brought for him from Peradur. Check shorts from Mysore. Satin jacket. Shirt collar covering the jacket's collar. Gold-laced satin cap for the head. Two quarters in his pocket. What more did Rama need to have fun?

Their enthusiasm knew no bounds as they neared the market-place. Appu warned, 'Rama, tell me everything you want at the fair right now. Don't kick up a row there like you did the last time.' What didn't Rama want at the fair? Sweetmeats, of both the hollow and solid varieties, hot and sweet sticks . . . these were absolutely necessary. If possible, some fried stuff at Kamath's. 'But, what if Mother finds out? So what? In any case, Appu is going to buy it for me. He did the last time.' Besides, there was another attraction for him at Kamath's. A big vessel that made pleasant sounds. To listen to that was a delight. He also wondered about how the sounds were made. Once he even asked Appu. Appu said, 'You know there is water in the vessel. They have put a coin in it.' Rama had a follow-up question. 'Why do they place a coin in it?' 'You ask me why?' Appu didn't really know. But he didn't want to display his ignorance before Rama. 'Why? You are still young. You will understand when you grow up.' Appu said this to show Rama his place and shut his mouth. Rama persisted: 'Grow up means what? As big as you?' Appu acted like an adult now. 'Yes. You shut up now!' He could shut Rama's mouth but not his mind that wondered and speculated about everything at the fair. Furthermore, he kept up with his whats, whys, wheres and hows about everything that caught his fancy. Appu might have been older than Rama, but he did not have the know-how to satisfy Rama's curiosity. He got annoyed and scolded Rama once again.

But his annoyance had another cause too. Rama's mother had given each two quarters. But that was nothing for a kid of his age. He had cajoled his sister into giving him two half-anna coins. His mother gave him a half-anna; and he pilfered a couple of coins from the kitchen box, his mother's favourite secret hiding-place. He had not even counted the money, but his pocket jingled with a bunch of coins. His big worry was how to spend all that money. He could buy a sweet dish with one quarter at Kamath's. If he were to grin at him, the owner might gift away a piece of some hot stuff. Why wouldn't he? Didn't he buy sugar, soap, etc. on credit from his daddy's shop? If that tribal vendor was here this time too, he should buy a small harmonica from her. When he was busy thinking of all this, wouldn't Rama's endless queries annoy him?

Somehow, they managed to reach the stall area. Rama had already complained of thirst to Appu. Appu took Rama to a sherbet shop. Rama saw rows and rows of sherbet bottles of varied colours. On top of each was a lemon. To the side, the soda-giver was opening the bottles with a ear-catching hissing sound. Appu asked what Rama wanted. Which colour should he choose? All the colours looked tempting. The lady shopkeeper asked him to hurry up and choose. Rama pointed his finger at a purple bottle. She washed a glass and put some jaggery syrup into it. But suddenly, red looked more attractive than purple to Rama. 'That red will do,' said Rama. 'Oh! you kids. Enough of you!' the lady grumbled and poured the red sherbet into the glass. She added a few cooling seeds, stirred it and held it aloft. In the meanwhile Rama's attention was distracted by the heavy man at the side who put a soda bottle on his chest and pushed the marble stopper down. When the bottled-up gas and water gushed upward, Rama stubbornly refused to drink anything but that. When Appu raised his voice and said, 'All right, all right. What a pest you are! I should not have brought you at all,' Rama, feeling helpless, drank whatever was given to him. 'Drank' is not the word for it! More than half of it spilled on to his jacket. A little bit went into his stomach. His mouth, cheeks, the jacket's front, were all red. 'Come on. Out with the quarter,' said the shop lady. Appu added, 'Get it out!' Rama couldn't help crying. How else could Appu respond to it but get angry. 'You . . . you . . . ,' he grumbled but gave the money anyhow from his own pocket, and then dragged Rama along. But Rama was unstoppable. As if to exasperate Appu, Rama queried, 'How do they put the marble in the bottle?' Appu thundered, 'You shut your mouth and follow me.'

What did these kids encounter next but a totally different world! Some fellow was singing to the beat of anklets, 'Come and see the city of Bombay, come and see its whores.' A group of children had gathered around him. Why children, several of the town's respectable couples were listening to the vendor without feeling shy or embarrassed. With such a throng around, what do you expect Rama to do but feel curious? How much time does it take for curiosity to become importunity? And isn't crying the only means when stubbornness doesn't produce results? Appu cursed not only Rama but Rama's entire family tree. But the truth was that he too wanted to see the Bombay show just as much. He had actually seen it once, but where did it say he shouldn't see it again? 'All right, you bugger, go and see the show,' said Appu. When Rama looked through the magnifying glass, shading both his eyes, he saw in that small box a fabulous fascinating world. 'Ho ho ho!' he laughed and refused to budge from the box even after the show was over. 'Just a little more. Just a little more,' he danced. Appu had to pull him away before he himself could take a peep.

Questions came down on Appu like torrential rain, after Rama had experienced the peep show. How did that woman in the show get into the box? What was Bombay? What was a whore? etc. etc. Appu felt nagged, invaded.

Appu noticed the sweetmeat shop at a distance and admonished Rama: 'Now, you have to listen to me. The quarter your mother gave you, give it to me. I'll get you whatever sweet you want. If you don't, you'll get nothing.' Rama said fine and put his hand in his pocket. Wasn't there a whole universe in it? How could one find a quarter with ease in that universe of marbles and stuff? They stood at the roadside near a stone bench. Rama tried to find the quarter. Appu felt frustrated and burdened, 'You have ruined everything! Where could it have disappeared in such a short time? Damn it!' Having said it bitterly, Appu thought of something. He suggested to Rama, 'Your pocket is filled with junk. If you remove every item from it, you may find your coin.' Rama took everything out and laid it on the bench. First to come out after a lot of struggle was his nail-less top. Next emerged

Grandpa's empty snuff box, rattling. After that. . . .

It was at this point that all hell broke loose. The secret was out. Appu screamed, 'Ho! You have stolen it!' and snatched the tin whistle from Rama's hand. Rama shouted, 'No! it is mine!' Appu challenged, 'How could it be yours? When you came to our house yesterday, you took it to try it just once, but you obviously never gave it back!' Rama protested, weeping, 'No . . . No! it's mine. My mother bought it for me.' Appu pocketed the whistle, asserting his ownership. Grief welling up in him, Rama kicked his hands and feet. A few kids gathered and a couple of elders came too. One of them scolded the older boy. Another tried to scare the little fellow. Rama pulled down Appu's hand. Appu, incensed, shook it free from Rama's hold. Somehow, in the scuffle, Appu got hit once. Appu retaliated with a punch on Rama's back. Rama picked up a big stone. Some good souls intervened and got Rama to drop his weapon. They wanted to know the facts. Appu told the story of the whistle with all the details. Rama interjected a few times with, 'No . . . no. It's mine.' He cried. Who could ever find conclusive evidence in children's fights? Doesn't justice favour the one who cries the most? Doesn't it go to the younger children? In a fight between a man and a woman, who would favour the man against the woman? The elders here decided that Appu was lying. Rama got the whistle. Appu even received a few words of warning. When falsehood is taken to be the truth, what else but exasperation and outrage could one feel! The grown-ups settled the dispute and went their way. Rama blew the whistle in Appu's face. Fighting started anew. Appu threatened: 'Come home and see. I'll tell my father.' Rama did not take it lying down. He said mockingly, 'I too will tell my father.' Appu felt annoyed, saying, 'When did you come to have a father?' Appu laughed aloud.

Just then an elderly woman held Rama by his shoulder and said, 'Your father is calling you, master.' Rama looked at her and felt scared. She asked him, 'Isn't Rama your name?' and Rama nodded. Rama wanted to know where his father was. She said, 'Over there, at the clothing store.' 'Which one?' 'Right there, come, let's go.' Rama figured that he stood to gain by going to the clothing store anyway and forgot all about his fight with Appu. Maybe he even forgot that Appu was still standing there. He clung to the stranger-woman and followed her. Appu muttered to himself bitterly, 'Thank God! The devil is gone. Good riddance! Now it is up to him and his grandfather!' He ran towards his father's shop.

Rama asked repeatedly, 'Where is Father?' The woman kept saying, 'Right here, right here,' and walked him by the shoulder. They finally reached the store. Rama's eyes searched for his father amongst the customers as soon as they entered. But where was he? The woman pointed at a man in a broken chair and said, 'Look there, that's your father.' How could that be? Rama was confused for a moment. Fear, laughter. 'Oh, no! that's not my father,' Rama said, smiling divinely, in a tone that implied that the woman knew nothing. When the man in the broken chair heard him, he jumped up. He had on a soot-covered white cap. Behind it a visible tuft of hair. Earrings. Over one ear, a bunch of flowers. An umbrella in his hand. A wrap-around piece of clothing from his waist down to his knees. A silver anklet. A pair of thick leather slippers. He said, 'Come, child.' Rama saw a bundle of new clothes next to him. 'This is for you,' the man said. He invited Rama three times. The woman pushed Rama forward, saying, 'Go, master, go.' Rama moved slowly like a tortoise, as if under a spell. He stood blinking before the stranger. The stranger stepped forward, took Rama by the hand and seated him in the chair. 'Do you know all these clothes are for you?' 'Do you like them?' Rama nodded his head. The stranger embraced Rama and said, 'Oh, my son.' He lifted Rama's face and gazed into the child's eyes. Rama felt happy even though the man's hand was rough. He also wondered why there were tears in this elderly man's eyes. Tears came to his eyes too. How come there were tears in the eyes of the woman too, standing at a distance?

All this happened in four to five minutes. The man asked the woman to pack. He picked up Rama and carried him out on his shoulders. They bought a big bundle of sweets at the sweetmeat shop outside. Wouldn't you guess that Rama's face broadened brightly. 'For me!' Rama held out his hand from over the man's shoulders. The stranger took a couple of hot-and-sweet sticks by making a hole in the bundle and gave them to Rama and said, 'For whom else? All for you, my dear boy.' With one leg resting against the man's chest and the other hanging over his back, and holding the man's head, Rama felt as if he was horse-riding. Rama even said so: 'You are like a horse, I am like a rider.' He even started goading the man-horse by kicking his chest and back. The man liked the pressure of tender feet on his body. After going some distance, he told the woman something. She said yes and walked ahead faster. Rama felt it strange that they were moving in the opposite direction from their house. Where were they going? He said, 'Let's go home.' The man replied, 'We are going home.' They reached the outskirts of the market-place; the man lifted Rama off his back under the *ganapakayi* tree. At the same time, there arrived a cart with an arched frame, drawn by a pair of bullocks. The man put Rama inside the cart from the rear side and the woman pulled him in from the inside. Rama started crying, really loud this time. The man climbed aboard and said, 'Hurry up!' The bullocks, their bells chiming, headed for Seethur via Musurehalla, red dirt splashing.

Though it pleased him to sit in the cart, going to an unknown place with strangers made him cry, his wails reaching a crescendo, screaming, 'Father . . . Mother.' The woman gave him sweets from the bundle, all the while caressing him on her lap and saying, 'Please, don't cry, master.' Though the crying stopped when he saw the sweets, his panting did not. The woman asked him, 'What is this?' when she saw a red spot on his jacket right below his lips. He said, 'That's from the sherbet I drank at the fair.' He asked her, 'Have you had it? It's really very nice.' She smiled. The man smiled too. Rama's back hurt when he hit against the swaying frame of the cart moving unsteadily. His joy vanished in a second and he started yelling, 'I am hurt! I am hurt!' He asked, 'Where are we going?' He asserted, 'Our house is not here.' The woman responded: 'We are going to your house. You know this gentleman. Don't you? He's your father.' Rama retorted, 'He is definitely not my father!' The man pleaded, 'Believe me. I am your father!' Rama was stubborn, 'No . . . No! My father is at home. Let's go home.' The man explained the best he could: 'Please don't cry, dear son. I am really your father. The one at your other house, Manjayya, he's your mother's father.' Rama was confounded. 'But, Appu said that I have no father,' he said. The man looked at the woman and the woman looked at the man. The man reassured the boy, 'Let's thrash that Appu. You be quiet now.' Rama rejoiced.

The woman and the man talked about a lot of things. As their conversation mentioned occasionally familiar words like Parvathi, Manjayya, Grandmother, Rama knew that it involved his family, but how could he make head or tail of the total converstion. He blinked at the man and the woman alternately, and shot an occasional glance at the bundle of sweetmeats.

The cart passed Balgadi and turned left. Its rocking motion lulled Rama to sleep. He fell asleep on the woman's lap. As a piece of the sweetmeat was still sticking out of his mouth, saliva trickled down one corner of his mouth. The woman let it be for fear of waking him. Saliva wetted her saree too. She told the man, 'What a beautiful child, master!' as she caressed the child's hair. The cart rocked this way and that like a cradle. The bells around the bullocks' necks played like a child's twinkle box.

Rama woke up with a start when the cart tripped over a big stone. He opened his eyes all of a sudden and screamed, 'Mother . . . .' He looked at the woman and then looked at the man. Feeling as though he was in a new world, he wept, crying, 'Where is Mother? Where is she?' The man and the woman felt exhausted trying to stop his wailing and appeased him by giving him some more sweets. The woman told the man, 'I am frightened, master!'

The cart must have travelled a furlong or two after Rama woke up. A motor car sped down from behind, honking. Rama was watching it. The car passed the cart and stopped in front of it, blocking its way. The cart-driver pulled hard at the reins and the bullocks came to a halt. They were breathing hard, their bells sounding. Rama saw his grandfather's face. He sprang up and shouted proudly, 'Appayya, I am here!' The woman asked the man, 'What do you do now, master?' You couldn't expect the man to be calm under these circumstances! He sat sullen, provoked and motionless, but screamed at the woman, 'Will you please shut your mouth, my dear woman?' Rama went to the edge of the cart and threatened to descend. The woman pulled him back.

Manjayya, Seetharama, shopkeeper Sadananda Bhatta, the owner of the car, Sheenappa, Bhatta's servant, Shambhu . . . all familiar faces. Rama was delighted. Biting a piece of sweetmeat, he called out, 'Appayya, I am here.'

Manjappa roared, 'Get him down!' The man responded without getting out of the cart, 'It's impossible!'

'What insolence! I'll strangle you. You . . . get him down. Now!'

'Let's see how you take him with you.' So saying, the man leapt out of the cart.

Manjappa said, 'What do you mean? Are you going to beat me up? If you touch me, you will become a corpse right here!' The two faced each other. Sadananda Bhatta came between them.

Rama tried to break free from the woman's grip and shouted, 'Appayya, I'll come.' The woman was at a loss and prayed to all kinds of gods while she held on to the child. Rama writhed under her hold. 'Let me go . . . let me go . . . ,' he repeated. She tried to calm him down by thrusting two kinds of sweets into his mouth. He snatched the sweetmeats from her, but didn't stop screaming, 'Let me go.'

Sadananda Bhatta spoke up, 'Shivarama, let me tell you. Don't carry on your quarrel on the road. After all, he is your father-in-law.'

Shivarama gnashed his teeth and shouted, 'Who? Him? He is my father-in-law? No . . . no. This is that hapless woman's, Parvathi's, father. Isn't that why he kept her at his place? All right. She's your daughter. This boy's my son. What right have you over him? Even if I have to spill my blood for it, it is fine. Let me see how you will take my son with you!'

Rama could make neither head nor tail of this adult battle. As the top in his pocket bothered him, he put his hand in the pocket. He caught hold of the whistle. His face blossomed. He told the woman, 'Look here, this whistle—it is mine. Do you know?' He insisted that she should blow it. She couldn't help laughing. She said, 'No, I can't. Please blow it yourself.' Rama felt proud. 'Oh! You can't blow it. I can.' His throat swelling, cheeks blooming, he blew the whistle loud. As he did, a herd of deer came down the hill to the road and stood like stones, their ears erect. Rama's attention wandered from the whistle to the deer and he exclaimed to the woman, 'Oh! Look . . . look. Over there.' He poked at the woman's face to make her see. Just one minute. The next minute, the deer vanished. They went over the slope of the hill and entered the forest. 'Do you have deer where you live?' queried the boy of the woman. What response could she make to him while her heart pounded away in pain?

At one point, Shivarama raised his voice and shouted, 'You will have to take him over my dead body.' Again, Sadananda Bhatta, Sheenappa and others came up to his deflate mood. Manjappa, meanwhile, hurried to the back of the cart. 'Woman, give him over to me!' he ordered. Shivarama warned her, 'If you do, you'll die here! Do you understand?' Poor woman, what could she do in this confusion? Rama sprang up. She turned around and caught hold of his hand. Manjappa gripped the other hand from below and pulled. Now Rama really felt the pain. 'Appayya, it hurts.' Shivarama came running and pulled his father-in-law's hand. The rest of them came. Somebody lifted Rama down. He did not know who it was. Anyway, he got caught in the midst of adult legs and feet. When he looked up, he saw only fat thighs and chins. They scared him like the demons in Mother's stories. He cried for Mother. He trembled saying, 'Appayya, Appayya.' Shambhu took him away and tried to quieten him. Rama was actually shaking. He kept on asking why they were all acting that way.

About ten minutes must have elapsed. Manjappa took Rama from Shambhu and went straight to the car. He dumped him in the car. Shivarama shouted all sorts of things from the cart. Rama got frightened by the changed surroundings.

Everyone sat in the car. It began the return journey. Rama found the soft seat of the car more pleasant than the grass bed in the cart. He looked back through the window. The cart, the woman, the man, everything slowly receded. Everyone got smaller. They all disappeared round a bend in the road. As soon as the cart became invisible, Rama remembered the sweets: 'Oho! I left the sweets back there.' Grandfather said, 'Sit quiet.' 'Will you get me sweets at the fair?' Sadananda Bhatta said to the boy, 'All right. You're smart. Stop talking.' Rama wouldn't stop: 'Where are we going?' Someone said, 'Home.' Rama pulled at his grandfather's chin and said, 'Appayya, Appayya, it appears they have deer at their place. Will you get me a deer, Appayya?' Manjappa got angry and said sternly, 'Sit quiet. Don't say a word more!' Rama felt let down. He said, 'This car is better than that cart.' He said many things, all kinds of things, but who had the peace and patience to listen to him?

'Manjappa, you won this time. What next?' Sadananda Bhatta

wanted to know.

Manjappa felt shrunk by the whole series of events that day. Things that happened in the morning, events that followed, the possible consequences to come, had wearied him. He remembered what that woman had said to him: 'You must be feeling great to keep your married daughter at home? What sort of a man and you!'

Manjappa expressed his resentment: 'Oh my God! What cheek! That cheap woman had the gall to mock me!'

Rama started saying something entirely different: 'Appayya, Appayya. . . .'

Manjappa paid no heed at all.

Rama's mind started wandering. He recalled the whistle. He took it out and blew it loud.

Manjappa was irritated: 'What a nuisance you are! You . . . little boy!'

Rama was nonplussed. But he was too young to obey orders. He went on blowing the whistle softly.

Sadananda Bhatta recounted everything with full details: Shivarama's visit to his shop, the abduction of Rama, himself pursuing the kidnappers, and so on to the present moment.

Manjuappa thanked him: 'It was nice of you to have helped us.'

When the car went past the stalls of the fair, Rama began saying softly, 'Appayya, Appayya.' Mainly because he felt sad to leave the fair ground.

Sounding the horn, the car came to a halt at the house. Rama saw that there was a real crowd. The gathering shouted in chorus: 'They are back. They are back.' One by one, the occupants of the car got down. Manjappa asked Rama to get off. Rama was reluctant to leave such a fine automobile, but because so many were especially watching him, he felt proud and got off regally. Parvathi broke out of the crowd, hugged him, pressed him to herself and cried, 'Where did you go, my golden boy? Where? It's a miracle that I am alive!' Though Rama was happy to see his mother, her smothering love made him ache, and he said, 'Let go, please, let go of me!' Mother and son leading the way, everyone else following, they all went into the house. From the inner room, Kalyani kept asking, 'Has the child come back? Is my husband back?' She rambled on. Appu, standing in the midst of the throng, called out Rama's name. Rama felt like going with him, but recalling the whistle incident, he responded reluctantly. His face was swollen with resentment. 'Go away. I don't want to come with you,' he said coldly, resting on his mother's waist.

Parvathi had umpteen questions to ask: 'Appayya, where did you find him? Where were you in the first place?' She was now seated leaning against the wall.

Manjappa threw away his wrap-cloth, sat on the swing and said sarcastically, 'Where was I? I was at the cemetery!'

People began leaving one by one, remembering their various responsibilities. Finally, the only outsider left was Sadananda Bhatta. He briefly reported all the events. Parvathi gazed at the lost face of her son lying on her lap and cried, 'Oh, my son! my son!' Rama too sobbed.

When the sobbing of mother and son had somewhat subsided, Sadananda Bhatta addressed Manjappa.

'Your son-in-law has shown, by kidnapping his son, that he is capable of any move. He is desperate and unpredictable. That's why I say, absorbed in your stubborn attitudes. . . .' Manjappa interrupted, 'Yes. That vagrant woman said that. Now you are speaking in the same tone. What should I do? Tell me that.' There was disgust in his voice—anger. But that didn't make Bhatta feel the same emotions. Instead, he felt that this was the right time to speak some sense. After all, Parvathi was right there. Her mother was in the bedroom. His words might reach her. It was good if they did.

Bhatta spoke up: 'Manjappa, did I say you alone were at fault? I have never spoken about your family affairs in Parvathi's presence. But today, all that can go wrong did go wrong. Therefore, I thought of saying something sensible. Parvathi should not misunderstand me. After all, I used to play with her when she was a little girl. To speak the truth, this is the first time after her marriage that I am taking a good look at her. I feel sorry that this well-built woman has become so thin.' Parvathi began sobbing, 'Oh, my cursed fate! My karma! This is indeed my karma!' Rama was scared and started asking her, 'Why, Mother? Why are you crying?'

'Come here, son. Let me see you once.' This was Grandmother's repeated appeal from the inner room. But Rama sat firm on his mother's lap, afraid of that dark room inside.

Sadananda Bhatta did not change the topic and continued, 'Manjappa, tell me, who is happy in your family now? Your wife is bedridden. Parvathi's fate, we know. Your mind is not an unthinking tree to feel happy when things are in such a mess. Let's forget us, old people. You and I are weakening. We are ready to go when the God of Death calls us. Think of what might happen afterwards. What will Parvathi do? What about Rama's future? When he grows up, he should not be forced to curse you all, including his mother.' Rama knew that Bhatta was talking about him because Bhatta often pointed his finger at him and so Rama grew serious, shifting his sight from Grandfather to Mother and back again, repeatedly.

Rama's grandmother interrupted Sadananda, 'Who's it? Is it Sadananda? Yes . . . yes. It is. By the way, Sadananda, is it true that your brother Venkatesh's daughter ran away with a waiter from the valley?'

Parvathi felt somewhat avenged by her mother's counter-accusation and gnashed her teeth in triumph.

Manjayya's head became hot, 'Why don't you shut your mouth and stay in bed? I lost because I listened to you.'

Kalyani retorted from the inner room, 'Tell me! Whatever happened because you listened to me?'

'Don't loosen your tongues. Do you understand?'

'Oho . . . ! Grandmother, keep quiet. Will you?' Rama imitated his elders and smiled at his mother.

Grandmother said some other things from the inside. Manjayya was horrified. When his grandma and grandpa fought like this, Rama's only support was his mother. He nestled further back into his mother's lap, feeling more scared than ever. But, when the remnants of the sweetmeats in his pocket pressed against his thigh, he remembered them and took them out. He showed them to his mother and asked, 'Mother, look here. Do you know who bought them for me? Do you want some?' He pushed a few bits into his mother's mouth despite her protests. She swallowed them eventually, murmuring, 'What a bother you are!'

Manjappa thundered, 'Sadananda, look here. Do you think I like any of this? Do you think I don't understand any of this? This daughter, this nonentity, she ran back home within three days of her wedding. I told her a thousand times, "This is not right, you shouldn't do this." Who listens to me in this house? The daughter wept, crying, " Mother . . . Mother." That woman— the one sleeping in the inner room, my daughter's mother—said yes to everything her daughter told her, danced to her tune. Once it began, there was no stopping it. When she was carrying Rama, my daughter came home for good. She swore she would never return. Well, her mother said that her daughter was no burden on her. What do they care—these women worth three pennies! I am the one who has to face the world out there!'

Parvathi pushed Rama aside and stood up. 'Appayya, why do you speak this way? Did I come here not wanting to stay with my husband? I can't count the ways he tortured me. Why me, no woman can live with him. Why talk now? A time will come when everyone will realize what he is.' She wept uncontrollably. She couldn't stand it any longer. She told Rama, 'You demon, come on. Let's go.' She dragged him along, heading towards her mother's room. She shouted, 'Let's not be a burden on anyone. Let's go. Let's go somewhere. To hell even!' Rama kept screaming, 'Mother, let go of me . . . let go of me!'

Mother and daughter spoke of many things. Parvathi said something to her mother in a raised voice. Kalyani could be heard sobbing. Rama ran back, scared, and climbed on to his grandfather's lap.

Sadananda Bhatta started where he had left off.

'Whatever you may say, Manjayya, your son-in-law isn't as bad or as cruel and heartless as you think. I saw for myself today. You saw it too. Would he behave the way he did if he didn't love his son? Didn't he say that we would have to take his son over his dead body? If he wasn't attached to his wife and kid, would he say such a thing? Besides, he does not have to worry about getting another bride. After all, with the money he has, he can find a wife just like that.'

The manner in which the stranger and Grandpa had played tug-of-war over him remained green in Rama's memory, even if he didn't remember other things. But this clear memory brought back the whole picture—the man, the woman, the deer, the cart, everything came back. He pinched his grandpa's chin and said, 'Appayya, really, that cart was beautiful. Appayya, Appayya, see.

It seems they have deer at their place. Appayya, will you buy me
a deer?' Parvathi returned from her mother's room just then,
grumbling, 'He wants the child but not me.'

Sadananda Bhatta started again, 'You say all this now. When
he came to your father four times to take you back, what did your
father say? What about you? Did you ask your husband, who had
come to your door, as much as "who are you?" Your mother, she
called him all sorts of names. Sivarama has told me all. He is
actually shedding tears over it.'

Parvathi was humiliated and incensed.

'Bhattare, look here. You may say anything you want about
me. But if you say a word about my sick, helpless mother, I won't
tolerate it.' She snatched her son away from her father and moved
towards her mother's room. Rama was suddenly frightened by
these adults who were tossing him around like a ball. Manjappa
was loud to Parvathi: 'Parvathi, shut up! Learn to respect your
elders.' Parvathi was emphatic to his face: 'If elders were to behave
like elders, they would get the respect they deserve.' 'What
arrogance!' screamed Manjayya. Parvathi felt like crying again:
'Yes, I am arrogant! Why? Because I have all that I want, right?
Oh . . .! What the hell should I live for?' She threw Rama to the
floor and started hitting her head against the door. Sadananda
Bhatta tried to stop her. Parvathi fought back: 'Leave me alone.
Don't touch me. I'll die. Am I not the cause of all this?' Rama was
shaking. He groaned, 'Mother, Mother.' He did not however feel
bold enough to go near her. Manjayya found the scene entirely
nauseating. His head was throbbing hot. He slapped Parvathi
twice on her cheek, screaming, 'You want to die? You slut, you
want to die!' Parvathi yelled, 'Ayyo! I am dying . . . I am dying!'

Sadananda Bhatta restrained Manjayya: 'What the hell are
you doing, Manjayya?' They all looked like demons to Rama. He
had no strength to go to anyone, even though he kept calling out,
'Appayya.' Parvathi turned against him now, 'As if I have no
worries, I have you round my neck. Come on! Let's go and drown
in a well or a river or a tank. Who wants this hell?' She tried to
grab hold of Rama. Rama found everything terrifying. Felt as if
he was in some strange country. Mother looked just like a *rakshasi*,
a demon in stories—dishevelled hair and a half-naked torso! He
started stepping back. He came close to the door, sobbing all the

way. He crossed the threshold. He put a hand in his pocket. Of all things, should his hand land on the tin whistle? He remembered Appu. . . . Remembered his mother's story. . . . 'If you steal, demons will come and. . . .' He felt that returning the whistle was the safest thing. He waited no longer. He started running towards Appu's house. Kept running.

— *Translated by P. Sreenivasa Rao*

Not Me

P. Lankesh

Hey, the hand is mine. . . . Midnight . . . the dull starlight oozing into the dark room and a hand lying flat on the bed. An itching desire to pull it back . . . was it someone else's? Inert, looking like a stiff, old stick. Could it be dead? No. No. I tried to lift my hand. I couldn't.

The wretched professor had teased her right in front of me; Rangiah had reprimanded her through me, mocking me all the while. Why brood on such worthless thoughts at midnight? I looked at my hand again. My eyes must be real. My hand must be real. But if what I suspected was true, there would be problems. There is no one in the house below. No friendly neighbour. The body will simply rot. A foul smell will seep through the cracks in the window. At first people would take it for a dead rat. Later there would be nausea and fear. Even then they would only exchange glances. They would refrain from pointless conjecture and wait for someone else to reveal the truth.

I struggled in distress on the bed.

It started in the morning: a strong wish to visit someone. But who? The lecturing Bhatta? The grinning LIC agent, Rangasami? Huseni, the chatter-box boys from Udupi? I laughed.

The soft light of dawn had floated in like the flowing robes of youth. The wind had thrilled. The world was kind to everyone and one could live in peace with others. Anyway, the weight of the world did not rest on me.

These were the thoughts with which I had set off towards the hotel, with soap and a towel, for a bath. The magic of youth brings that sudden surge of zest. I might meet, perchance, a friend on the way and exchange a few pleasant words! Or perhaps please a lovely girl with a persistent flattering gaze! I might even find an unexpected letter in the room on coming back! What joy! I walked on, puffing on a cigarette I had bought at the corner shop.

The corpse lay on the wide road right in front of the hotel.

I stopped. Thoughts whirled inside my head. My father had written to say he would come. My friend might have come here too. Or maybe the hotel owner had fallen under a bus, or it could be the father of the girl next door or Bhatta or Huseni . . . or the enemy had killed a brave warrior of ours and thrown him off an aeroplane, or it could be Rangiah or . . . or . . . or . . . I ventured nearer, puffing the cigarette.

A corpse in the middle of the road. An age of flashing swords. Only a few people walking here and there. Not looking at one another. Not stopping. (Surely I'm not the only one who can see the corpse.) The oncoming rickshaw slows down and goes round. Even a bus does the same. The dead man's face cannot be seen. The body is lying stretched out, face downwards and half-naked. I couldn't bear to stand there. I felt like asking someone as to what had happened. But everyone was going around with hard cruel faces, as if I belonged to the CID, as if they were not concerned in any way. No discussion. No interest. Not the least bit of attention. Who knew what sort of a man he was? By evincing interest, one might have to go to court or even be imprisoned. . . . Why get mixed up? Heads bent, as if on the run, one goes on. Content at home, obedient at work, just a good citizen of India. Why go near the corpse? Why ask people. My concern has no meaning. Suppose I touch the corpse? I can only make sure he is dead, not carry him. Corpses are very heavy. Then why bother? Why invite trouble? If I tell the police or ring them up, they'll come and ask all sorts of questions. What do I gain by that? He cannot be brought back to life anyway. Even if it mars the beauty of a road in Malleshwaram, what business is it of mine? Why get involved? So, people will be able to breathe more easily if the corpse were removed. But who am I to help them breathe? Why get involved?

I got into the hotel and started bathing. My thoughts were still on the road below. Were the people afraid? Had they never touched a corpse? I would surely have gone near, unafraid, had anybody asked me to. But there was suspicion among us. I was a stranger. Who knew what they might do? Anyway, was there no one around who knew him? Was he utterly alone? Was there no person who could come forward and claim him? Suddenly, the helplessness terrified me. The bathing hole was enough to stifle all breath. The stupid proprietor was only interested in the money he got—couldn't care less about the customers. Heartless people. Stones in rice. Filthy bathroom. Murderers. I came out wanting to cry. I was in a dilemma. I wanted to see the corpse before I ate. I felt uneasy, as if I had cheated someone. The half-naked body haunted me. I left the bathroom, galloped down the stairs and looked around curiously. The corpse wasn't there. I looked around. It lay under a tree, quietly by the roadside, out of everyone's way. Somehow, I felt better. I thought it didn't matter if its insides began to rot. I didn't know why it was better that the corpse had changed places. People moved about, just as before, expressionless. A man was standing right near me. He pretended not to look that side and spoke to me: 'What's the matter, sir? You are standing here, wearing nothing but your briefs.'

'Oh, why should you be so interested, all of a sudden?' I asked sarcastically.

'I merely asked.'

'So you did.'

He walked away quietly. I ran in ashamed. What a disaster! I raced to the bathroom, put on my shirt and pyjamas and walked through to eat in the restaurant. I wanted to chat with the waiters. 'By the way, Subramanya, what will happen if you die suddenly at night, in your sleep?'

He answered laughingly, 'That wouldn't matter in the least. Someone will carry me away and cremate me.'

'It's all very simple then,' I said.

'What else, sir? Don't our soldiers die everyday?'

Eating thoughtfully, I remarked, 'Like the man who died in the street today, Subramanya?' He turned serious. A young waiter nearby suddenly said, 'He was staying in our hotel, sir.' As I sat up, interest mingling with fear, Subramanya dragged him away. Terrible thoughts flooded my mind. I spat out what I was eating. I was sick.

As soon as he came back, I asked him what it was all about. 'Nothing at all, sir. He is a stupid fellow,' he said, trying to evade the issue. I couldn't leave him at that. I started reprimanding him loudly, firing all sorts of questions.

'Subramanya, why do you work like a dog here for two meals

a day? Why don't you get back to your God-forsaken Udupi and do something there? You know me so well. Yet you don't come out honestly with what you have on your mind. If that man really stayed here yesterday, how come he died so suddenly? Cholera? Plague? A fight? Or was he rich? Was he run over by a bus? I'll feel much easier in my mind if you tell me all there is to tell. It's better for you too.'

'How can I possibly tell all I know, sir?'

'Then hang yourself!'

I should not have gone so far. Subramanya stiffened like a log. 'Wait, sir, I shall call my boss.' He went up and I waited below. He never came down. I got up in disgust. Something would certainly have been done about the corpse. A big crowd must have gathered there. I looked around at the tree. The corpse had disappeared. I didn't know what to make of it. I just stared at the tree and the shadow it cast. If the corpse still lay there, I could at least have felt some remorse over other people's indifference. But there was nothing now. So far I had kept myself from much involvement. I hadn't shown much curiosity nor done anything courageous. I hadn't even gone very near the body. But where was the satisfaction over a good deed done? Since he was a compatriot, I could only stand in the thick shade where the corpse had been and pray that his soul rest in peace, as was the custom when elderly, respected people died. It was neither beyond one's means nor difficult. I felt disgusted with myself for harbouring such thoughts and spat on the ground. As I steeled my resolve to do something more humane, Subramanya spoke from behind.

'Sir, the boss is calling you.' The hotel owner stood grinning at the entrance, displaying all his teeth. 'Hello, sir. It is already the eighth today. You owe us money for a month's meals.' Sensing that I was upset, he added, 'Don't you worry, sir. Take your time. Mutual trust is the most important thing. Life in Bangalore is no joke. Obviously you have problems too. Please come in. Have some coffee. Waiter, bring him some coffee, quick.'

'I don't want coffee now. I shall settle your dues and go somewhere else. You know why?' I added meaningfully.

'You shouldn't go off like that, sir. You are still very young. We shall talk later. We must have trust in each other. And trust in God Almighty.'

'I know. That's why I'm going. I'll come back in the afternoon.'

Now, something had to be done. I counted the possibilities. Forty rupees to clear the debts. Money for eating in another hotel. Above all, moral support for bringing up the subject of the corpse. Hard times ahead for reward. After making these plans and calculations I set off to see my friends from Udupi. They had gone out somewhere. Anandaramu was sitting with his buddies around him, turning this way and that, laughing ostentatiously, talking of Lawrence, feeling on top of the world. But the moment he started off on the similarity between Adiga's and Eliot's poetry, I left him. I went to Bhatta. He never allowed me to talk, glorying in his own imaginary love affair. The minute I mentioned what I owed the hotel for my meals, he got scared and started a long harrangue on metre and rhythm in poetry. In the end I told him about the corpse.

'It'll make a splendid story. But it's got to be written in the modern way, using the modern technique,' he said in his tinkling voice. After visiting him, I felt like seeing my writer friend, Lokeshi. He was an idiot. I was sure he would smile crookedly and tell me to get lost. I wandered around aimlessly.

The hot sun drained me of all feeling as I walked on alone. People moved all around me. Despair and darkness enveloped me. I must be a true bourgeois—among those that cry about a dead dog in the street, among those who would hang its photograph on the wall. People keep dying for ever so many reasons. But that haunting corpse tumbled headlong, helpless, symbolic to my early-morning mind; it would not leave me, howsoever hard I tried. The corpse and I were one, I had absorbed the corpse. . . . As my weary legs carried me towards the hotel, I stopped—startled—to look at the crows that had gathered around, pecking at the rubbish outside the shops, flying on to telegraph wires, sitting in a row, cawing hoarsely, swirling close above my head, as if they came to smell me, spearing one another with their beaks. I walked briskly and came near the hotel. I did not want to go in, but stood outside trying to think. Wanted nothing. Wanted no one. Nothing was there at all.

'Come in,' said the proprietor as I walked slowly in with eyes closed.

He didn't ask for money. 'It is trust, sir, that makes the world go round—trust and confidence.' I weighed his words and said 'yes'. He laughed. He meant something else, quite different. He shouted for Subramanya: 'Look, the gentleman has arrived. Serve him his meal. He is tired.'

'I don't want a meal,' I said.

'Have some snacks at least,' he said and brought me a dosa from the kitchen. Should I eat it or should I not? I went in to wash my hands, my mind racing all the while. The crows were still milling around outside. People were strolling about as usual. With a mind blank and tired, I walked to the table and looked down at the food. I was terribly hungry. I closed my mind to the onrush of thoughts. I breathe, I talk, I should eat. I should be trustworthy, I should live in harmony. I took a mouthful and reflected. Pushing out all thoughts of the corpse, I swallowed the food.

I slept early that night but woke up sometime later. The hand lay over there in the dim light of midnight. A multitude of feelings—Bhatta, Anandaramu, Adiga, crows, the sun, people with tightened faces, a stench, memories.

I sat up in bed. I touched my hand, looked at the place where it lay, smiled and closed my eyes as I rolled back into bed.

— *Translated by Padma Ramachandra Sharma*

Tabara's Story

K. P. Poorna Chandra Tejasvi

Tabara Setty has gone mad, said the people of Padugere. Among the twenty-five or so lunatics living in the town at the time, Tabara Setty was the most recent to go mad. The people of Padugere were not greatly upset when someone went mad, for it was not as if those lunatics went mad one day suddenly without any forewarning. Rather, they would go mad little by little, almost predictably. One watched them go mad, pitied them when they had gone completely mad, and then one just accepted the fact as though that was how things happened in this world. Yet, it seems that there is a story behind every lunatic.

Tabara Setty had been a familiar figure in the town for years. He had joined the Government service years ago when the British were still ruling the country. Of the two persons in Padugere who kept their memory of the British fresh, talking admiringly of their discipline and rigour, one was Dr Silva; Tabara Setty was the other. Often, when reminiscing to people about the old days, each would refer to the other for affirmation of what he was talking about.

When, during the British rule, Tabara was put in charge of collecting the excise revenue at the Customs House, he walked on air. Not only was he deemed respectable in the eyes of the people, but those who brought vegetables, fish and such other items for selling at Padugere, in addition to paying the toll, gave him gifts in kind.

It was around the same time that an agitation of sorts broke out in the country. It was the Independence movement. Tabara Setty had been newly married to a girl called Appi or Appamma from the Mangalore region. The couple sat at the toll gate and often talked about the Independence movement. They had frequently heard the name of Gandhi—the man who was leading the struggle against the British. But the precise nature of the struggle was not clear to them except that it was to drive the British out of the country. Though not a patriot, Tabara began to wonder why the British did not stay happily in their own land, among their own people, instead of grotesquely gadding about here in India among the dark natives. He could see that there was some truth too in what Gandhi was saying. But when the Satyagraha agitation turned into activities such as the no-tax campaign and cutting the telegraph wires, Tabara found himself in a quandary. He couldn't just excuse himself from taking sides on the pretext that he had no views on the subject, nor could he silently watch the people who went about defiantly without paying the tax. Tabara became worried. 'Devil take this Gandhi!' he grumbled. He managed to escape the Customs House job by somehow getting himself a caretaker's job at the Padugere Circuit House. There, as a result of serving and waiting on the white sahibs from near, Tabara came to realize that though they looked different they too were human beings like us.

The fervour of the freedom movement kept increasing and it spread even to the countryside. Tabara, too, began to have qualms about serving his white masters devotedly. Besides, the Anglo-Indian butlers who accompanied the visiting British officials always treated him with contempt and suspicion. Seeing how humiliated he felt by this, Appi suggested that he get a transfer, this time, to the Taluk Office.

By the time Tabara became an attendant in the Taluk Office, India had gained independence. One by one, the white faces were disappearing and the Government was now in the hands of his own countrymen. In addition to the Taluk Office it already had, Padugere now got offices like the Taluk Development Board, the Coffee Board, and the Excise Department.

At first, there was a dispute as to which department Tabara belonged to and what his present job title and salary should be. After shunting him from one department to another, at last it was decided that he was to be an employee of the Town Municipality. A few more years lapsed, however, before he was given the livery that would emphatically identify him as an employee of the Padugere Municipality. By then Tabara had neared the retirement age. Sometimes, Tabara would feel the pressure of work; and there would be moments of anxiety and confusion. But this was due largely to the style of functioning of the Padugere administration.

Twenty-five years had passed since the country got independence. Gandhi was little more than a memory in people's minds.

A few days before he was to retire, Tabara was put in charge of collecting the excise tax on coffee at the Coffee Depot. On the very first day he presented himself at the Coffee Depot, he found himself in the midst of a dispute between the Manager there and the Town Municipality. The Manager contended that because coffee was considered an 'export' item it was exempt from the excise tax which the municipality wanted to levy. Meanwhile, Ramanna, a coffee merchant in the town, protested that he was being taxed twice—once at the time of buying the coffee from the coffee growers, and again at the Coffee Depot. The coffee growers themselves refused to pay the tax. All this was confusing to Tabara. It seemed that though Gandhi had been long dead, his style of agitation still lingered on. While the dispute was still unresolved, Tabara issued a couple of receipts to some coffee growers who refused to pay the tax.

The president of the municipality blamed Tabara for issuing the receipts without actually having collected the tax and ordered him to pay a fine of three-hundred-and-sixty rupees, equivalent to the amount for which he had issued the receipts. Tabara had to pay the fine from out of his monthly salary of sixty rupees.

His wife Appi's health had been deteriorating steadily all this while. Tabara himself had often said to his neighbours that the poor woman had taken it to heart that she was childless. 'What can we do?' he had said to them, 'God didn't will it. He kept me too busy to give children to my wife.'

To make matters worse, someone put a suspicion in Tabara's head that his wife had been poisoned by somebody who bore a grudge against them. Tabara subjected her to all kinds of tests like dipping tamarind seeds in her urine, smearing her hand with *nugge* extract; but to no avail. In the end, he gave whatever money he had to one Jubeda Bibi who claimed that she had an antidote to the poison. The medicine induced vomitting and Jubeda Bibi pointed to a substance in the vomit as the poison. Then she gave some powder saying, 'Let your wife eat this, and in just four days you'll see the colour return to her cheeks.' Appi finished taking the powder. But the only colour she got was when she had blushed at what the medicine-woman said.

Tabara had noticed in the course of these tests that ants were gathering around her urine and he suspected that her ailment had something to do with it.

It made him wonder that he should love her so much as to fret over her in this manner. The thought had never occurred to him before she had turned into an invalid.

When at last he took her to Dr Silva he at once suspected diabetes and the tests confirmed it.

'Do you know this is a disease of the wealthy?' Dr Silva joked with Tabara. 'In our time, I've seen one or two white men who had it. I wonder how your wife got it? Probably it means you are about to become rich.' He gave a prescription for some tablets and said that if she didn't improve, she would have to have injections. Tabara said to his wife, 'Did you hear? It seems that what you've got is a royal illness. We should be glad that if not the white sahibs' prestige at least you got their illness.'

From the white sahibs' disease to the subject of British rule, Dr Silva and Tabara chattered on for a long time. Appi didn't follow much of what they were talking about.

On the way home Tabara worried that far from bringing them wealth, the illness had cost them every paisa they had, and had reduced them almost to begging.

The Padugere Municipality Board had been dissolved, its term having come to an end and it was time for fresh elections. The Tehsildar had assumed the charge of interim affairs.

Tabara received a notice from the Taluk Office according to which he had failed to pay up the money with respect to two or three tax receipts he had signed, and if he didn't pay it up immediately, his salary would be withheld. Tabara went running up to the Taluk Office and explained what had happened. The Tehsildar told him that though at present the charge against him was one of misappropriation of funds, he would write the amount as arrears still to be collected by Tabara. This meant that no matter how he looked at it there was no way out for him but to pay the three-hundred-and-sixty rupees out of his own pocket.

Never in his life had Tabara felt so humiliated. He was an honourable man, he protested, he had served under the British rule and under many important officers; Government servants weren't falsely accused like this in those days.

The Tehsildar was so preoccupied with his own professional world of appeals, litigations, notices and signatures, that the old man's tales about the past had no interest for him. Besides, by praising the British rule, Tabara had unwittingly denigrated the present rule.

In any case, Tabara didn't get his salary that month. There was no money for even his wife's medicine. He had to scrape together money from here and there so he could feed his wife some *raagi* gruel.

At that point, someone suggested that he might be eligible for his pension money. Tabara once again went running to the Tehsildar's office. 'Give me a petition in writing. I will send it up to the higher authority,' said the Tehsildar and buried his head among the files.

With the municipal elections just a few days away, there were many candidates bustling about, on the look-out for causes. One of those candidates, Bantappa, found in Tabara his opportunity to serve society. 'Come, let us find out why you are not getting your pension money,' he told Tabara. 'We'll take the Government to court, if necessary.'

When the two met the Tehsildar, the latter told them that it was not clear whether Tabara belonged to the provident fund scheme or the pension scheme and that he was going to write to the higher authorities to get the matter clarified.

Bantappa made a swift calculation and told Tabara that if he belonged to the provident fund scheme, he had about six to seven thousand rupees coming to him. Tabara was overjoyed. 'My wife's illness must be a royal one after all, if it should bring us all that money,' Tabara thought and hoped that the money would come soon so he could buy the medicine needed by his wife.

Buoyed by the anticipated pension money, Tabara began to run up small debts with all and sundry. He made the rounds of the Tehsildar's office routinely. All the while, his wife's condition was deteriorating. At first Tabara ignored it. 'All she was losing in her urine was a little sugar. So what?' he thought. But before long it got to a stage when she had to be confined to bed.

Some time before, Appi had hurt her big toe while doing the household chores. She applied some herbal juice on it and went about her work, limping. Tabara hardly noticed it, as he had received some good news that day. A clerk at the Taluk Office had informed him that there was a reply from the higher authorities and that he was likely to get approximately seventeen thousand rupees as his provident fund. The Tehsildar had asked him to collect proofs of employment from whatever departments he had previously served. Not realizing the enormity of the task before him, Tabara gloated over the prospect of getting seventeen thousand rupees.

'Dr Silva tells me that there is some injection which would cure your illness in no time,' he told his wife apprising her of their imminent prosperity. 'Let us see what you have got in your luck.'

Tabara began making the rounds of all the departments he had served previously and everywhere it was the same litany he sang: 'Sir, my wife is ill. My money is with the Government. To get it, I need your certificate.' With each certificate he acquired, his file grew bigger.

Bantappa, the candidate in the municipal election told Tabara that if there was any delay in getting his money, he would take him to Bangalore to the Minister to get the money sanctioned expeditiously and Bantappa even offered to bear Tabara's expenses himself. Tabara was worried that if he went to Bangalore, there would be no one to feed the rice gruel to his wife, especially since the leg wound had deteriorated to the extent that she could not even walk around. When he took her to the Government hospital, he was told that she had gangrene and her leg would have to be amputated.

Tabara got scared. 'The devil take these doctors,' he thought. 'The wound is in one toe and they want to cut off the whole leg. Next they will chop off the man's head just because he has a headache.' He brought Appi back thinking that may be he could find some native doctor who could come up with a cure for her.

By now, his file was close to completion. The clerks and the attendants at the Taluk Office, who had watched his frenzied running around and his obsession with the case, concluded that he was losing his mind and that he was surely possessed by the devil to have turned so patently greedy.

Tabara went to Subbu Setti, the loan shark of Padugere, and asked him for a loan on the strength of his expected pension but was greeted with derisive laughter. 'You expect money from the Government? You might as well expect a dead body to come back from the grave,' said Subbu Setti prophetically. 'You should consider yourself lucky if you get your money before your own death, let alone your wife's.' Still, on seeing his sad face, Subbu Setti offered him four rupees.

'Sir, I swear to God,' he said as he walked away, 'I didn't come here to beg money for beedis. Of what use are four rupees to me? If you find it in your heart to lend me a bigger sum, you will do me a big favour.' Tabara left with a heavy heart, but he began to see the truth of Subbu Setti's words. It seemed to him as if his slow-moving file was in a race against his wife's rapidly worsening leg wound. Appi was whimpering in pain as the wound had now spread to the whole of her foot.

The Tehsildar had told him that his file was forwarded to higher authorities for approval. However, Tabara was back in his office the very next day to enquire after the file's progress. The Tehsildar flew into a rage. 'Do you think your file was sent to the backyard that it should be returned in a day?' he shouted. 'It has to go up to Bangalore before it can come back to us.'

Bantappa renewed his offer to take him to Bangalore, all expenses paid. In return, all he needed to do was to canvass for Bantappa among his neighbours. But since Tabara wouldn't leave his wife uncared for even for a day, they decided that before making the trip to Bangalore they would visit the Deputy Commissioner's office at Chikamagalur to check on the file's progress. When they went there enquiring after the file, the clerk fumed at them: 'How dare you come poking around here? Don't you know that everything has to come through the proper channel?' They were asked to leave the office.

As they were leaving, the head clerk called back Tabara and cautioned him about associating with politicians like Bantappa especially where matters of money were involved. He also told him that there might be a delay in clearing the file, as they were all busy with the preparation for the silver jubilee of Independence.

When Tabara returned home in the evening, his wife was howling in pain. She told him that she wanted to poison herself. A harried Tabara tried to comfort her by saying that his pension money was due any day now, and as soon as it came he would take her to Bangalore and spare no expense to get her the best treatment.

The following day, with the help of Bantappa, Tabara took Appi to the hospital. The doctor took one look at her leg and said that if she was not taken right then to the Sakaleshpur Hospital for an amputation, she would not live. Tabara, stunned, was taking her back home when the attendant from the Tehsildar's office met him and said that the Tehsildar had sent for him. His file had arrived.

With flickering hope that he might still be able to save Appi from dying, he went to the Tehsildar's office. It turned out that the file had been sent back from Chikamagalur with a remark from the concerned clerk that the certificates of residence from the Shanubhog and Patel were required.

Back at home, Appi was screaming in agony: 'I can't bear this pain any longer. I don't want medicine or anything. Just get me four annas worth of poison.' The irony was that Tabara didn't have even four annas with him that day!

More days went by as the file kept moving back and forth. How true were Subbu Setti's words, Tabara thought. He had now lost all hopes of either saving his wife from dying or getting his pension money from the Government.

A few days later, the Tehsildar sent for him again. His face contorted in pain, his voice choking in anguish, he went and stood before the Tehsildar.

'There is a police report against you,' growled the stern-faced Tehsildar. 'It appears that you have been hobnobbing with that Naxalite communist, Bantappa, and making trouble at the Chikamagalur District Collector's Office.' Then, softening a little he said, 'Look, I feel sorry for you. You don't seem to have learnt anything from all the trouble God gave you. Anyhow, I'll write a favourable report on you today. But I would like you to contribute something to our fund to celebrate the silver jubilee of our nation's Independence.' A strange smile spread across Tabara's face. 'You can take all of it,' he said, 'all of my pension money as my contribution to your fund.' The Tehsildar thought that there was something odd about Tabara's behaviour.

Slowly, Tabara began to perceive all around him a pitiless and meaningless system that snared human beings and transformed them into policemen, officers, Shanubhogs, Patels, attendants, and so on, a system that guarded, at its heart, a heap of files with nonsense written in them. It seemed as though the devil had spread this snare to entrap humanity, chew it up and spew forth the pitiful remnants. The Tehsildar, like a fiend stuffing his victims into the folds of the file like so many dried fish, was making grotesque, meaningless gestures. Hopping from desk to desk the battered human souls entered the files that closed themselves on them. As Tabara looked at this infernal machine at work, tears rolled down his cheeks. He felt sorrow for the sake of his wife, for his fellow human beings, the Tehsildar, for the attendant Javara.

The attendant led him by the hand out of the office. Outside, for quite some time, he stood dazed, just the way the attendant had left him.

Later, he somehow managed to take his wife to the hospital in Sakaleshpur. There, he was asked to produce a certificate attesting that he was a former employee of the Government, along with some documents clarifying whether an employee of the Municipality could in fact be considered a Government employee.

When Tabara brought his wife back, she was on the verge of fainting from the excruciating pain. She was frothing at the mouth. He went to Yusuf, the butcher, and asked him whether he could chop off his wife's leg from the knee down. In the shop, dangling from the ceiling, four or five chopped heads of sheep were staring at the sky with a blank look.

'Planning to cook a stew out of your wife's leg?' laughed Yusuf teasingly. A few onlookers there joined in the laughter.

A dog that had grown fat on raw meat was chewing on a bone. The carcasses of the sheep hung from the ceiling, dripping red drops. Next to the butcher shop sat a skinny girl trying to sell the pods of a cut jackfruit, all the while swinging her thin arms mechanically, to chase the flies away.

Tabara began to suspect that he had been dead for some time and had been wandering among the ghosts of the dead.

They say that when his wife died, Tabara was laughing

hysterically. The people of Padugere were anxious to conclude that Tabara had gone mad. For, once he was known as mad, his problems could be considered as belonging to another world. Only a very few could see in him the appalling reflection of our own system. It shook them with an unknown terror.

It was just a coincidence that Tabara went mad on the same day as the twenty-fifth anniversary of our nation's Independence. When all the speakers were lavishing praise on Free India, Tabara was babbling about the greatness of the British rule. Everyone laughed at his craziness.

The only man worried by the news of Tabara's madness was the Tehsildar. There was still the question of collecting three hundred rupees from Tabara. The Tehsildar was hoping to deduct the money from Tabara's provident fund. Besides, he had already sent up a report on Tabara vouching that he was of a sound and dependable character, and put the blame for the arrears he owned on the vagaries of the administration.

And now this? thought the Tehsildar. It was enough to make him go mad.

—Translated by Narayan Hegde

A Story Like This

Veena Shanteshwar

Ten years ago it had been an evening much like this. The rainy season had begun. The city of Bombay, which had literally blazed during the day in summer, had become cool and salubrious after a drizzle. After office, she had normally scampered for a local train or a bus like everyone else, but on that day she had plodded her way in the gentle shower, getting deliberately drenched. Her body had cooled. She had come from Malanad. Though she had come to Bombay several years ago to take up a job, she had found the heat unbearable. She had forever longed for the rains, and when they had come, she had felt happy and augmented. But as soon as the rains had vanished, there had lingered in her a residue of dissatisfaction.

After every season she had told herself that it hadn't rained enough and she hadn't had enough of a drenching. Despairing and expectant, she had spent the years waiting for the rains.

'Hello, madam,' a scooter had suddenly stopped beside her and she had turned to see who it was.

It had been the same chap who had come from their Delhi Head Office to receive training as a Probationary Officer. His dignified mien had attracted her.

'Hello,' she had replied with a tender smile.

'Do you like getting drenched in the rain, madam?' he had queried in English. Though he had spoken to her for the first time, he had put this question—without the prefatory pleasantries—directly to her, as if he had known her for a long time.

'Yes, I like it very much,' she had agreed without a hint of hesitation.

'Then you come along with me. Instead of these crowded streets, the deserted beach is an ideal spot for getting soaked. I too would like to get soaked with you. Are you coming, please?' His offer had lacked emphasis, but had the drift of extreme gentleness.

She had stared at him for a moment. But the next moment she had hopped on to the pillion. And they had gone off together.

*

Years ago when she had joined her office as a clerk, several men on several occasions had asked her, 'Are you coming with me, madam?' And the same offer had been repeated when she had become an officer after passing several departmental examinations. Her bosses, her colleagues and office visitors had invited her at the office, on the roads, in the parks. Never at anytime had she felt like going out with any of them. She had spent all those years in this vast city of Bombay alone.

It was this juncture that he had arrived in her life. During the next ten years she was never alone. He always hung around her—in the room, at the office, in the streets, at the market, in the theatres, in the restaurants, on the beach, at office meetings, during office picnics. Here, there and everywhere, they spent days, months and years together.

His training lasted a year. Afterwards, for her sake, he got himself transferred to Bombay. And their life together went on in an orderly manner. During the first few years he went every year to Delhi for three or four days to look up his people. She too visited her home town, but invariably returned disgusted as her relatives soundly reproached her for leading that kind of life. Hurt, both stopped visiting their relatives. Instead, they made trips to holiday resorts and spots. This sort of congenial co-existence brought them supreme happiness. They made no demands on each other. Since there were no expectations, there weren't any disappointments either. They were made for each other—he and she.

As usual people around gossiped about them. How long could their tongues wag? The gossip ceased. The two cared two hoots for others' small talk. Their indifference didn't have a chink.

Having spent years without bickering and bitterness, and in fact in a happy manner, she of late felt the stirrings of discontent. Fatigue and discomfort fretted her. She consulted many a lady doctor. At last a doctor whispered into her ears, 'You are pregnant.

It's two months now.'

'Really?' was all she could say and lapsed into silence. Consternation, surprise and a sense of fear gripped her. But above all there was a feeling of triumph. Till now she had been under the impression that she was devoid of such emotions, but now she realized that she was a centre of a variety of such cross-currents.

Since the lady doctor knew of her position, she advised, 'Take your time to consider, and then we'll see.' Patting her back affectionately, the doctor sent her home.

At home, for the first time she realized that she was waiting for his return. In a fit of agitation, she tried in vain to imagine what feelings she would have had if she had been married; what would have been his reactions to her shy disclosure; what they would have said about their impending baby. Soon she said to herself, 'How stupid of me! How sentimental I have become.' Her normal impersonal self tried to reassert itself.

That night he returned home late. He said, 'I have received a telegram from Delhi. Mother is seriously ill.' They both had dinner. They cleared the table. They even washed a few dishes. In tune with their routine, they did everything together. As she was going through the chores, she felt a flurry of apprehension. The more she tried to suppress it, the greater was the agitation. That a long-standing companion like this had failed to recognize her condition galled her. Simultaneously she felt ashamed for getting angry inside at his indifference towards the fulfilment of her expectations. She asked herself: 'Why do I despair so much? Am I not wrong?'

When they were in bed, he noticed the change in her and asked, 'Are you tired?'

'No, not really,' she replied.

What followed was the habitual act—as expected. Wanting to sleep and drawing the blanket up, she said, 'Today the doctor told me that I'm going to be a mother.' But she didn't say, 'You're going to be a father.'

'What, what will you be?' he said this with an inflection of disbelief. Understandably he was surprised. 'Husband', 'wife', 'mother', 'father', 'children'—the two of them had never ever used these barren words.

Correcting herself she said, 'I'm supposed to be pregnant.'

'Oh,' he said. The impersonal tone as usual. Without having any ability to imagine what was happening in his mind, she was ruminating over the ideas that came inside the region of her understanding. Before falling asleep he remarked, 'I'm expected to be in Delhi tomorrow.'

'You may go,' she said, contented.

Since he had full faith in her abilities, he slept peacefully. With equal ease he left for Delhi the next day. Returning after a fortnight he asked, 'Did everything go off well?' She didn't reply.

For the first time his complacency was shaken and agitation took root. 'What is this? Why didn't you go to a doctor for an abortion?'

'Because I didn't feel like it!' Though he was shocked for a moment, he regained his self-possession and said with a smile, 'Well, were you waiting for my return? All right. Let us go in the evening.'

She didn't say a thing. In the evening she told him that she wouldn't go to the doctor and didn't approve of abortion. On this point their differences, arguments, debates, misunderstanding and animus originated.

'What kind of madness is this? Will you have a child? What'll you do with the child? Won't we lose all our freedom? Besides . . . besides . . . ,' he expressed his doubts.

'Besides what?' she spoke sharply.

'We have no right to have a child. Legally we aren't husband and wife. Don't you know that?' he said this with great unease.

She laughed. 'You too talk about laws like ordinary people. It is the woman's birthright to deliver a child. This is my belief. Your opinion is uncalled for.'

'Which means you are suggesting that I should marry you,' he said this in distress.

'Nonsense,' she thought. She felt indignant. 'He is slandering me. Does a man lose his mental balance in the face of difficulties? Isn't there a limit to misunderstanding me?' Keeping her self-control she said calmly, 'No. So far I haven't bothered you with anything. It's not so now. Nor will it be in the future.'

'Then? What is the meaning of all this?'

'Nothing. It's very simple. A baby is growing in me. I want the baby to live. That's all.'

'But shouldn't you get married to become a mother?'

'Don't be silly. What is the relation between the two?'

'Meaning . . . would you like to be an unwed mother?' In his voice there was despair, shrillness.

A man who had spent ten years with her, living beyond conventions, accepted norms, regular relationships, a man with whom she had worn out the prime of her life, how could anyone imagine that such a man would think in cliches? Fatigued by their tedious arguments and counter-arguments, she said in a decisive voice, 'Look, I intend to become a mother. I'm not seeking your permission. So I'm not in need of your advice or guidance. I just want to be a "mother". And leave it at that.'

'What does it mean? What will people say?'

'People?' For the first time she was really disgusted with him.

Perhaps he too was aware of his mistake. If she had been another woman, he thought, she would have flung at him umpteen questions—where were those "people" till now? From where did they appear suddenly? and so on. But she was quiet. That made him feel small before her. He added in a conciliatory tone, 'Look, it isn't as if I am afraid of people. But everything has its own limits—including fearlessness. As it is, we are happy. Why ask for gratuitous trouble? A headache.'

'Well, I've already told you. You don't have to worry. Mirth or melancholy, it is all mine. You be at peace.'

'When I live with you in the same house day and night and work with you in the same office, how can I be at peace and be indifferent? Aren't I human?'

'Is that so? Then you don't have to live with me. Get a transfer to Delhi. You'll be with your mother during her last days. You needn't worry about me.'

'You make it sound so simple. Don't you ever feel for me? If it's so, all right. The kink in your head about the baby is too much for me to bear. I don't know how to react to your decision about becoming a mother without being married. I find it intolerable. If I leave, don't blame me.'

'Definitely not,' she said in all honesty. Actually, she didn't feel the necessity of analysing the rights and wrongs of his attitude. What pervaded her consciousness was something very different. It had an intoxicating effect on her. And he left.

During the first few days after he left she really felt the heaviness of his absence. While having food, getting ready for the office, going out for a walk, and specially while going to bed, she felt awfully bored. But as days lapsed a strange kind of animation took root in her and blanketed all her sundry sorrows. A being all on its own was taking shape and quivering within her—what an astonishing sensation! 'All these years I've been alone. Yes, even when he was around, I was alone. But now it isn't so. Now in a true sense with me there's another human being. When it's born it will lean on itself. It'll call me, "Amma". It'll run to me and put its arms round my neck with a pure heart, without expectations, and with total devotion it will love me.' This fantasy of love brought tears to her eyes, which hadn't happened for years.

'Does every woman about to become a mother feel this way? The only real love is the one between a mother and her child. This is the only true relationship and the rest is unreal, empty and meaningless—is this a universal experience? How can we find fault with a baby's birth when it gives one a sense of such great fulfilment? How is it an impropriety? How can it be a sin? It cannot happen that way. I need this baby which has helped me experience truth, beauty and God. Under no circumstances will I lose this child. The very idea of conceiving and begetting a child is very beautiful. Honestly I don't want anything else in life.

'Don't I need anything else? Don't I need him either? When I felt cold, he brought me warmth; when I felt hot, he made me cool; and also he helped me cross the crowded streets, he gave me the water of life when I felt thirsty, and for ten long years he was my inseparable companion.'

But he wrote her letters regularly. Every second day he telephoned her. 'I hate to be away from you, but my mother is on her deathbed. My mother has been pressing me to marry her brother's daughter. My mother says your caste is different, your language different and we can't afford such discordant notes. She tells me to forget Bombay. How can I forget?' And so on.

When her baby was born, she was tired. Even then she opened her eyes and looked at her child and at herself. It was a very pretty baby girl. In the eyes of her child, she could see the cosmic vision and the significance of life.

A week later there was a call from him. His voice was filled with zeal, 'A piece of good news for you. At last my mother has permitted me to marry you. I can't live away from you. Let's get married. Besides the child will have a place in society.'

She cut him short, and unrelentingly she said, 'I don't need anybody now. I have whatever I wished for. You fend for yourself.'

—Translated by Basavaraj Urs

Cruelty

S. Diwakar

Alamelu, the only daughter of Prof. Tiruchandoor Srinivas Raghavacharya and his good spouse Kalyanamma, died the other day. The sun was burning hot, powerful enough to pierce the skin and drill though the bones. Alamelu lay dying near the Kodambakkam station, on the melting and fuming tar of the road.

A knife, thrown with some force, had unexpectedly plunged into Alamelu's back. Palanichami, the one who sold salt heaped in his push-cart, held her to his naked breast, while the crowd waited for an ambulance.

Whenever Alamelu opened her eyes wide, she could see only the infinite blue that threatened to envelop in a moment the circle of black heads around her. The train whistled even as the dogs barked. She widened her nostrils as if the fragrance of flowers had beckoned her from her home garden on Habibulla road. She didn't understand what the people around her were saying as everyone was speaking at the same time. She felt that time moved along with the moving train, making a rolling sound. She didn't mind the bilious smell coming from the mouth of the man who held her to his breast.

Though Alamelu was thirty-six years old, she hadn't grown up as a woman. It was true that Professor Tiruchandoor Srinivas Raghavacharya married Kalyanamma at the age of eighteen. It was equally true that Kalyanamma, devoted to the Vadagali tradition, became his fond wife. But it was only when the professor was forty or so that Alamelu was born. They had waited for a son who would carry on their family name but Alamelu was born and was down with polio soon after birth. Not being good-looking, she was no favourite of her parents.

Alamelu spent most of her life in the Andal Mandir on Habibullah road. And she thought she would die there too. It was an ancient, but huge, house. If you opened the gates and went in you would find flowers on either side of the driveway. A portico on two pillars stretched out of the house. The hall was rather dark even with the windows open. The double-storeyed houses that had come up on either side had cut off the light. There was a mirror in one corner next to the door leading to the bathroom. To its left there were two cane chairs and in the right corner there was a table. Up on the wall were photographs of grandfathers and forefathers hung in a row. Whenever Alamelu returned home from outside, she used to set her things on the table and then slip inside for a chat with her mother. Both the professor and his wife kept their eyes on everything she did, the books she read, the clothes she wore, and so on.

In the evenings Prof. Tiruchandoor Srinivas Raghavacharya and his wife would sit on the two cane chairs and discuss Vishishtadwaita philosophy. The professor, dressed in a thick lungi and a short-sleeved shirt, would open an ancient and musty book and cast a sidelong glance at his wife. He would then smile, showing his two protruding front teeth, and stare at her. Kalyanamma's face, with the sunken cheeks, would then bloom and her left hand fingers would squeeze the tip of her left nostril.

'Look, Kalyanu, in Tirukovilur, the place where Poihaiah Alwar slept was just enough for him, and when Poodattalwar came Poihaiah had to get up and sit. When both of them were sitting, lo, Peyalwar came and they all had to stand up as there was no space for three. They then realized all of a sudden that there was a fourth one there.'

'Oh, there were great people, really great ones,' said Kalyanamma, rubbing hard the tip of her nose and opening her lipless mouth. 'How beautiful is Poodattalwar's statement,' she exclaimed with half-closed eyes. 'Devotion is the bowl, desire the ghee, and worry, which burns away with joy, is the wick. In this way my soul worships God Narayana with the light of my knowledge.' There was wonder in her eyes as she quoted the words of Poodattalwar.

During such occasions of communion, the Professor would frown with annoyance if he spotted Alamelu around. He would shout, 'You shameless girl, how many times should I ask you to cover yourself properly with the *pallu* of your saree?' Professor

Srinivas Raghavacharya who had retired as Professor of Philosophy from the University of Madras after long years of service, found his peace of mind these days in the thinking of Vishishtadwaita. At one time he had been fascinated with Schopenhauer's Philosophy of the Will, but now he was convinced that nothing excelled Bhagwan Ramanujan's Karmayoga theory. He remembered with great pride and thrill the religious devotion and piety which characterized the lives of his father and forefathers. No wonder Alamelu was an outsider in his world. Alamelu, of course, longed for the love of her parents. But, not possessing the qualities which her parents would have valued, she had little freedom at home. She was not allowed even to open the windows of her room when she liked.

When Alamelu was twenty or so, two mischievous fellows who walked past her house had called her an old hag. By the time she was thirty, she had really grown into one.

Alamelu had a thin longish face with dark rings under her eyes and a nose which was rather long but flattened at the tip. Her dark hair was thin and had never grown beyond her neck. Her right cheek had a scar, the result of branding when she was struck down with polio. When she walked, she first kept her short stick-like right leg on the ground and then would lift her left leg high. . . .

The fact that, once upon a time, Alamelu had fallen in love, was not known to anyone on Habibulla road, not even to her parents. Her love was, of course, short-lived. She often wondered whether the chap who had loved her was still alive. This was something which happened when she went—the only time she did—to her mother's ancestral home in Kanchipur. The occasion was her aunt's wedding and Alamelu had gone with her mother. The house next to the temple was full of relatives, unheard of and unknown to her. There was plenty of freedom to walk about with boys and girls of her own age. Yes, what was his name? Was it not Ramanujan? He had held her hand and helped her cross the raised threshold of the temple. When pretty girls were reluctant to be seen with her, he had walked with her, eyes brimming with love and compassion. When some fifteen of them went to see the film, *Nenjil Oru Aalayam* (The Heart is a Temple), it was Ramanujan who had sat next to her. In the darkness of the theatre his hand had wandered all over her body.

Alamelu had loved him secretly and, in keeping with her youth, she had been coy and shown some reluctance. After her return from Kanchipur, she had been miserable for some time. The boy never showed up again and she had thought he must be dead. It was left to her then to help her mother in domestic chores like getting vegetables and some knick-knacks from the shops. . . .

Now, Alamelu, who was thirty-six and without any grace or beauty to arouse sympathy or pity, lay dying on the road. The plastic basket which had jumped out of her hand when she collapsed at the edge of the road, lay at a distance. Her saree, which was in some disorder, revealed the thin sticks of her legs stretched out in different directions, right up to her knees. Palanichami pulled her up so that she sat straight against his body. He put the saree in some order to cover her legs.

He had run to her as soon as he'd heard about the knife plunging into her. Before that, he was probably lying down at home with only a lungi round his waist. Strong and sturdy, his body was as dark as charcoal, with black hair covering his chest. In his bulging eyes popping out of his swollen face, Alamelu saw some brown spots. Though she was aware that he was from one of those huts, she felt snug and comfortable. Her face lost its confused misery for a while and became a little more cheerful. She felt that his deep breath was filling her lungs with life. . . .

'Water,' Alamelu said, weakly.

'Water, bring some water,' shouted Palanichami to the people crowding around. 'Not water, bring some soda,' said someone from the crowd.

Alamelu felt a strange happiness. The love that she saw in the eyes of the black guy was the type she wanted from her parents. She knew that a whole world separated her from him. If she were black and that man's daughter, he would have loved her. If he were fair and were her father, he would have looked after her with love and care. When her mouth twisted to the right in an effort to smile at her fancy, the slum-dwellers around thought that she was grimacing in pain. She saw in her benefactor's eyes the kind of compassion that she had never experienced before in her life.

For the last three years, morning and evening, Alamelu had

crossed the same street on her way to Pondi Bazaar to purchase things for home. She could have gone straight to the bazaar after taking a turn to Masilamani Mudali road from Habibulla road. But what she usually did was to avoid Masilamani Mudali road and go to Kodambakkam station, then walk along the track by the lane that went through the slum. The reason was that once, when she had gone dragging her leg, a stranger had gone past her, brushing her arm. Although her feet had shaken in fear, what he said had made her pale face blush. She had never been able to forget this little adventure in her life and since then she had always gone to Pondi bazaar via Kodambakkam station. That particular morning a snake-charmer had attracted a whole host of people to his little corner of a square, and she had found it strange that a lot of people had run from all directions to see what was happening. Even though she had kept an eye on the crowd, she felt that someone had actually brushed against her arm. He was a dwarf with squinted eyes and was dressed in a torn half-pant. The sweat that poured down from his tousled hair had made deep lines on his cheeks. The hair on his chest, too, had been shining with sweat. His lower lip had a carbuncle on it. When Alamelu had turned towards him, he had pretended to have lost his balance and veered to the left. He had said with widened eyes, 'Oh, my little Aiyar girl!' Alamelu, who had held her purse tightly to her breast, had felt as if the dwarf had giggled and winked at her rather meaningfully. It was true that she had frowned at him then, but the very next minute she had felt as if there was some affectionate softness in his words: 'Oh, my little Aiyar girl!' She had walked away fast and turned her eyes to the meat shop to the left which had never caught her eye before. She had fixed her gaze on the mutton ribs. She had been aware of people staring at her and, blushing like a bride, she had slid away. . . .

When she had stepped into the living-room, Professor Srinivas Raghavacharya had been disturbed, since he was profoundly immersed in explaining to Kalyanamma the various stages of the non-aligned consciousness—Yatamana, Vyatireka, Ekendriya and Vashikara. Alamelu had come in quite noisily and, above all, she had a smile on her face. 'What happened and why are you laughing, mad girl?'

Alamelu had slipped inside and disappeared, leaving the professor to take up the incident related to Adal, who had resolved to marry God, adorned himself with flowers picked for His worship and looked at his own reflection in the mirror, asking himself, 'Will God accept me now?'

As soon as she had entered the room, Alamelu had felt like opening the window. It was not right to look into the mirror at night, was it? She had quietly taken up the mirror kept in the window and said to herself, 'Oh, my little Aiyar girl!' What she had seen in the mirror was a blooming face with shining eyes and the nose was not flat at the end. There had been no sign of the scar on the right cheek. And waves of hair had kept rushing over her neck. Oh, it must have been Ramanujan himself who had brushed her arm that evening. 'No, that man was different. Whoever it was, there was someone who loved even her. She was not bad-looking, after all; in fact, quite nice-looking, wasn't she? Alamelu who had all the time been looking into the mirror had heard the street-door close. Why should their discussion on Vedanta end so early? Alamelu had been a little frustrated.

Later, in the dining-hall, as the professor sat in front of his plate, Alamelu had not felt self-conscious when she sat down in her odd fashion as usual, planting her right thigh on the floor first, keeping her left thigh erect and supporting it with her left hand. And Professor Raghavacharya was not happy to see the change that had taken place in her face. He stared at his wife in scornful seriousness.

After dinner, it was usual for Kalyanamma to sit scanning the paper *Kalki*, and the professor *The Hindu*, for the second time in the day. Alamelu, lying on her stomach on the bed, which had looked wider than usual, had recollected the snake-charmer, the crowd surrounding him, the man who had brushed against her and winked, and the faces that had stared at her from the meat shop. As usual, she had also recollected the days she spent with Ramanujan. She had felt for a while that she was buried in his arms and that his hands had pressed the soft parts of her body. And she had slept soundly.

It was from that day that Alamelu, instead of going to Pondi bazaar via Masilamani Mudali road, had taken the road along the Kodambakkam railway track. She felt happy to be in a thick crowd. On the side of the road, along the footpath, there were huts, and on the other footpath lots of people. It was but natural, wasn't it, and not a matter of disgrace if her body brushed against someone else's? She had not been scared of the quarrels and thefts so common in that area. She had even experienced a thrill when people whistled at her with curious eyes after their bodies brushed hers accidentally.

It was during the thirty-sixth year of her life that a knife entered her back. It was eleven o' clock. There was a big crowd at the meat shop. A half-naked hefty man was beating up a boy of sixteen or seventeen, holding the boy's hair and pounding him again and again. The boy's mouth was bloody and his shirt was in tatters. Two women, sitting with their dung baskets, chewing paan and betel nut, were eagerly watching the fight. One of them, with twinkling nose rings on either side of her nose, bit her lips every second, and shook her shoulders every time the hefty fellow hit the boy. The other woman sat with her legs stretched in front of her, scratching her arm-pits. Alamelu looked at them and limped along the edge of the road without looking behind her. She had barely walked ten yards when the boy gave the hefty fellow the slip and shouting, 'Wait, you son of a widow, I'll show you. . .,' ran towards Alamelu. A chap from the crowd tried to hold him as the hefty fellow chased the boy. The boy held Alamelu's shoulders with both his hands and let out a stream of abuses at the hefty fellow. Alamelu's face blossomed with delight at the intimate touch of the boy who had pressed his body against hers as he held her by the shoulders. She shuddered when she noticed the blood oozing from his mouth.

By this time, the hefty one, who had been held fast by two people, screamed wildly and took out a knife. The blade had gleamed in the hot sun. The boy bent in the nick of time and the knife, thrown by the hefty one, had gone straight into Alamelu's back. The boy had run away and Alamelu had heard the words, 'Somebody hit her,' and moaned. The hefty one ran past her after the boy. Even as Alamelu collapsed gasping for breath, and as her eyes dimmed, she saw the man and the boy disappearing among the huts.

The crowd rushed towards Alamelu. Someone shouted, 'Ring up the police.' From somewhere Palanichami had come running, crying, '*Ayyo, ayyo.*' The woman with two nose rings had quickly picked up the knife which had fallen to the ground after striking Alamelu, and slipped it into her basket. The other one had picked up Alamelu's purse and, in the twinkling of an eye, both of them had disappeared from the scene.

A boy brought a bottle of soda and Palanichami held it to Alamelu's lips. Alamelu sipped a little, turned her eyes towards him and suddenly turned her head to the right. She wondered why the water stuck in her gullet like sand.

'Don't know whether she will still be alive when the ambulance comes,' someone said.

The crowd, seeing Alamelu's condition and her blood drenching Palanichami's chest, had gone quiet.

Alamelu lay leaning heavily against Palanichami's chest. She breathed with great difficulty. Palanichami shouted, 'Move, let her have some air.' Though her eyes were closed, Alamelu felt the pressure of his muscles against her armpits as she heard the tick-tock of Palanichami's heart. Whenever she opened her eyes, she saw compassion in his bulging eyes. His bilious breath and the sweat dropping from his head had brought real life to her, she thought. She imagined she was rocking in the cradle of his arms.

The police van came and, as three policemen disembarked, the crowd started dispersing. Palanichami said something to Alamelu. Though she did not understand what he was saying, she knew that the words had something in them which every human being should feel for another. Even as the policemen held Palanichami up and scanned the wound on Alamelu's back, she moaned for the last time, sobbed once and closed her eyes. One of the policemen turned to Palanichami and asked, 'Where have you kept the knife?'

Their enquiry into the incident had begun.

— *Translated by Shantinath Desai*

Akku

Vaidehi

Akku has a large vermilion mark on her forehead although she has no husband. There are black beads around her neck, but sometimes she leaves them in her box when she goes out. She has often devoured people, whole, who have asked about her husband's whereabouts. Not always, though. Sometimes she sits silent and tight-lipped. At other times she bursts out laughing through a crooked mouth and nose-tip, shaking her head and looking at you from the corners of her eyes.

She always has a towel in her hand—actually a handkerchief, a man's handkerchief. No one knows how it came into her possession, nor is it worth bothering about. It is enough to say that Akku is never without it. And to her nothing is of greater consequence than misplacing it and looking for it all the time. Let domestic chores go to the dogs; she will carry on searching every nook and cranny for her towel.

Here, in Ajjayya's house, no one is free. Perhaps Uncle Vasu is allowed a voice, and Bhanu Chikki actually dares to speak up a little. Doddatte, as Ajjayya's sister, and 'Great Aunt' to everyone, fears nobody. However, it is Akku alone who is under no obligation, no duress. She is merely chaff, empty. 'Let her wander around as she likes. She has to while away her time somehow.' Perhaps she wasn't always like this—without substance. But she is excused now. The rest of the household is there to churn butter, add spices to food, wear new sarees and jewellery at weddings, or whatever. The men look after the business and report to Ajjayya. They are all like the pillars of the house, never saying anything, however heavy their burdens.

Akku held back by nothing, was not one to miss festive meals at other people's houses. The right side of her face seemingly squashed in, her dimly lit eyes moving, her lips forever trying to hide her jutting teeth, she stood a mere four-and-three-quarter feet. She would fill her nose with snuff and then rub her towel sharply across it, this way and that, like a saw. She would pass her hand over her face and then wipe it on her saree which fell free from her shoulder and then walk along, brandishing her towel. There was no shortage of people who spoke to her in riddles: 'O Cloth that Spreads, Fan that Sways, where will you eat today?' 'Where is the banner off to?' they would ask her to her face. She would answer if she felt like it. Otherwise, she would snap, 'To your grandfather's death anniversary,' and leap away nimbly, like an evil spirit.

When she sat down to eat, she just slurped away quickly, head bent, oblivious to everything around her. She would clutch some of the delicacies in her left hand, wrap them up in the same towel that smelt of snuff and come home to sit alone in the veranda, stuffing herself, ungenerous even to a crow. She was expert at this.

She never missed the festive meals specially prepared to satisfy the whims of pregnant women, or to celebrate the naming ceremony of a baby. Once there, she wouldn't stir from the side of the pregnant woman who sat wearing strung flowers of seven kinds; weight upon weight. Akku, sitting there like an idiot, would be sighted by strangers, or people from the husband's family. 'Who is this dishevelled creature, Devamma? Get her away from there.' The girl's relatives would come and plead timidly with her to sit elsewhere. But Akku was deaf to everything. It was the same at naming ceremonies too. She would let go of the ropes that held up the cradle only when she left for home. Sometimes she even sang a couple of lullabies after all the guests had left. And it seemed that people could never sleep in peace until they had finished mocking her: 'Akku, a whole flock of crows came to sit by the window to hear you singing like a cuckoo.'

Then Siriyatte got married. What happened on the day of the wedding is best heard in her own words:

'The bridegroom's party had arrived. No one had stayed with me, they had all rushed off to the *pandal*; I was very nervous, scared. Then Akku came in. "O, Akku," I said, feeling relieved. "Either Akku or her shadow," she retorted, sharply. She stood at some distance and stared at me. "Why have you dolled yourself up like this?" she asked. I didn't say a thing. Her voice sounded cracked and rasping. I just sat, numb, looking at her. "Come here," she said. "Why?" I asked. "Do as you are told," she said. I wanted to shout, call someone. Then I thought I'd better not. "Akku, aren't you well?" I enquired. She rushed straight at me and in a flash tore off the flowers from my hair. "This will do," she said, "No one who marries you for your beauty alone will keep you happy. You may write that on a wall." I tell you, honestly, I felt as if I couldn't breathe. Akku is attractive in her own way, although she is a bit short. But then she looked like a demon, just for a moment. I was very upset. Not because she tore off the flowers, but because of the way she stared, not blinking once. "How terribly hot it is," she said as she went out, fanning herself with one hand and wiping her face with the towel which she held in the other. If I had told this to Vasu, would he have left her alone? He would have thrashed her and locked her up in a room. Anyway, Doddatte came in then and told me off properly regardless of the fact that I was a bride. She redid my hair and put the flowers in once again.'

Akku created a rumpus on the day Siriyatte left home after the wedding. 'Where has my husband gone and perished? Bring him back this instant.' Not a word other than that. She threw her towel into the air over and over again, repeating the same thing. Uncle Vasu who was standing there, cleaning his teeth with a small stick, said, 'Look there, in that enclosure,' and pointed at the cook, Babu Bhatta, who lay snoring beyond the bamboo screen, totally unaware of the commotion about him. Bhanu Chikki added,'There's your husband. Nobody knows when he arrived, no one saw him. I heard him shouting, "Akku, Akku," so I brought him in.' But Akku's tantrums didn't subside. The louder she shouted, the funnier it seemed. Satyamani, a boy just so high, couldn't control himself and ran to Babu Bhatta and woke him up. Giggling away, he said to him, 'Babu Bhatta, they say you are Akku's husband.' 'I, married to her?' asked Babu Bhatta. 'Good heavens, she would break my limbs and put me in the fire—she'd sell me for a handful of puffed rice.'

We were ecstatic, intoxicated with laughter. Meanwhile, Thammaniah, black as coal, who was sitting learning against the wall, breaking areca nuts and watching the drama unfold, joined in the fray. He was used to taking female roles in Yakshagana and now came swaying and beating his chest. 'Beloved, I am here, your husband. What do you want of me?' He looked around theatrically, smiling at everyone, but leapt back in pain as Akku rushed at him and bit him. She ran inside, got herself a glass of water and gulped it down. 'Thammaniah, get lost! Mind your own business. Don't interfere in mine. Shall I tell you now who your wife slept with the other day?' Her voice was as sharp as a flashing sword. Thammaniah's laughter was put out by the heightened merriment of those around him.

'Never mind, Thammaniah. Everyone knows she has lost her senses. Don't get upset,' Uncle Vasu said in an effort to console him. Thammaniah's wife, who had till this moment been watching happily, head resting on her bent knee, suddenly got up and ran inside, saree stuffed into her mouth as if she was holding back sobs. 'Bhanu, go in and see to her. Decent folk will be compelled to hang themselves because of this wretched creature,' said Uncle Vasu. 'Wandering all over the place and picking up filthy language!'

Akku who had shut herself up appeared only the next morning after the cowherd had taken away the animals for grazing. Anthanna who was around asked her, 'What happened, Akku? Did you find your husband or not?' This, in spite of being told that Akku should be left alone. 'I've just buried him,' she replied. Her face was distorted because of a sleepless night. She did indeed look as if she had washed her hands and feet after burying someone. 'What happens to your children then?' someone asked. 'What else is my lover for? He will look after them,' she spat out. 'What a predicament! The poor man,' someone else whispered and laughed. She appeared not to hear this.

Akku sat leaning against a pillar, her hair dishevelled, the vermilion mark bright on her forehead. Dodatte saw her and started rocking back and forth as she sat slicing green stems in circles. She was well known for composing songs on the spur of the moment and she sang now:

Akku's red mark on her forehead is lovely
and so are her curls.
She is indeed the lovliest
among all on earth.

Doddatte had dragged home her wandering husband and lorded it over him. Eventually he'd died. 'It would have been dreadful, had he lived. It's blissful now,' she had pronounced. She spent her time teasing Akku, slicing vegetables and earning her keep by doing chores; she was nearing sixty. Bow-legged Doddatte looked all right when you saw her sitting down, but her back hunched when she stood up.

Akku listened to the song and blew her nose. She wiped her fingers on her saree and asked, 'Where is my towel?' 'I saw it going past the gate this morning. I was told it was on its way to Manja's hotel for a cup of coffee,' answered little Satya and took to his heels. Akku laughed, but did not make an effort to chase him. Then she sniffed and turned towards Doddatte. 'Bow-legged Subbi! I'll break your back and carry it over my shoulder like a bow. Just you watch out!'

'My husband is in hell now, blessed woman. I would like to stay in one piece as long as I live. Don't harm me in any way,' Doddatte said in a tone of mock surrender. 'Poor soul,' she added later, to herself.

'Why do you say that? Poor soul indeed! Why do I need your pity? I'm not a widow like you. Are you pitying me because my husband went off to eat what he could beg at the roadside, leaving me behind? Remember I was the one who pushed Thimmappiah of the long house off me right into the pond. You just listen to me, witch. . . .' She would have gone on but for the arrival of Doddajjayya. People ran helter and skelter as they heard the sound of his breathing and the tapping of his walking stick. 'Hey, Vasu!' Uncle Vasu came flying like Hanumantha, the Monkey God. 'Go on. Thrash her and cool her down a bit.' Akku screamed as she sprinted away to shut herself up in the corner room, as if Doddajjayya's words alone had raised welts on her body.

Akku was Siriyatte's sister, but she was 'Akku' to everyone. Even a newborn baby could call her that and not look for a kinship term corresponding to the relationship. There must have been a big age gap between Akku and Siriyatte, but all the same Siriyatte looked older than Akku. And Akku had been as she was ever since Siriyatte was old enough to be aware of such things. 'It doesn't matter what you lose, so long as it isn't your sanity. Otherwise you are held in contempt not only by your own parents, but by the entire town,' Siriyatte used to say.

Akku had feigned pregnancy ever since her husband went away with a sanyasi. Of course it never seemed anything but absolutely real to her. On one occasion she went around complaining loudly of a stomach-ache. She made such a fuss about it that everyone who set foot in the house was told of her pain. 'I'll get rid of your pain once and for all,' offered Doddajjayya, brandishing a broom. 'Appiah, my baby will die. The sin will be on your head,' she screamed as she bent down and made sure her stomach would not be hit. After she had been thrashed, she stayed in her room, curled up, for a fortnight or so, without saying a thing. Her corner room was where all the junk was dumped. A broom had never been used there, it was filled with cobwebs. It stood in a corner, all alone. They even said that evil spirits lurked in that room.

Once, when we were all playing house, we heard a jangling sound from inside the corner room. Our throats went dry. We dragged our unwilling feet to tell the news to the others, and Uncle Vasu and Anthanna came hurrying to investigate. We were told off when we followed them. 'How dare you girls be so forward! Get back at once or else. . . .' We were pushed back like cattle. We pretended to go away, but came back stealthily. Uncle Vasu pushed the door open slowly with one finger. 'Anthanna, what sort of ghost is this?' he laughed. We peeped in too. Akku was sitting by the brass cradle. The chains had been removed and placed inside. She was shaking them in an effort to rock the cradle. 'Quiet,' she warned, 'the baby has just dropped off after its feed.' Uncle Vasu laughed, screeching like chalk on a blackboard. Doddatte who came in swaying, said, 'Ask her if she has plenty of milk,' raising further shrieks of laughter. And Uncle Vasu did ask, shamelessly. Akku arranged the folds of her saree and said, 'Yes, it will do for now.' 'Utterly mad! Well, never mind. When did you give birth to the baby?'

'Last night.'

There was talk the whole day about the ghost that had given birth in the corner room. Uncle Vasu was afraid that if Akku was left there in that state, then a real ghost might come and strangle her. 'Don't you worry about it,' said Doddatte, 'This creature has already pushed away the ghost that really came to catch her.'

Akku was pregnant the next day. Now the pregnancy was a permanent one. And her husband still did not return.

Then, one day, at last, news spread of Akku's husband's arrival, reaching even the people who were sitting upstairs in the house, reading quietly. Apparently he had been told of Akku's pregnancy the instant he arrived and very nearly went away, shocked. However, on being assured that it was only a story, he changed his mind. Now he sat in the veranda with Doddajjayya, talking in a phlegm-ridden voice. He had neither a fat belly, a large moustache, a short body nor a rough face as we had imagined. Indeed he was skeletal, with limbs like sticks of wood. He sat hunched, wrapped in a dhoti which had enough mud on it to be able to sprout seeds. Doddajjayya sat stiffly in his big chair with an utterly joyless face. Even the tips of his moustache looked askance at this man, as if he were worth nothing.

Akku's husband was not able to sit still. He was squirming away like a water-snake. He had left her behind to follow the wretched swami, remember? He had just walked off. The swami had gone to Kashi and the Himalayas. So had he. Now he went on and on. . . . He should not be considered a good-for-nothing. One could earn a tidy sum by staying with the swami. . . . Doddajjayya was not responding in any way. He wasn't even looking at him.

And then, where was Akku when she was sent for? She was not to be seen anywhere inside. 'Look for her. How can you say you can't find her?' the order came. Uncle Vasu, who went looking for her, had found her near the tank by the woods. 'Don't jump into the tank. Your husband has arrived,' he had said. 'Give him his bus fare and send him back. I came here because I saw him,' she had replied, quite indifferently. He had moved heaven and earth to cajole her to meet her husband. He now warned, wiping the sweat off his face, 'If you scold her and she jumps into the tank, there'll be nothing that I can do.'

Akku entered the house through the backdoor, but would not move from there for anything. She stood by the gaping paddy pounder, right heel against the wall, all crooked and wide-eyed. Doddajjayya, for his part, waited in the front veranda for a while, and then brought Sankappa, Akku's husband, inside.

'Akku . . . ,' called Doddajjayya.

'Akku died three days and three nights ago. Did this wretch come to perform the last rites? Ask him that,' Akku said in a voice like a blazing fire.

Sankappa stood with his head bent, his face looked as if it had been partly consumed by cockroaches. Doddatte needled him further, 'So you have come back at last! Have you run through all the girls in town, or what?'

Sankappa stayed for two days. Akku continued to sleep in her corner room; and she did not come inside the house. Sankappa slept in the veranda all curled up; a simpleton who knew nothing.

The next morning, Doddatte whispered to Uncle Vasu, 'Last night, I sat by the bottom step, waiting to see if this creature was really a sanyasi. Would you believe it if I told you the fellow got up around midnight and quietly found his way to the corner room? It was only after watching him that I went inside to sleep.'

We girls were sitting there stringing flowers for worship and could not help hearing this. We felt like plugging our ears though when she added more loudly, 'These girls, they are all ears when they are growing up.' Was this not the same Doddatte who had goaded Uncle Vasu into asking Akku whether she had enough milk? She was the one who said whatever she chose, whenever she chose, unmindful of who might be around. And now she was being so sanctimonious. Was she not herself a woman too? These speculations began to mix with the flowers we were stringing.

Then Akku's voice exploded like a demon's.

'Hey, you whom they call Doddatte! Come here quickly. There is something I have to tell you. Bring some betel leaves with you. . . .'

Doddatte heard the excitement in her voice and rose to go, saying that the slut was probably going to die. Behind her went the rest of the household, the servants and us. Akku sat there, rocking herself, one leg laid on the other. 'Hey, listen. He caught hold of me as soon as he came in. "Much better than a woman by the roadside," he said. "Get lost, scum," I said, "don't touch me, I'm pregnant." "Who's responsible?" he asked me. "Thimmappiah of the long house," I said. He wouldn't leave me alone even then. I'll teach you, I thought, and pulled out the cradle chains. I hurled them at him over and over again. What do you think the wretch did? He wrapped a thin towel around himself and ran for all he was worth. Whatever you say, Doddatte, Thimmappiah was any day better than this creature. His chest . . . his lips. . . .'

We could hear Doddajjayya's walking stick. Uncle Vasu put his hand over Akku's mouth and dragged her along to the large kitchen where he pulled out a stick from a bundle of firewood and started beating her with it as if he were beating out clothes on a stone slab. 'If this fool wanders about all over the place, not only Thimmappiah, but his father too will get hold of her. Then the wandering will come to a stop once and for all.' The beating continued.

'He might not even have laid a finger on her, for all we know. If we believe this mad creature and go after him, we might very well get our faces slapped,' said Anthanna, rolling the betel nut from one side of his mouth to the other. 'Really! Thimmappiah of all people! Has any seed that he has sown ever sprouted?' His laughter grated.

'Drag Sankappa here. Let them both get out of here and hang themselves.'

So even the pillars of the house had found a voice. Doddajjayya came in, trembling in anger. 'What did I do to deserve this,' he cried out, as if in pain. 'Hit her harder. Let her die. None will regret it.'

'Appiah, Vasu is thrashing me. He is killing me and my baby too. Appiah, ask him who he was after when he was sitting on Thimmappiah's veranda the other day. . . .' Vasu hit her hard on the mouth as she screamed on. No one stopped him. No one asked him to let go. No one pulled Akku away. The audience grew; it seemed it wanted the scene to go on indefinitely, as if it were prepared to listen endlessly to the perfect dovetailing of screams and blows. Bhanu Chikki stood, hands at her waist. 'She's nothing but a raving lunatic, and she turns everyone else into one.' She sounded as if she was sobbing.

'If I was beaten like that, I'd surely be dead by now. People say the mad are really strong,' a female voice spoke up.

But Akku's screaming did not stop. Neither did her accusations. And she did not die. It was Uncle Vasu who came out, defeated. 'Get away, everyone,' he cried, and bolted the door.

We thought she might run up behind him and scream for the door to be opened! We were wrong. Our desire to open the door for her surreptitiously, when no one was around, lost its edge. Akku stayed inside the room shouting and waving her towel.

'Thimmappiah's wife is waiting for you. Run to her. Run quickly, you shameless wretch. There! Are you going to beat me now?'

—Translated by Padma Ramachandra Sharma

A Revolutionary Incident

Ramachandra Deva

Whether you have been to this village or not, I don't know. Well, there is nothing in it to write home about. Though one would expect a few people to talk about some riot or commotion, one wouldn't hear anything because the people are scared of any disturbance, and the village is known for its peace and quiet. Yet even here, three or four years ago, an incident happened. It almost grew into a wrangle. It is this incident I am narrating now.

The village is Puthur. It is about five or six miles on the bus route that takes you to Subramanya. Though it is an ordinary village, yet it is not like any other village. It has its own customs and beliefs. Its own local legends. Those who visit the village believing it to be like other villages would get lost here. And even those who visit, do so rarely. On the way to Subramanya, if a bus breaks down near this village, around nightfall, and if it is inevitable for the passengers to rest somewhere and look for lodging, they may then end up in the village and have a glimpse of it. Likewise, those who come from a city hardly visit once in a year or two. The ones who come here don't stay more than a night. So their idea of this village is the same as a blind man's vision of an elephant.

Entering this village for the first time is like entering a deserted capital. A six-foot wall encircles the village. Seeing a portion of it from a distance, one gets the impression that it is a ruined building, but its solidity and height make it look like a prison. Locating the road that takes you to the village is quite a puzzle. The village is always surrounded by an empty silence. Even at midday when the sun blazes away, its silence haunts one. The scorching glare of the midday sun hurts your eyes so fiercely that you can't identify an object that is before you. Besides, you can't see a single human being either at noon or at dusk. When a stranded bus passenger walks its streets looking for shelter, he hears the sounds of his own footsteps, and off and on the long wails of street dogs, and gets anxious for a chat with another human being. But what he sees first are the ancient buildings lining the streets on either side that speak of a bygone glory and these towering buildings and their domes stare down at him. The bats that hang on to the edges of these domes enhance the eerie emptiness of this place. Some of the bats try to fly at dusk and knock against the domes. Further down there is a *dharmachatra* built by the kings of the past. A peculiar distinction of this village is that by looking at things from the outside no one can say what they are like. For instance look at this *dharmachatra*—its arched doorway. . . .

If you go inside it hoping to seek shelter, you see a moss-covered floor and decaying walls and the place is desolate. For over two hundred years, it has survived intact. But no one knows, including the village leader, Shyamachar, why this *dharmachatra* has a spire like that of a temple. If you insist on getting an answer, they reply, 'Our forefathers made it and let it be so.' Some say a god's icon had been installed there and a few others believe that it was built to be made into a temple but the god's image couldn't be set up.

The people who lived here long ago built a clean water-pond, which is now blackened and moss-laden, and they built one more *dharmachatra*. Also surviving are a bull's sculpture, which looks alive at dusk, and a stone chariot. Seen alongside the stone chariot is a temple, and near it a peepul tree. But the central structure that shapes the life of the villagers is the shrine lying at the edge of the village. A faceless ball-like object of a god is all that remains in the shrine. When you question the villagers about this, they, with their eyes closed, reply that, once upon a time, it appears it was a beautiful bronze figure of Lord Gopalakrishna, whose smiling face was marked by a certain cruelty, and who looked as if he was rising from his sitting posture, with one hand raised to bless, the second in normal position, and the other two hands bearing a conch, a disc, a mace and a lotus—all of which were meant to protect his devotees. What shape and origins can the Formless and Featureless Brahma have? Yet the villagers have named him Lord Gopalakrishna. Once upon a time the village was about to be struck by a plague. People in the neighbouring villages had died like worms. Then the inhabitants of this village installed this god and the plague didn't touch the village; and, legend says, since that day this deity has been worshipped. Well, whatever may have been the significance of this shrine to the village, the following narration of mine centres on this deity.

When I delineate the visual side of this village, one may wonder whether there are any people in it at all. In a way it is possible to believe that this village looks uninhabited. Walking its crooked and convoluted streets, if one starts looking for houses and human beings, one discovers that the streets have led him back to where one had started. These villagers find one thing amusing—the way visitors throw up their hands in despair as the domes and buildings of one part of the village look exactly like those in the other parts of the village. According to the villagers, some strangers came to this village, married and settled down to its obscure ways. Some years later a hot-blooded youth arrived and, as expected, raged against the ancient domes and images. But he too, within a few days, turned into a conformist. Now if you enquire about him, you learn that he knows every inch of the village, and has married and settled down. Today he looks like an old man.

If one is on the lookout for houses, one may not locate them. One doesn't seem to run into habitation. It might be tucked away within the folds of a huge temple, a *dharmachatra* or a monastery. Only one man's house lies nestling at the farthest end of a narrow gap between a big dome and a small dome. A house of another man called Sadashivaiah is situated below the *dharmachatra*, and as one climbs down the steps of the *dharmachatra*, one sees it with a desiccated tree next to it. Shyamachar's house is located right behind the bull's sculpture. One notices that these houses are of recent origin. Besides, they are all puny. These houses almost disappear from view because of the towering presence of those mighty old structures and domes that disseminate in ten different directions the regal pageantry and magnificence of a bygone era.

I said that these people are afraid of a riot or a brawl—even before it turns dark they eat and go to bed.

During the day they don't make much noise either. At best one may vaguely hear the muffled sounds of prayers, *mantras* and temple bells, thinly emanating from behind closed doors. The speciality of this village is that even the children are not given to making a noise. They are put through a regimen of iron discipline. Around the age of ten or twelve, they shed the playfulness of the young and behave like the aged. So the interests and inclinations of those about twenty are around the same as those of their elders. The so-called generation gap doesn't exist here. They learn reading and writing in the village school under the peepul tree, and are taught by the village priests. The Government school has not yet made its presence felt. Writing on sand, a one-line hymn to Lord Ganesh, they, after their thread ceremony, begin their writing lessons. The priests feed them with stories of the past kings and their pomp and prodigality. Their blood and bones are inextricably laced with the magnificence of the erstwhile era. It appears that once a Shudra boy entered the shrine, stood on the dirt and danced, guffawing loudly. The boys who had accompanied him to the shrine stood aghast and reported it to their parents. The lashes the Shudra boy received and the punishment—suspension by a rope—are ingrained in their minds even to this day. This particular incident happened many years ago. If the boys play games and enjoy them, they are reminded of what happened to the Shudra boy, and they run home in sheer terror and cower and crouch in fear.

In fact, there are people who lived here for a while and left forever. However, right from the beginning one or the other of these people showed signs of independence. One of them even left the village, declaring, 'Nothing could be done here. I'll go elsewhere. For me, all that matters is life.' But he returned inside three months. When Shyamachar recounts this incident in the context of the glorious ethos of his village, his face becomes a beacon of happiness. He adds, 'How can anyone find the kind of happiness and grandeur there that one finds here? When one is young one indulges in a bit of madness.' Now he is married, has children and lives in perfect harmony with his fellow villagers.

Just before ten in the morning, one hears the din of human existence in this village. A river flows past the village. Its origin is traced to a cave on a mountain near the village. It is said that during the Treta Yuga, Swayamprabha performed penance here, and Hanuman, Jambuvantha and their retinue came in search of

Sita and entered the cave by chance to find Swayamprabha there and received her blessings. It was after meeting her that Hanuman felt he was no ordinary monkey and realized that he was a hero and could fly to Lanka. People of this village believe that the river is the incarnation of Ganga. Anyone in the throes of death has to have a sip of water from the river.

Early in the morning, men and women are seen at the river washing clothes, cleaning dishes or bathing. Even there one hardly hears any noise, conversation or laughter. On the river-bank are seen huge black boulders forming a fort. The burning sun at noon and the silence of desolation make these dark men working among the black rocks look like the rocks and the rocks look like the men. Once they retire to their homes after washing and bathing, you don't come across a soul in the village.

Shyamachar is the uncrowned village leader. He is the oldest of the lot. Next to Lord Gopalakrishna, the villagers run to him for advice. They cast their responsibilities on Shyamachar. His grandfather's grandfather was a famous man, it appears. Among worldly men he was a saint, and among saints a bohemian observing silence for weeks on end and being friendly and not so friendly simultaneously with the old and the young; he lived among his people as impersonal as a star. The villagers believe that Shyamachar has inherited the same attributes. However, Shyamachar is a lazy man. 'This world is God's creation. According to His wishes everything has to happen. Our sole business is to watch His frolics,' he opines, sitting on his haunches on his dais.

According to Shyamachar, four or five hundred years ago, this village was a king's capital. Wiping his wrinkled face, he, with pride, shows you the vestiges of the king's palace and the place of outing which the king and the queen used to visit. Finishing their chores at work and repairing their torn sarees in a half-asleep and half-awake state, the married but forlorn women and the widows of the village, sitting in their kitchens, gossip about the king's harem, the beauty of his queen and the dazzling diamonds that brightened his harem. The peepul tree was planted on the day of the king's coronation. Its shade spans half the village. The villagers point at the path the king walked. The king made the Ganga flow here through the cave. This was when the whole village had been devastated by a famine. None had any life in his eyes, a smile on his face, or a touch of liveliness. The large capital looked like a sepulchre. The times were such that people felt as suffocated as prisoners and despaired that they hadn't died, and yet nothing of life remained! The rocks stood out of the now full-flowing river, and from a distance the rocks could be likened to human beings. Realizing the agony of his people and abandoning all protocol, the king walked stark naked into the cave and performed penance—standing on one leg in front of Goddess Ganga. He woke up from his penance only when he felt the Ganga flow past his leg. Considering this a miracle, the villagers even now feel happy within. But the people in the neighbouring villages say that this is a piece of fiction believed by those who are unable to sort out truth from falsehood, and they contend that the famine vanished because of the rains and the river started flowing because the king dug a tunnel there. Now that the people use the same river for washing their bottoms after defecating and worshipping God, the water has got polluted. Besides, the village doesn't have any other water source. At noon the village blazes away and the sand looks like glass. But for some old trees, one doesn't see many plants or any greenery.

The wall that girdles the village like a fort, was built by the same king. He built it to safeguard the freedom of his subjects. The wall was necessary to protect the capital. The people had no fear of insecurity. The wall that was erected for his subjects' protection now forms the village boundary. The erection of the wall involved a lot of time and labour. I say this, because, from my description, one may get the idea that this is a small village, but actually it isn't so. It is not possible to describe how big this village is. Shyamachar says, 'If you measure from the sacrificial altar at one end where will you stop? At the temple? At Lord Gopalakrishna's shrine? Or the peepul tree beyond it? The river?' I mention this so that you understand the problem the builders of the wall would have faced. Because of this complexity, I have never bothered to measure the area of this village. Since the buildings and domes in one part of the village look the same as those in the other parts of the village, and it is difficult to determine one's direction, how can one estimate the village limits? Maybe on account of this they call this a huge village. Yet, whichever way you go, the wall confronts you like an obstacle.

However, the most important thing in the village is Lord Gopalakrishna. Well, I have been meaning to talk about this God. But I seem to have got carried away by my own gibberish and seem to run in circles. Whenever you begin to talk it is always like this—you intend to say one thing, but you end up saying something else. And the meaning will be wholly different. At the end tedium sets in between the talker and the listener and this might even snuff out conversation. The story I want to recount is about a man who had a dialogue with God and about the .possibility of such a dialogue.

Like, I mentioned before, ever since the threat of the plague, Lord Gopalakrishna has become the village deity. Without consulting him, no one moves a step here.

He directs the entire gamut of life in this village. Once a year there is a fair when he is taken in a procession and is worshipped on a grand scale. All the villagers gather in one place to celebrate the event. Attended by women and children, the occasion swells in a crescendo of din and bustle. The chariot procession, the offerings of coconuts and fruits and elaborate prayers mark the moment. This is the only eventful happening in their lives. Those who know say that the present celebrations are almost comparable to the ones held by the kings of yore. At the end of the week the atmosphere of desolation returns to the village. As before, people troop to the river in the morning, return home after washing in silence, remind their children of the Shudra boy if they are up to mischief, eat, read religious books and sleep—the village is engulfed by the blazing heat at noon and the howls of the street dogs at dusk. Through the year people remember now and then the god's procession and keep fussing over the trinkets they bought at the fair. This dream world haunts them and permeates their lacklustre existence. The whole year they gladly cling to this illusion.

The legend about Lord Gopalakrishna has a similar ring to it. When Garudachar begot his son and was about to have him blessed in the shrine, the lamp was blown out. Within a week his child died. Shyamachar has another story to add. There was a man called Ramachar and one day Lord Gopalakrishna appeared in his dream and told him that his birthday, the star under which he was born and the day of his death would fall on the same day during the month. Ramachar died the same day. What is important is that all the villages are mortally afraid of this god. Due to this no one violates the village customs and beliefs.

Govinda's story is directly related to this. Govinda had lost his parents. Govinda was found lying by the roadside near a village and he was picked up by someone and brought to the village. What persuaded that someone to bring him here and how the villagers accepted him is still a mystery. But soon Govinda learnt the ways of the village and became a typical boy of that village. Yet Govinda was different from the other boys. He used to amuse the dour-faced boys by saying that the tuft on Venkatayya's bald head resembled a lizard's tail. He used to share bawdy jokes with them. The villagers, used to the rigours of their homes and the priests' school, found Govinda novel. As Govinda grew up, he started feeling he should leave this village and start his life elsewhere. When he was around thirteen or fourteen, he left for Mangalore. None in the village interfered. They were as silent now as they had been when someone had brought him to the village.

In Mangalore, Govinda found a job in a hotel. Besides, he joined school and, later, college, for his B.A. In school and college he made some friends. All of them had revolutionary ideas. Of these friends Rama Bhatta and Govinda were closest. Rama Bhatta had been brought up in a highly traditional Brahmin home. Soon after coming to Mangalore, he consigned his sacred thread to the flames. He ate meat and drank beer. He even exorcized the fear of God in Govinda. Both of them believed that God swallowed up everyone's individuality and it was for everyone to rebuild his own individuality. They held the view that standing away from society they should develop their individual potential. They generally read Marx and Camus. They desired that the established social order undergo a change. As he read and had discussions Govinda would remember his village. Govinda wanted a fundamental change in his villagers' abject submission to God, their fear of God, their inveterate superstition and their pre-occupation with their past glory. He wanted something new to happen. He understood that unless he rebelled against the past, the wheel of routine would grind on inexorably, stifling all creativity.

Even if I claim that this transformation came about in Govinda suddenly, in actuality it did not happen that easily. It evolved by increments, bit by bit, in about five or six years. But I mention all this in a hurry just to tell you how it gained in content and form. The result of this was that he was furious with the world. Naturally he felt everyone was oppressing him. To mention one instance—he quarrelled with his hotel proprietors. They were Udipi Brahmins. They treated their workers like slaves. They clamped their stamp of authority on them. For their eight hours of non-stop work, the owners paid ten rupees as monthly wages and fed them three meals a day. And the quantity of each meal was rationed and the owners kept a watch on the amount eaten. One day Govinda ate beyond his quota and the proprietor started scolding him. Govinda was sick of this slavery. He picked up his cup filled with chilli curry and flung it at his master's face. This led to a riot in the hotel. The other workers, frightened by Govinda's cruel technique, sided with the proprietor. They held Govinda by his neck and threw him out of the hotel. The workers returned to their work. Without knowing what to do, Govinda, in shame and anger, went to Rama Bhatta's room. Rama Bhatta consoled him for hours. Govinda was sad, because, in spite of his protest, things went back to normal. Govinda was studying for his B.A. examination, but now he had to abandon his studies. Rama Bhatta suggested to him to return to his village. After some initial reluctance Govinda left for his village.

He returned to the village after a period of four or five years. Nobody else had left the village for so long to live in another place; and to them any contact with a city had been unknown. The villagers were all born in the same village, drank water from the same river, sang paeans to the same god and ended up in the same crematorium. When Govinda returned none said a word to him. The village boys, used to tufts and ash marks on their foreheads, gaped in wonder at Govinda's close-cut hair and sandals. After he returned to the village the villagers' mouldy customs enraged him further. He felt he was tethered to something without the hope of freedom. About this time another incident occurred. Govinda's sister—not actually his sister, but the daughter of his foster parents—went mad. In the village, before a marriage, the horoscopes were scanned and compared and flowers strewn on the idol. If a white flower fell, it meant the god consented to the marriage. Every marriage in the village had taken place like this. Govinda's sister also had been married to one Gopalakrishnachar's son. By the time this boy was ten or twelve he could faultlessly recite *rudrajates*. But he died of a snake-bite inside of six months of his marriage. His wife—a girl of thirteen or fourteen—shaved off the hair on her head and wore a red saree. In about three months she went mad. The villagers, talking among themselves, believed that Lord Gopalakrishna had laid a curse on her. They said that this was on account of her father having brought to their village a boy of another caste. Now a nemesis had been cast over his daughter.

Govinda came. His sister's madness drove him to uncontrollable fury. Under a blazing sun she ran to the shrine, sat on its steps and hit her head against them. Initially the villagers wanted to restrain her, but soon they felt that there was nothing unusual in her behaviour. When Govinda returned, he didn't, to start with, visit anyone's house in the village. Later, occasionally, he would go to someone's house for an afternoon meal. Some of the villagers even invited him home. But Govinda feared that if he accepted their invitation, he might return to the routine ways of the village. Those who invited him were happily convinced that he, too, had gone mad. Govinda could see now how the youth behaved like the old, how age caught up with them and how they led their stale existence. He felt he should burn their customs and beliefs once and for all. The whole village needed a change. His sister's shaven head, red saree and fear of God had contributed to the drying up of her youth, he believed. These villagers given to abject submission to their dilapidated temples, their rickety customs and their god, were fuddy-duddy Brahmins and Govinda was convinced that all their gods had to be flung on a dung heap. But the villagers said, 'In what way are we responsible for others' sufferings?'

It was then that what follows happened. Before daybreak, when everyone was asleep, the villagers were woken up by the sputtering sounds of fire and the peals of temple bells. When they rushed out they saw that Lord Gopalakrishna's shrine was on fire. Most of it had already been gutted. It looked as though the darkness itself was on fire. Since they were yet rubbing away sleep from their eyes, it took a while for the incident to seep into their minds. Still stunned, they scrambled around like blind men for water, but the shrine had already been razed to the ground by the fire. They saw the shrine's bamboo sticks falling and turning into embers and ashes. Tongues of flames were reaching for the skies. Morning was breaking. In place of the god's image they now saw a melted bronze ball. The simmering lava of the melted conch, disc, mace and lotus was flowing on the floor. The golden rays of the sun glinted on the hot flowing metal.

The villagers were totally helpless. They despaired—they were in a wilderness and their Hanging Garden of Illusions had cracked into shreds; their habits crushed. The god had been disfigured beyond recognition. They felt like someone, who, on waking up from an enchanted dream, had to face the cold realities of a dark night. As they had been mortally scared of a disturbance, they were now writhing in pain, apprehending a calamity. Their agony was comparable to the agony of those who couldn't bury a rotting corpse lying in their midst. Women, children and all the others gathered in front of the shrine.

On the other hand, Govinda felt he had been relieved of an oppressive burden. The villagers' tragedy brought him happiness. He felt that now the life of the village children and youth would bloom without being nipped in the bud. A few days passed. Rudely jolted out of their habits, the villagers felt they had fallen into an abyss and became distraught believing that their daily life had lost its focus. Without the daily prayers to their god and deprived of his daily blessings, they saw there was total confusion in their relationship with other villagers. Having run from pillar to post for sometime like this, one day the important members of the village gathered in front of the gutted shrine for a meeting under the leadership of Shyamachar. The women and children stood at a distance to watch the event. Shyamachar stood up and held forth, 'Govinda has set fire to the shrine; it is true that the God's icon has lost its original beauty; and it is equally true that we couldn't figure out for three days what we had to do under the circumstances. But when we analyse the event in calmer moments we realize that we shouldn't have panicked at all. I feel that Lord Gopalakrishna would have willed it that way. Otherwise why should Govinda return so abruptly to the village after having left it for so many years? Having come here and without creating any other nuisance, why would he resort only to this? Having done this why should he disappear all of a sudden? I believe that Govinda was only carrying out the wishes of the god.' Everyone in the village agreed with him. In accordance with the other villagers' suggestions, certain decisions were taken. First, they should find out whether Govinda had a dream to that effect. Secondly, they should rebuild the shrine. Thirdly, they should retain the god's image in its present form and not tamper with it. They should continue their traditional prayers and forms of worship. Fourthly, they should bring back Govinda and see that he became one of them. It was contrary to God's wish to hate someone without reason and they didn't know what motivated him to perform the act. Suppose God had appeared in Govinda's dream and told him so? Having made these decisions, the villagers felt that a mighty burden had been taken off their chests. They were convinced that they could now return to their original ways. The same day Shyamachar ran into Govinda. Shyamachar asked him whether he burnt down the idol according to the wishes of God who appeared in his dream. Govinda stared at him and walked away without uttering a word.

With the help of the strong men of the village, the villagers rebuilt the shrine. Worship of, and prayers to, the god continue as usual. The annual procession is also held on a grand scale. Living in their frozen present, the villagers look lost in their dream world. Revelling in their remembered dreams amidst the realities of their lives, they carry on. Only the god's face is disfigured. But the villagers don't consider it a defect. If you ask them about it, they reply that 'it is God's will'. Now they believe that Govinda did it at the behest of God and that Govinda had a dream. As in the past, even now the god directs and guides the lives of the villagers. People are afraid of him.

After a few days Govinda felt he should get out of this vicious labyrinth. He was tired. He said to himself enough was enough. Thinking he would run away he went to the river. The sun above blazed away like a tyrant. Govinda felt his eyes darken and sat down on a rock. Everything looked murky and Govinda saw only one thing moving. Govinda felt as if something had arrived after travelling a long distance and was enveloping him and crushing his bones. What is it? The wall? The dome? The kings? Some ineffable being? Possibly it will remain ineffable for ever. Govinda's eyes sparkled once, batted their lashes and gradually shut. Overcome with fatigue and in utter helplessness he lay on the rock fully stretched. The crows up in the sky circled above him making their cacophonous calls like they do on the day of obsequies. Slowly his head sank on his chest.

The village, as was its wont, slept in perfect peace.

— *Translated by Basavaraj Urs*

Tar Arrives

Devanoor Mahadeva

An Overview of the Village

The dirt track, that's just good enough for a bullock-cart to amble along, starts like an alley from the village and winds for three miles before joining the main road on which the buses ply. The same route back from the main road, dips down to the village, hedged in on both sides by cactii, meanders around the banyan grove in which the spirits reside, forks into three, and then runs into the village. On either side of the forked alleys are houses, so close together that at first sight they seem to choke each other.

It is not a village that's known for anything. If one counts, there would at the most be some eighty households. There's not even a little hotel there, like everywhere else. You can judge the place from that. And then there are some four young men who have studied up to high school, either at the neighbouring Nanjangud or Mysore. Lakuma, Rajappa, Madu and Shambu are their names.

The relation between the above names and the story to be told is as follows: the village patel doesn't quite like these characters. After all, who could suffer these twits, born before one's own eyes, strutting around with their heads held high? As we've seen, it's been the same story since our fathers' times. These boys, heedless of upper caste or lower caste, run around with that Untouchable, Lakuma, as if they were born out of the same womb. They had been warned through their fathers. You think they'd listen to their fathers? Everyone is waiting for those boys to be caught molesting some girl. That will be an opportunity to drag them to the village hall, strip them down to their underpants, tie them to a pole and flog them. There is the hope that the boys will certainly oblige.

A Road is Ordered

It was during such times that the order sanctioning a road for the village came from above. The patel's body puffed up even more. The news spread through the village like a wild fire. It may be recalled in this connection, that some seven or eight years ago when the Minister had visited the village, the patel had personally garlanded him and given him lemon-fruit, and had said that a village to be considered a village should at least have a road, and had pleaded with the Honourable Minister to be magnanimous and sanction one. It was evening by the time the same patel returned from Nanjangud that day. Along with him he brought the news that the patel himself was to be the road contractor and that, from then on, for months together, no one needed to look around for work, and also that with the excess Government money the village temple was to be renovated; every house in the village was agog with all this news.

In Front of the Village

It's been many days now since all this has happened. Now the village is a regular battlefield. The banyan trees that once stood spread against the sky, as high as the eye could see, have all been cut down to the ground. To those who once saw the village hidden behind the dense mat of banyan trees, it must now look like a desert. There's not even a trace left to show that they were once there. Where they once stood, there are now machines running around. At the sight of these machines, with their stone wheels that reach man-high, running around belching smoke, let alone the village kids, even the men and women forget themselves as they watch, fascinated. The clamour that rises from there crosses the village and goes beyond. To anyone seeing the village from a distance, it will look as if there is an upheaval going on there. But if you come closer, it is the same people, from the same village. If you talk to them you will know them to be the same people. But they *have* changed beyond recognition—with the black tar that is spread on the ground smeared all over them—the way they look!

The way they move!

On one side, ten or fifteen young women sit and crush the gravel with their sarees tied around their heads. One among them raises her thin voice and sings, 'Come, come soon, Chenna Basavayya.' Others prod her on, joining her in a chorus, which is heard even by those working at a distance. With the workers engrossed in their work, the whole place, for as far as a furlong, has a festive air about it. Measuring and digging, digging and levelling, levelling and sprinkling water, sprinkling water and bringing the blend of gravel and tar in a barrow and filling it in, filling it in and spreading it—all this on the other side. A machine that goes backwards and forwards. A *"dhug   dhug"* machine that levels. A fire-spitting machine that mixes the gravel, sand and tar together. For everything a machine. How many of them! Each one a black, black weird form.

The patel is standing with his hands tied in front of him, where the measuring is going on. Suddenly he turns back. He takes a few steps forward. From the look on his face, even a child can say that the work is going on well.

Hands and Mouths Tarred

Kids, everywhere, are the same. The moment they leave the hamlet they gather around the tar. When the elders scold them they retreat; when they've turned away, the kids are back again. On the whole, all the kids spend their evenings where the tar is melted. Even after night has fallen they do not return to their houses. The elders have to come, spank them and take them back. But then, even the elders who come to take the kids away, can't help spending at least a few moments watching the miracle of road-making before they go back. And if, while going home, they hold the hands of the kids, the tar from the kids' hands will smear theirs. That's what happened when one Rangappa came to take back his son. Angered, he spanked his son, saying: 'Is this what your master taught you in school?' The kid who opened his mouth wide and started to cry didn't stop. When Rangappa, losing patience, hit the kid on the mouth, the child cried even louder and put his hands into his mouth. The tar on his hands stuck to his mouth. The mouth was sealed and the crying stopped. And many such things, every evening.

And then, it has become a habit with the women to bring home a ball of tar when returning from work. Apparently, some woman tried to plug a leak in a pot with the tar, and it worked like magic. Since then, in whichever corner of the village there is a leaking pot, the tar finds its way there. It has also become a practice to borrow tar from the households that maintain a ready stock of it.

A Letter to the Editor

The driver, who ran the big machine, commuted every day back and forth from Nanjangud. One day word spread that the paper he brought along with him carried news of village. Everyone, without getting down to work, crowded around the driver. The patel was fuming. The news the paper carried about the village, read like this:

> Sir,
> This is with reference to the road that the Government in its magnanimity has sanctioned to our village and the construction that is presently going on. We have learnt that the road contractor, who is also the village patel, plans to utilize Government funds for the renovation of the temple. This is misuse of public funds. It is our prayer to the concerned authorities that they should ensure that no such thing takes place.
>
> — Aggrieved

Call for Justice

One cannot say with certainty whether the road work went on that day or whether it did not. Shall we say it went on like it didn't go on? What had started off as one thing had begun to turn into something entirely different. The fear as to what would be the outcome of all this spread through the streets of the village. As evening approached, the plot grew thicker and thicker. The patel had the drummer announce that every household should send one person to the village hall for a meeting of the Village Council. Night had just begun to fall and darkness had just enveloped the village. Outside it was so dark that people couldn't see each other's faces. The dim light from within the houses fell out of the windows and was lost in the darkness.

The Village Hall

In the Village Hall the lantern was spewing out abundant smoke and light. Already a few men had spread themselves out as if they had nothing to do with what was going on. People started dropping in one by one. As the crowd grew, the bustle grew with it.

In a moment, the din that rose from there began to drown the village. The patel was seated in the centre. The light from the lantern was falling straight on his face. You could see his face sweating lightly and his forehead rhythmically wrinkle, unwrinkle and wrinkle again. You could see who was sitting in which far corner as their faces lit up when they struck a match to light a beedi. There was such a mob of people there.

The First Man: Why don't you start?

The Second Man: Everyone knows it. What is there to start, except the dressing-down?

Rajappa: What does that mean, brother?

The Third Man: You are the ones who know about meanings and things like that. Have we gone to school, like you?

The Shanbhog: Be quiet for a while. Patel, why don't you speak?

The Patel: What is there to say?
The Shanbhog: Everyone knows that you are the ones

who wrote the letter to disgrace the village. Are you people inclined to accept that?

(The Shanbhog looks towards Lakuma, Rajappa, Shambu and Madu. They nod their heads as if to say yes. An uproar, that pounds the chests of those standing outside looms from within.)

The Patel: What wrong did you people see in that?

(The Patel's words are heard like a crack. Not one opens his mouth.)

Rajappa: If you put the money that's meant for something into something else, what else can happen?

(The clamour rises again. The Shanbhog waves his hand. The noise dies out gradually.)

The Patel: Did I swallow the money for my children's sake? Or did I do it for the sake of the village and for God's work?

Madu: You might do it for anything, sir. You didn't use it for what it was meant for.

(The clamour rises again. This time louder than before. The Shanbhog as usual. This time one or two even stand up.)

The First Man: Don't you fellows have anything like gods, elders and things like that?

The Second Man: If they did, would they get into this business?

The Third Man: Enough, keep quiet. Why does everyone have to say something?

The Fourth Man: Flog them. That'll set them right. They will talk straight.

Rajappa, Shambhu and Shambu's father: Who's that man? Come beat us then. We'll take care of that too. Your writ runs only till the tip of your nose.

The Patel *(raising his voice)*: Yes. What you did was the right thing to do, I say.

Shambu: And you think what you did is right. Why talk of it?

The Patel: What did you say? You have the audacity to talk back to me like that! Have I become so decrepit as to take it from you?

So saying, the patel clenched his fist and rose up like a shot. His head hit the lantern, broke the glass, and the glass pieces fell tinkling to the ground. The lantern flame flickered until it finally died out, plunging the whole place into darkness. Pandemonium immediately filled the place. Everyone struggled to get out of the Village Hall as soon as possible. It went on like this for a while, then everything was quiet. The houses in the village closed their doors shut.

News from Hosur

The village slept; dreaming, perhaps, of what happened last night. As if to spoil the dream, a man from neighbouring Hosur passed by in the early hours of the day. The words he left behind, began to creep along the alleys of the village:

Sir, I am from Hosur. In our village there was a seductress. It had been her practice to seduce all the teenaged boys of the village. How long could one try to talk her out of it? She went about her own way. They tried scolding her, but she went about her own way. Finally they did what had to be done. They called a Village Council meeting and dragged her there. Even there she went about her arrogant way. Furious, they didn't leave it at that. They stripped her down to her birthday suit, flogged her with a tamarind branch, and made her rue the day she was born.

Yet, she wouldn't let it go at that. She carried the same face straight to the police station. They say she told the police everything in detail: they did this to me, they did that to me. The police van arrived and rounded up all the landlords. Nobody knows what happened after that.

The news from Hosur blended with what was already brewing in the village, and the ferment rose higher and higher. They talked of what had happened.

The Patel: 'Hmm.' The Shanbhog: 'Ha.' The Foursome: 'My sons! They were lording it over. Now they've been shown their place.' The First Man: '*Ayyo,* Siva!'

Tar in the Pit, in the Pitch of the Night

Even after all this had happened, things just didn't stop at that. Remember the tar drums that had been heated and kept in front of the village? Next morning they were not to be seen there. If you followed their trail, it led you outside the village, where round a pit, with their mouths wide open, they were gorging out the tar from within in thick lumps. As the sun rose higher and higher the tar continued pouring out into the pit, stretching gently out of the mouths of the drums. Those who had gathered round to see, kept watching. Those who hadn't seen it yet, came to see it in flocks. After they had watched and watched, and the blackness of it had filled their eyes, they would slowly move away. Nobody had a word to say.

Even the patel didn't have a word to say. One man said to the patel: 'You should have just said yes, we would have beaten the daylights out of them last night.' Even at that, the patel only clenched his teeth. Didn't say a word. He went to the police station straight from there. It was evening when he came back. It became known that the next day, early in the morning, the police would come to carry out the investigations and that no one could now say what turn it would all take.

The One who Went to the Hamlet Hasn't Returned

As one thing added to another and the plot grew darker and darker, and as the village waited for night to fall, there was yet another thing waiting to add to it further. Although it was dusk and every house had closed its door, and there was not a soul stirring in the streets, Rangappa's kid hadn't still come back home. Apparently he had headed towards the hamlet after lunch. They asked the school-master. He said he had himself seen him walk homewards; he was the kind of dumb kid that headed straight wherever he was going. With a lantern in hand, they knocked at every house in the village. They asked his playmates. Everyone said that they had not seen him. Not a single street, not a single alley was left unsearched. How long could this continue? His mother's cry was the only sound in the silent village and she wailed on throughout the night.

Investigations

At dawn the police van came bumping along with difficulty and stopped in front of the village. The Inspector sent the man who had come out to see, to bring the patel along. The patel rushed out in a hurry and came and stood there. Everyone came over to the pit outside the village to see, and froze the moment they saw. The tar in the pit had grasped Rangappa's kid by his feet. The tar drum clasped both his hands. His hands, his body and face were all covered with tar. And if you took a closer look, in that child's body there was life still throbbing.

— *Translated by Manu Shetty and A. K. Ramanujan*

Notes on the Writers

Ramachandra Sharma (b. 1925)

One of the pioneers of the Modern movement in Kannada literature, Ramachandra Sharma has written poetry, short stories, plays and criticism. He has some twenty-five books to his credit, including *Gestures,* a collection of poems in English. He has translated one hundred English poems of this century into Kannada and has translated both prose and poetry from Kannada into English. He has received the Karnataka Sahitya Akademi Award. He now lives in Bangalore after having worked abroad for over two decades.

Bagalodi Devaraya (1927–1985)

Essentially of the Masti tradition in story-telling, Bagalodi has left behind just two collections of short stories. He had been India's Ambassador to various countries, like New Zealand, Laos and Bulgaria.

Yashwant Chittal (b. 1928)

A distinguished writer of fiction, Chittal has a number of novels and collections of short stories to his credit. His contribution to the development of the short story as a literary *genre* has been considerable. He has received the Sahitya Akademi Award for his collection of short stories, *Katheyadalu Hudugi.* The story, which gave the collection its title, has been included in this volume. He lives in Bombay.

Shantinath Desai (b. 1929)

A writer of fiction, Desai has a number of novels and collections of short stories to his credit. He gave the first modern novel to

Kannada in the early '60s. A reputed critic, he has translated both prose and poetry from Kannada into Marathi and English. He was, till recently, the Vice Chancellor of the Kuvempu University in Karnatka and has been a member of many cultural delegations sent from India.

A. K. Ramanujan (b. 1929)

Internationally known for his able translations from Tamil and Kannada, Ramanujan has written original poetry both in English and Kannada. He has received the prestigious McArthur Award and is the Professor of South Asia Languages and Area Studies at Chicago University. He has been a visiting professor in many universities all over the world. Though he has written only a handful of stories, every one of them has come in for considerable praise.

U. R. Anantha Murthy (b. 1932)

Anantha Murthy is one of the most important writers of fiction in Kannada and is famous both for his short stories and novels. His novel, *Samaskara*, which was made into an award-winning film, has been translated into many European languages, including English. As a critic, he played an important role in interpreting the writings of the Navya school. Widely travelled, he has been a member of many cultural delegations from India. He was, till recently, the Vice Chancellor of the Mahatma Gandhi University in Kottayam, Kerala.

Raghavendra Khasaneesa (b. 1933)

Not certainly a prolific writer, Khasaneesa has just one collection of short stories in which he has included all the stories he has written over the last two decades. He was a librarian with the University of Bangalore and has now retired.

K. Sadashiva (1933–1977)

A master writer of short stories, Sadashiva has left behind him a number of excellent stories. His influence on younger writers has been considerable. His premature death in 1977 was a loss to the world of Kannada short stories.

P. Lankesh (b. 1935)

Critic, playwright, poet and writer of novels and short stories, Lankesh has also made some award-winning films. After having taught English in the University of Bangalore, he took to journalism and is currently the Editor of *Lankesh Patrike*, a leading weekly in Kannada. The *Patrike* has discovered a number of talented young writers.

K. P. Poorna Chandra Tejasvi (b. 1938)

Once a Navya writer, Tejasvi turned his back on the movement in the early '70s. He has written some excellent stories, some of which have been made into good films. He has written two novels, the second of them, *Chidambara Rahasya*, winning him the Sahitya Akademi Award. Tejasvi is a farmer.

Veena Shanteshwar (b. 1945)

Shanteshwar has one novel and a number of collections of short stories to her credit. She teaches English in one of the colleges in Dharwar. The story included here is typical of the feminist view she has been expressing over the last few years.

S. Diwakar (b. 1946)

A journalist by profession, Diwakar is currently with the United States Information Service in Madras as the Kannada Editor. He has one collection of short stories and has translated the stories of all the Nobel laureates into Kannada.

Vaidehi (b. 1947)

With three volumes to her credit, Vaidehi is one of the best writers of her generation. She has written some poetry also.

Ramachandra Deva (b. 1948)

Formerly a journalist, Ramachandra Deva is currently teaching English in the Kuvempu University. He has written some very good stories. His translation of Shakespeare's plays received considerable praise.

Devanoor Mahadeva (b. 1949)

One of the most gifted writers of the day, Devanoor Mahadeva has written about the Dalit experience. His long, short story, *Odalala*, was a virtual *tour de force*. He has one collection of short stories; and a novel, *Kusuma Bala*, which he published recently, is remarkable for the experiments he conducted with language and the mode of narration he employed. The novel won him the Sahitya Akademi Award in 1989.

Notes on the Translators

Basavaraj Urs

Formerly a teacher of English in the University of Bangalore, he is now a senior officer in the State Bank of India. He lives in Bangalore.

Manu Shetty

Till recently Shetty worked at the University of Chicago, and is currently in Mangalore doing doctoral reserch. He has collaborated with A.K. Ramanujan in translations of prose and poetry from Kannada into English.

Narayan Hegde

Professor of English in the State University of New York, Hegde recently spent a number of months in India translating Kannada short stories into English. He lives in Brentwood, Long Island.

Padma Ramachandra Sharama

A teacher by profession, Padma Ramachandra Sharma has taught English in Ethiopia, Zambia, Malawi and England. She has translated the stories of many of the leading writers in Kannada. Her translation of two novels by Poorna Chandra Tejasvi into English have been published by Penguin Books, India.

P. Sreenivasa Rao

Professor of English in the La Salle University in Philadelphia, USA, Sreenivasa Rao has written original stories and poems both in English and Kannada.

See *Notes on the Writers* for information on Ramachandra Sharma, A.K. Ramanujan and Shantinath Desai.

MORE ABOUT PENGUINS

For further information about books available from Penguins in India write to Penguin Books (India) Ltd, B4/246, Safdarjung Enclave, New Delhi 110 029.

In the UK: For a complete list of books available from Penguins in the United Kingdom write to Dept. EP, Penguin Books Ltd, Harmondsworth, Middlesex UB7 0DA.

In the U.S.A.: For a complete list of books available from Penguins in the United States write to Dept. DG, Penguin Books, 299 Murray Hill Parkway, East Rutherford, New Jersey 07073.

In Canada: For a complete list of books available from Penguins in Canada write to Penguin Books Canada Ltd, 2801 John Street, Markham, Ontario L3R 1B4.

In Australia: For a complete list of books available from Penguins in Australia write to the Marketing Department, Penguin Books Australia Ltd, P.O. Box 257, Ringwood, Victoria 3134.

In New Zealand: For a complete list of books available from Penguins in New Zealand write to the Marketing Department, Penguin Books (N.Z.) Ltd, Private Bag, Takapuna, Auckland 9.

FOR THE BEST IN PAPERBACKS, LOOK FOR THE

AFTER THE HANGING
O.V. Vijayan

Translated from the Malayalam by the author

Each of the stories in this collection is a small masterpiece, shining and enchanting in its perfection. These are extended allegories of terror and loathing (inspired by the Emergency imposed on the country by Indira Gandhi), strange stories of the supernatural, glowing stories of love and the joys of growing up in the country, stories of loss, separation and death, and mystical stories of ordinary men and women breaking out of the crude husk of their earthly existence to become one with the Creator.

'It is easy to walk into the brooding world he brings to life, but difficult to emerge from its charming snare without wanting to continue...'

— *Bombay*

'A major writer of our times.'

—*India Today*

SEASONS
Jacquelin Singh

The last thing Helen wants to hear from her Sikh lover is that he already has a wife. After the initial shock, however, Helen's innate optimism reasserts itself and she carries on with her preparations to follow Tej back to India, a country she has known only through history texts...

How will she cope with the other wife and, most of all, will the huge and unfamiliar land awaiting her prove too much for her?

As this carefully constructed, beautifully written first novel unfolds we are treated to a new and refreshing love story as well as a magnificent and arresting portrait of India.

FOR THE BEST IN PAPERBACKS, LOOK FOR THE (🐧)

DELIVERANCE AND OTHER STORIES
Premchand
Translated from the Hindi by David Ruben

Premchand was an extraordinarily versatile writer who first began publishing around the turn of the century. Equally at home in Urdu and in Hindi, he wrote some fourteen novels, three hundred short stories and several hundred essays. Although he was influenced by Tolstoy, Maupassant and Chekov, his strength was his ability to capture village and small town India in minute and glittering detail. This collection brings together the finest stories Premchand wrote—including classics such as *The Chess Players, The Shroud, Deliverance* and the wonderfully comic Moteram Shastri Stories.

'Probably the greatest figure in modern Indian literature.'
                                                    —*The Scotsman*